THE MAN IN THE MOONE

broadview editions
series editor: L.W. Conolly

THE MAN IN THE MOONE

Francis Godwin

edited by William Poole

broadview editions

Library and Archives Canada Cataloguing in Publication

Godwin, Francis, 1562-1633
  The man in the moone / Francis Godwin ; edited by William Poole.

First published in 1638.
Includes bibliographical references.
ISBN 978-1-55111-896-3

  1. Voyages, Imaginary. 2. Godwin, Francis, 1562-1633—Criticism and interpretation. I. Poole, William, 1977- II. Title.

PR3478.G7M36 2009   823'.3   C2009-903613-4

Broadview Editions

The Broadview Editions series represents the ever-changing canon of literature in English by bringing together texts long regarded as classics with valuable lesser-known works.

Advisory editor for this volume: Martin Boyne

Broadview Press is an independent, international publishing house, incorporated in 1985. Broadview believes in shared ownership, both with its employees and with the general public; since the year 2000 Broadview shares have traded publicly on the Toronto Venture Exchange under the symbol BDP.

We welcome comments and suggestions regarding any aspect of our publications—please feel free to contact us at the addresses below or at broadview@broadviewpress.com.

North America
Post Office Box 1243, Peterborough, Ontario, Canada K9J 7H5
2215 Kenmore Avenue, Buffalo, NY, USA 14207
Tel: (705) 743-8990; Fax: (705) 743-8353;
email: customerservice@broadviewpress.com

UK, Ireland, and continental Europe
NBN International, Estover Road, Plymouth UK PL6 7PY
Tel: 44 (0) 1752 202300   Fax: 44 (0) 1752 202330
email: enquiries@nbninternational.com

Australia and New Zealand
NewSouth Books
c/o TL Distribution, 15-23 Helles Ave., Moorebank, NSW, 2170
Tel: (02) 8778 9999; Fax: (02) 8778 9944
email: orders@tldistribution.com.au

www.broadviewpress.com

FSC

Mixed Sources
Product group from well-managed forests, controlled sources and recycled wood or fibre

Cert no. SW-COC-003438
www.fsc.org
© 1996 Forest Stewardship Council

This book is printed on paper containing 100% post-consumer fibre.

Typesetting and assembly: True to Type Inc., Claremont, Canada.

PRINTED IN CANADA

Contents

Preface

The first work of English science fiction that can claim some title to that status was published in 1638, pseudonymously, and five years after its genuine author's death. *The Man in the Moone* of "Domingo Gonsales," a midget Spaniard who flies to the moon by geese power and there encounters an advanced lunar civilisation, had an enormous impact on the European imagination for centuries after its initial publication. There are scores of references to it in the contemporary literature, and it was translated into at least three other languages; indeed, its first English edition was literally read to bits—it is now so scarce that only a handful of copies are in the public domain.

"Domingo Gonsales" was not the author, however, and although the work itself claims to be a genuine travel narrative, starting plausibly enough in the real historical setting of the Dutch Revolt, and ending in the much-discussed kingdom of China among identifiable members of the Jesuit Mission, it was actually written by Francis Godwin (1562-1633), Bishop successively of Llandaff and Hereford, and a celebrated antiquary. But the hoax was perpetrated even after Godwin's death: when *The Man in the Moone* was entered into the Stationers' Register it was even then described as a translation from the Spanish, although when it finally appeared in print its prefatory epistle left no doubt that the following work was one of "fancy" as well as of "judgement." Further confusions resulted when it was translated into French by Jean Baudoin, who was thereafter often assumed to be the original author, and its own afterlife in English was principally as an abbreviated, even bowdlerised text.

Godwin's work is important for two reasons, not entirely separable. First, it is a work of literary sophistication. It is narrated by a slightly implausible figure who does a number of very implausible things, not least fly to the moon and back. But it is carefully situated in recent, familiar history, and the device of employing a narrator whose nation was the principal enemy of England in its supposed time-frame further heightens readerly problems about who and what to trust in this text, and why. Such a technique spawns an interesting set of interventions in the heterogeneous traditions that literary and scientific historians have retrospectively labelled as travel writing, utopianism, and the discourses of experimental philosophy.

This brings us to the second reason for *The Man in the Moone*'s importance: its finely integrated discussion of various state-of-the-art ideas about astronomy and cosmology—magnetic attraction, diurnal rotation, and the possibility of interplanetary travel and extraterrestrial life. The dramatisation of these discussions in *The Man in the Moone* is at once a form of popular science and also a form of popular fiction. This is the age-old problem of fiction—the probable impossible intermingled with the possible improbable—but in Godwin the intersection between elements generically marked as fictitious (the picaresque overtones of the slightly ridiculous Spaniard adventurer) and elements familiar from contemporary natural philosophical discussion (the magnetic power of the earth, the arguments for real diurnal motion) is particularly troublesome, because hitherto picaresque and natural philosophy had not been at all close bedfellows.

Despite the literary and historical importance of Godwin's posthumous publication, it has not been edited adequately. Grant McColley's laudable edition of 1937 did much to put Godwin back on the literary map, and with his interests in the interactions between scientific and literary history McColley was ideally placed to comment on the positioning of *The Man in the Moone* in the history of ideas. Marjorie Nicolson too wrote extensively at the same time and in a similar vein on Godwin's importance, tracking the aftershocks of his text up to H.G. Wells and beyond. But attention since then, with a few notable exceptions, has been desultory, and the editions that have appeared in recent times have set themselves modest standards. Accordingly, this edition seeks to provide a text based on the first and only authoritative edition of 1638, along with an extensive introduction and commentary, a discussion of the printing of the text, and primary and secondary bibliographies. Godwin's mysterious unsigned Latin tract on telegraphy, the *Nuncius Inanimatus* (1629), is also supplied in the contemporary translation included in the second edition of *The Man in the Moone* (1657), as are a series of extracts from ancillary texts pertinent to the interpretation of Godwin's work (see Appendices beginning on p. 125).

Acknowledgements

I am first of all indebted to the previous commentators on this text, especially to McColley, whose 1937 edition was a landmark in the rehabilitation of Godwin's fiction. Subsequent editorial ventures are best passed over in silence, with the exception of Amartin-Serin's 1984 effort, which places the English and French editions in parallel with a good deal of useful commentary in French. Anglophone commentators have almost entirely neglected Amartin-Serin's edition, and although I have been able to correct and augment many of her notes, I have silently and gratefully taken over a few details from them too. Her edition also contains excellent commentary on Baudoin's performance as a translator. I recall with fondness supervising two undergraduate dissertations over the last few years on Godwin, one in Cambridge and one in Oxford, and so I thank Christina Hodson and Dorothy Feaver for giving me the excuse to think about this text properly. A late but timely intervention came from my fellow collegian Frédérique Aït-Touati, also a scholar of seventeenth-century science and fiction, who pointed out to me Amartin-Serin's edition and some of my own errors. I am also very grateful to those at Broadview Press, notably Leonard Conolly, Marjorie Mather, and Martin Boyne. I should note here that all translations from languages other than English are my own unless otherwise acknowledged.

Introduction

Francis Godwin (1562-1633), Bishop successively of Llandaff (1601) and of Hereford (1617), was himself the son of a bishop and married the daughter of another. As his grandson Morgan wrote in a begging letter to Archbishop Sancroft in 1681, he derived from a "most Loyall & Episcopall Family; My Grandfather & two Great-Grandfathers, being all three Bishops ... And my Father, sometime Arch-Deacon & Canon of Hereford."[1] Francis's father Thomas had been variously an academic and a schoolmaster. Upon the accession of Mary he retrained as a physician, but he was nonetheless harassed for his Protestantism by the authorities and, as one chronicler claimed, was frequently forced to change his abode or go into hiding.[2] The same chronicler also credited Godwin senior's swift ecclesiastical promotion after the accession of Elizabeth to his imposing physical appearance; certainly the surviving portraits of him and his son Francis suggest massive frames, or perhaps appetites.[3] The day Thomas died, his eldest son Thomas, who had been meddling with his father's wealth for some years, carried off with other family members all the furnishings in Thomas's properties before they could be seized for debt. Francis does not appear to have been entirely innocent of this business, and later he was twice ordered to investigate the matter.[4]

---

1   Sources for the life of Godwin include his acquaintance Sir John Harington's notice (British Library MS Add. 46370, fol. 44r and see p. 13 n. 2 below); Thomas Fuller, *The History of the Worthies of England* (London: Thomas Williams, 1662), 284; Anthony Wood, *Athenae Oxonienses*, ed. Philip Bliss, 4 vols. (London: Rivington *et al.*, 1813-20), 2.555-59, 882; Bodleian Library MS Gough Eccl. Top. 52, life (1734) by Thomas Delafield, following a printed copy of Godwin's *Catalogue*; Joseph Foster, *Alumni Oxonienses*, 3 vols. (Oxford, 1891, 1892), 2.584; D.R. Woolf, "Godwin, Francis," in *ODNB*. He had at least three brothers and three sisters. His grandson is cited from Bodleian Library MS Tanner 36, fol. 16, letter of 23 April 1681.

2   Roger Lea/Ley, *Gesta Britannica praesertim Anglorum* (1664), British Library MS Stowe 76, fol. 245r-v.

3   Mrs Reginald Lane Poole, *A Catalogue of Portraits in the Possession of the University, Colleges, City, and County of Oxford*, 3 vols. (Oxford: Clarendon Press, 1912-25), 2.20-22, 3.22; John Jones, *Portraits of Balliol College* (n.p., 1990), portrait numbers 51-53.

4   Phyllis M. Hembry, "The Death of Thomas Godwyn, Bishop of Bath and Wells," *Proceedings of the Somersetshire Archaeological and* (Continued)

Francis, born in Hannington in Northamptonshire, was the second son of Thomas and was to become the first Elizabethan bishop younger than Elizabeth herself.[1] He too went to Oxford, to Christ Church, where in 1578 he was elected to a junior Studentship, graduating as a Bachelor of Arts in 1581 and proceeding to his Master of Arts in 1584. If he attended the geography lecture in the college, his tutor would have been none other than the celebrated geographical editor Richard Hakluyt (1552-1616).[2] A hard-working scholar, Godwin then went into the church, attaining the higher degrees of Bachelor (1594) and then Doctor of Divinity (1596).[3] In 1586 he had been appointed prebendary of St Decumans, in the cathedral church of Wells, and was made subdean of Exeter the following year; various other ecclesiastical appointments accrued. At this time Godwin presumably developed his taste for antiquities, and in 1590 he accompanied William Camden on a historical foray into Wales; he is numbered by Camden's biographer as among the more famous antiquary's closest friends.[4] In the *Britannia*, Camden salutes Godwin as a practising if amateur antiquary, "a passing great lover of venerable Antiquity and of all good Literature."[5]

Early in the 1590s, Godwin started compiling a biographical register of all the English bishops from the beginning of Christianity in Britain to the current day. This appeared finally in 1601, Godwin excusing his passion for "the study of histories and antiquities" as "somewhat greater, then was needfull for a man

---

Natural History Society 96 (1951): 78-107. Thomas's motto suggests that word-play was a family trait: "Godwyn - wyn God wyn all" (98).

1 MS Stowe 76, fol. 245v.

2 Lesley B. Cormack, *Charting an Empire: Geography at the English Universities 1580-1620* (Chicago and London: U of Chicago P, 1997), 30, 45, 59-62.

3 Anthony Wood, *Fasti Oxonienses*, ed. Philip Bliss, 2 vols. (London: Rivington et al., 1813-20), 1.215, 224, 263, 271.

4 Thomas Smith, *V. Cl. Gulielmi Camdeni et Illustrium Virorum Ad G. Camdenum Epistolae* (London: Richard Chiswell, 1691), lxxiv; Smith also printed two letters from Godwin to Camden (pp. 109, 308, from British Library, MS Cotton Julius C. V, fols. 57v, 197v); and see MS Cotton Julius F. VI, fols. 296r-300v for further letters. Godwin's name does not however appear in the earliest lists of the London-based Society of Antiquaries (British Library MS Stowe 1045, fols. 4v, 5r), although the presence of a MS of his *Annales* in the Cotton Library, the hub of antiquarian scholarship in the earlier seventeenth century, may be significant; see p. 13 n. 6 below.

5 William Camden, *Britain*, trans. Philémon Holland (London: George Bishop and John Norton, 1610), 637.

that had dedicated himselfe and his labours unto the seruice of Gods church in the Ministery."[1] The *Catalogue* won Godwin immediate if not immediately lucrative preferment, as he was promoted to the very poor see of Llandaff in the same year.[2] Godwin republished the catalogue with additions in 1615, but the press made a mangle of it, and of the two editions the first remained the most reliable. The next year a corrected translation into Latin appeared, in which Godwin took occasion in the article on himself to complain about the second English edition, with its "multis ... flagitantibus."[3] This publication exposed Godwin's work to the international market and aided his translation to the bishopric of Hereford in late 1617, where he succeeded Robert Bennet, a zealous suppressor of Catholic recusants.[4] Hereford was a richer establishment, and it also boasted a celebrated library dating back to the eighth century, containing (as it still does) many important manuscripts.[5] In addition to the publication of the Latin *De Præsulibus*, 1616 also saw the publication of Godwin's *Rerum Anglicarum ... Annales*, a chronicle in the vein of Camden of the reigns of Henry VIII, Mary I, and Edward VI.[6] This was not as weighty a work as Godwin had

---

1 Godwin, *A Catalogue of the Bishops of England* (London: George Bishop, 1601), sg. [A3]r.

2 Harington is back-handed: "Doctr Francis Godwin hauing yt yeare newly published this worke, and the same being in great request, & highly commended to ye Queene for a godly, learned, & necessarie worke, shee gaue him presently this bishoprick, not full two months vacant, & would as willingly haue giuen him a much better in her owne disposition, as maie well appeare in that shee gaue doctor Cooper ye byshoprick of Lincoln only for making a dictionarie, or rather but for mending yt which Sr Thomas Elyot had made before" (British Library, MS Add. 46370, fol. 44r).

3 Godwin, *De Præsulibus* (London: John Bill, 1616), 642.

4 It seems initially that Godwin was tipped for Dean of York, as John Chamberlain reported to Sir Dudley Carleton in January 1617: letter quoted in John Maclean, ed., *Letters from George Lord Carew to Sir Thomas Roe, Ambassador to the Court of the Great Mogul 1615-1617* (London: Camden Society, 1860), 88, note b.

5 F.C. Morgan, *Hereford Cathedral Library* (Hereford: The Cathedral, 1958), 7; R.A.B. Mynors and R.M. Thomson, *Catalogue of the Manuscripts of Hereford Cathedral Library* (Cambridge: D.S. Brewer, 1993), xv-xxvi.

6 There is a fair manuscript of this work: British Library MS Cotton Titus C. XI; the title of the work is said to be in William Dugdale's hand. The copy itself is not a printer's copy and appears to be scribal: compare the autograph inserts for a revision of the work preserved in the Scudamore Papers, British Library, MS Add. 45140, fols. 6r-9v.

hoped, although it was soon being recommended as part of the accepted cursus of national historiography.[1] It was popular, reprinted in London in 1628, followed by a translation into French in 1647, and a continental edition of the Latin text ("nunc primùm editi" ["now first published"]!) from the Hague in 1653—although the continentals seemed largely unaware of who had written the original. Godwin's son Morgan also translated the *Annales* into English in 1630, reprinted in 1675 and 1676, this last impression coupled with Francis Bacon's far superior *History of the Reign of King Henry VII*.

Godwin remained Bishop of Hereford until his death in 1633, occupying himself in ecclesiastical matters—and in nepotism, as we shall see below.[2] Despite his promise at the conclusion of the *Annales* that he would continue into the reign of Elizabeth, he published no further significant historical works. Evidence from George Hakewill's *Apologie for the Power and Providence of God*, however, demonstrates that Godwin was working in the late 1620s on Roman coinage values.[3] Godwin was also named early in the long printed list of recipients—in reality a begging letter—produced to accompany John Minsheu's polyglot etymologicon *Ductor in Linguas* (1617), but as the list is not strictly a subscribers' list we cannot tell if Godwin did indeed finance this notable philological venture. Godwin's own library must have been large, but it no longer survives as a collection.[4]

Otherwise Godwin lived a professional and family life in Hereford. Some time in the early 1590s he had married a daughter of

---

1 D.R. Woolf, *The Idea of History in Early Stuart England* (Toronto: U of Toronto P, 1990), 125-28; Degory Wheare, *De ratione et methodo legendi historias dissertatio* (Oxford: John Lichfield, 1625), 54.

2 Kenneth Fincham, *Prelate as Pastor: The Episcopate of James* (Oxford: Clarendon P, 1990), 60, 321; Kenneth Fincham, ed., *Visitation Articles and Injunctions of the Church of England Vol. 1* (Woodbridge: The Boydell Press/Church of England Record Society, 1986), 152.

3 George Hakewill, *An Apologie for the Power and Providence of God*, 2nd ed. (Oxford: printed by William Turner, 1630), sgs. Yy2v-YY3r, Aaa6v, Bbb3v-Bbb4v; coinage paper shifted to the front of the volume in the 3rd ed. (Oxford: printed by William Turner, 1635), sgs. [b6]v, e1v-e3r. Sg. Zz1v of the 1630 edition notes the great new discovery of the *Nuncius Inanimatus*.

4 David Pearson, "The Libraries of English Bishops 1600-1640," *The Library* (6th series) 14 (1992): 221-57, at 231, 241, and see p. 125 n. 2 below. Godwin appears to have died intestate; Pearson notes that administration of the estate was granted to Godwin's daughter in 1633.

John Wolton, Bishop of Exeter (c. 1537-94), and the couple had had at least six children. His sons largely joined the family business: amongst their various appointments, Thomas Godwin became vicar of Newland, Gloucestershire; Morgan, who trained as a civilian, archdeacon of Shrewsbury; Charles held a benefice at Monmouth; but Paul was apprenticed to John Bill, the powerful London stationer and printer to the King. (This, as we shall see, provides an important hint concerning the posthumous publication of Godwin's work.) Godwin's nepotism proved an irritation. In 1625 his son Thomas had to be ejected from the Chancellorship of Hereford on the grounds of inappropriate qualification.[1] A decade earlier, as Bishop of Llandaff, Godwin had appointed his son-in-law to the Chancellorship of that diocese, despite the fact that, as Godwin knew, his son-in-law was lying about his qualifications in civil law. Doctors' Commons petitioned James I in protest, and Godwin was forced to sack his incumbent.[2] In 1627 Godwin was also apologising to the government for failing to apprehend two Catholic priests in his diocese; Godwin claimed the order to do so had arrived seven weeks late, allowing the priests ample time to vanish. Overall, Godwin does not appear to have been the most assiduous of diocesans, and his children did not manage to continue the episcopal line, most of them falling on hard times with the collapse of the Laudian church. In the 1680s Godwin's grandson Morgan, however, published some interesting works on evangelising Negro slaves.

Godwin passed the last years of his life as an ill man; as he wrote to Camden in as early as 1620, they were both growing "old and sickly."[3] But it is to this period, and not to his youthful student days, that the work for which he is now best known, *The Man in the Moone*, must be assigned. Fuller claimed that Godwin was "a good *Man*, grave *Divine*, skilful *Mathematician*, pure *Latinist*, and incomparable *Historian*."[4] The detail about mathematics is interesting, as it chimes with Godwin's interests in mensuration and astronomy in *The Man in the Moone*. No doubt much of the basis of such learning was acquired in Godwin's student days. But *The Man in the* Moone makes use

---

1   See the *Calendar of State Papers Domestic* (22 November 1625); Fincham, *Prelate as Pastor*, 164.
2   Brian P. Levack, *The Civil Lawyers in England 1603-1641: A Political Study* (Oxford: Clarendon P, 1973), 63-64.
3   Smith, *V. Cl. Guilielmi Camdeni*, 308.
4   Fuller, *The History of the Worthies of England*, 284.

of texts published perhaps as late as 1628, when Godwin was in his late sixties. Godwin's posthumous reputation was high, although not as stratospheric as Wood's later comparison of Godwin with Selden would have it. Historians used his work as a foundation for their own research well into the eighteenth century. Even in Godwin's own lifetime the Catalogue was used as a base text for further productions, notably the "Supplie" of Sir John Harington, a composite volume presented by Harington to Prince Henry in 1608, in which Godwin's printed text was reannotated by hand, and followed by indexes of these annotations and then Harington's own manuscript expansion of Godwin's catalogue to the year 1608.[1] Godwin also inspired an Irish imitator, James Ware (1594-1666), who published similar catalogues of the Irish clergy.[2] He was appropriated too by William Prynne as an authority, ironically, for how badly some former bishops had behaved, and hence Prynne used a catalogue written originally to bolster the claims of the English episcopal Church to undermine them.[3] Godwin's catalogue was republished as late as 1743 at Cambridge in a large folio edition, with emendations and additions up to that time. But the work that has had the longest influence, cropping up in dozens of writers from Aphra Behn to H.G. Wells, is the slight, posthumous *Man in the Moone*, and today it has a much more immediate claim to fame than can be made on behalf of any of Godwin's antiquarian or historical works. His writing on codes and moon travel also excited the young John Wilkins (see Appendix H), future founding father of the Royal Society, and this work would shape Wilkins's enduring interests—the new astronomy, and the possibility of constructing an artificial language. It would have surprised Godwin's contemporaries that it was this aspect of Godwin's work that was to endure; they had

---

1   British Library, Royal MS 17 B XXII. The imperfect autograph of Harington's additions is British Library MS Add. 46370, first printed 1653 (Harington supplies a biography of Godwin himself: fols. 43v-45v). See Jason Scott-Warren, *Sir John Harington and the Book as Gift* (Oxford: Oxford UP, 2001), 219-22, 226-27. The work has been edited with an introduction by R.H. Miller (Potomac, MD: Studia Humanitatis, 1979).

2   James Ware, *De Praesulibus Lageniae* (Dublin: Societas Bibliopolarum, 1628); *De Praesulibus Hiberniae Commentarius* (Dublin: Samuel Dancer, 1665).

3   William Prynne, *The Antipathie of the English Lordly Prelacie* (London: Michael Sparke, 1641), e.g., 3, 68, 83, 187, etc.

little idea the learned bishop was occupying his last years with such fripperies.[1]

Date and Sources

When Francis Godwin wrote *The Man in the Moone* is not obvious. The persistent assumption[2] that it is a student work (hence c. 1578-84) is quite impossible, as Domingo mentions in passing real events such as the battle off the Isle of Pines (1596) and concludes in China in late 1601 in the company of identifiable members of the Jesuit Mission. The work's scientific awareness also places it squarely in a seventeenth-century context: the moon has spots invisible to the unaided eye; diurnal rotation of the earth can be viewed from space; the fall of bodies to the earth may be compared to the attractive force of the loadstone; this attraction is exerted by the moon too; lunar attraction is weaker than that of the earth, because the moon is smaller; and such attraction varies with distance.[3] Godwin's fiction thus follows firmly in the wake of William Gilbert's *De Magnete* (1600), and probably Bacon's posthumous *Sylva Sylvarum* (1627) which also discusses flying by means of birds.[4] We might add that Godwin's mention of "Motes in the sun" refers to sunspots, another post-telescopic discovery of around 1611.[5] Flying by means of birds, however, was an idea as old as the myth of Alexander the Great's bird-powered flight, and we might

---

1 We may note, however, an intriguing entry into the Benefactors' Book of Sion College Library in London, made in 1630. A man calling himself simply "Anonymus Musophilus" donated "The Description of the King-dome of China. MS. fol. with the manners thereof," "Benedictus de Re Chimica MS 4°," and "Nuntius inanimatus, de Philosophia. MS 4°." Surely this was none other than Godwin himself, making a last, typically clandestine gesture! Sion College Library (deposited in London, Lambeth Palace Library), Benefactors' Book, 1629-1982 [Arc L 40.2/F 64], p. 10.

2 Wood, *Athenae Oxonienses*, 2.558, repeated as recently as *The Oxford Dictionary of National Biography*.

3 Grant McColley, "The Date of Godwin's 'Domingo Gonsales,'" *Modern Philology* 35 (1937): 47-60; Anke Janssen, *Francis Godwins "The Man in the Moone": Die Entdeckung des Romans als Medium der Auseinandersetzung mit Zeitproblemen* (Frankfurt: Peter Lang, 1981), 21-25.

4 Francis Bacon, *Sylva Sylvarum* (London: William Lee, 1627), 11-12, 235. We might note, though, that Bacon's discussion itself derives from Strabo, *Geography*, 10.2.9.

5 Martin Beech, "Resolving some Chronological Issues in Bishop Godwin's *The Man in the Moone*," *The Observatory* 121 (2001): 255-59.

compare a boast in Robert Greene's *Friar Bacon and Friar Bungay*, acted in 1589, about flying by geese:

> Marrie sir, Ile send to the Ile of Eely for foure or fiue dozen of Geese, and Ile haue them tide six and six together with whipcord, Now vpon their backes will I haue a faire field bed, with a Canapie, and so when it is my pleasure Ile flee into what place I please; this will be easie.[1]

As noted, Godwin's knowledge of China also serves as a dating agent. Gonsales' concluding Chinese adventure derives its detail ultimately from accounts such as the 1588 English translation of Juan Gonzáles de Mendoza's *Historie of the Great and Mightie Kingdome of China*, and possibly Nicholas Trigault's Latin redaction of Matteo Ricci's journals, *De Expeditione Christiana apud Sinos* (1615). Godwin may have read the former.[2] But if Godwin read the relevant sections of Trigault, he was most likely to have done so in the popular redaction of Samuel Purchas, *Purchas his Pilgrimes* (1625). Indeed, Purchas also redacted other accounts of China, notably that of the Jesuit missionary Diego Pantoja, a colleague of Ricci's, who started out teaching harpsichord to the Chinese Emperor's eunuchs and ended up in charge of the mission to Japan.[3] Gonsales names "*Pantoja*" on the final page of his account (126) as his confidant, and we might also note that Pantoja's letter home was dated 1602, the very year in which *The Man in the Moone* concludes. Gonsales names a further genuine Jesuit missionary, Francesco Pasio ("Father *Pacio*" [38]), likewise a figure who appears in Purchas.[4] By contrast, Gonsales does not mention the famous Matteo Ricci, on whose papers Trigault's book was based, at all. It is proposed therefore that Pantoja in Purchas (potentially backed up by other travel writers such as Jan Huygen

---

1 Robert Greene, *The Honorable Historie of Frier Bacon, and Frier Bongay* (London: Edward White, 1594), sg. C2v.

2 Takao Shimada, "Gonzáles de Mendoza's *Historie* as a possible source for Godwin's *Man in the Moone*," *Notes and Queries* 34 (1987): 314-15, argues that Godwin's knowledge of an alternative name for Peking, "Suntien," proved his knowledge of Mendoza's text. But in fact "Suntien" was also available in Purchas, as the relevant note below shows.

3 Samuel Purchas, *Purchas His Pilgrimes*, 4 vols. (London: Henry Fetherstone, 1625), 3.166-209, 316-411, especially 350-79 (Pantoja's letter); Joyce Lindorff, "Missionaries, Keyboards and Musical Exchange in the Ming and Qing Courts," *Early Music* 32 (2004): 403-12, at 405. We might note that Pantoja's letter was available in Spanish (1605) and French (1607), but Godwin surely just went to Purchas.

4 Purchas, *Pilgrimes*, 3.321-22.

van Linschoten and Richard Hakluyt)[1] provided Godwin with everything he needed for the terrestrial prelude and postlude to his lunar journey, although as we have seen Godwin may have owned a manuscript "Description of the Kingdom of China" too.[2] If this is correct, then 1625 becomes the *a quo* date of composition, and as Beech put it, *The Man in the Moone* was the work not of a young student, but of "the solemn head of a quinquagenerian Bishop."[3]

Godwin's physics, therefore, relies on William Gilbert's *De Magnete* (1600) and his knowledge of China probably on Samuel Purchas (1625). A third source will allow us to propose an even more precise date of composition. Godwin's Christ Church was—closely followed by New College—the centre for Oxonian geographical scholarship in the period, with a library well stocked for such study.[4] William Camden, the greatest of English chorographers, had been a member, as had Richard Verstegen the Saxon scholar, Edmund Gunter the geometer, and Richard Hakluyt the geographical anthologist. And although not usually thought of as a geographer, the most famous Christ Church literary figure of the years of Godwin's maturity steeped himself in geographical literature: Robert Burton (1577-1640), whose celebrated *Anatomy of Melancholy* was published in four ever-expanding editions within Godwin's lifetime (1621, 1624, 1628, 1632). One section in particular appears to have caught Godwin's eye: the "Digression of Ayre," in which Burton encyclopaedically rehearsed contemporary astronomical hypotheses. Indeed, it is possible that Godwin took his literary rise from Burton, who mused that

> ... some new fangled wits, me thinks, should some time or other finde out: or if that may not be; yet with a *Galelies* glasse, or *Icaro-menippus* wings in *Lucian*, command the Spheares and Heauens, & see what is done amongst them.[5]

---

1 See further Jan Huygen van Linschoten, *Discours of Voyages into the Easte and West Indies* (London: John Wolfe, [1598]), 37-44; Richard Hakluyt, *The Principal Navigations*, 2 vols. (London: George Bishop *et al.*, 1599-[1600]), 2.68-80, 88-98.

2 See p. 17 n. 1 above.

3 Beech 259.

4 Cormack, *Charting an Empire*, 59-66, with a booklist of contemporary holdings at 234-36.

5 Robert Burton, *The Anatomy of Melancholy*, ed. Thomas C. Faulkner *et al.*, 6 vols. (Oxford: Clarendon Press, 1989-2000), 2.2.3.1 (2.48). Throughout, Burton is cited in the form partition/section/member/subsection, followed in brackets by volume and page references keyed to the Clarendon edition, but the text quoted unless otherwise indicated is the 1628 edition. See Appendix G for an extract from Burton's "Digression of Ayre."

Godwin indeed put on the Hellenistic ironist Lucian's "*Icaro-menippus* wings"; that is, he explored the heavens via fiction rather than the telescope.

Burton's "Digression," which expanded significantly between the four editions available to Godwin, contains many details that crop up in Godwin too, including a number not immediately pertinent to his astronomical context—the height of El Pico, bird migration, seasonal somnulence, Tenerife, locust swarms, devils in the air, and so forth. Individually, many such details are of course not convincing markers of genetic debt. Yet some of the astronomical details do get us closer to such an assertion, notably the exact figures in both texts on the planetary periods:

> Burton: "and so the Planets, *Saturne* in 30 yeares absolues his sole and proper motion, *Iupiter* in 12. *Mars*, in 3, &c." compared to the "30 or 26 thousand yeares" required for the firmament.
>
> Godwin: "The *Moone* performeth it in 27 daies; the *Sunne*, *Venus*, and *Mercury* in a Yeare or thereabouts, *Mars* in 3 Yeare, *Jupiter* in twelve Yeares, and *Saturne* in 30" compared to "no lesse, I trowe, they say, then 30 thousand" for the firmament.[1]

Had Godwin taken these figures from Gilbert, say, he would instead have produced a Martian period of two years.[2] This passage only occurred in the 1628 and subsequent editions of Burton, and so were the general case of influence to be proved, this is the most likely edition Godwin consulted, and hence the most accurate and indeed the latest date marker we have.[3]

The conclusive marker of genetic debt happens to illuminate some crucial literary aspects of Godwin's text too. Burton's text is by nature derivative, and the figures for planetary periods can be found reproduced in other vernacular texts, such as Josuah Sylvester's popular translation of the French hexameral epic of Du Bartas.[4] But one anecdote reported in both texts—and con-

---

1 Page references to *The Man in the Moone* are to the original pagination, indicated in the text of this edition by numbers in square brackets. Burton, *Anatomy*, 3.1.2.2. (2.51); Godwin, *Man in the Moone*, 59.

2 William Gilbert, *De Magnete* (London: Peter Short, 1600), 6.3. Gilbert is cited throughout by book and chapter.

3 Godwin's debt to Burton is more fully excavated in William Poole, "The Origins of Francis Godwin's *The Man in the Moone* (1638)," *Philological Quarterly* 84 (2005): 189-210.

4 Josuah Sylvester, *Bartas: his Devine Weekes and Workes* (London: Humfrey Lownes, 1605), 127-28.

textually incongruous in both locations—settles the matter. This is the account of the Green Children of Woolpit. In the middle of his "Digression," Burton recalls the account preserved in the twelfth-century chronicler William of Newburgh's *Rerum Anglicarum* of two green children, a boy and a girl, found in a cave in East Anglia in the reign of King Stephen. Green from head to toe, the children spoke an unknown language and wore clothes of an unknown material. Later in life the girl, who remained in the community and learned English, explained that they were from "the land [*terra*] of Saint Martin, who in the land of our birth is held in the highest veneration." The land of the Green Children was Christian, but a place where the sun barely offered any light at all, although they could see a certain lucid body not far off, separated by water from their own *terra*.[1]

Burton introduces these green children in the context of alien life and, unlike William of Newburgh, whom he cites as his authority, states that they "fell from Heauen." He does not tell us anything else about them. But Godwin marked Burton's reference carefully and wove it into his fiction, where Gonsales declares that the green children reported by the twelfth-century chronicler are in truth the rejects of the lunar society Gonsales has just discovered (106). Godwin also derived from the chronicler the curious detail in *The Man in the Moone* that the Lunars venerate "*Martinus*," their term for God (83). Again, the green children's unknown fabric is the source for the similarly mysterious clothing of Godwin's Lunars, which resists Gonsales' attempts to describe it (71). William Camden, Godwin's friend and fellow antiquary, had also recalled the tale in passing in his *Britannia*, and Godwin certainly read William of Newburgh in the course of his antiquarian work.[2] But it is the coupling in both Burton and Godwin of contemporary astronomical debate with the twelfth-century anecdote that points overwhelmingly to genetic debt, and the chronology of printing permits such a borrowing to run only from Burton to Godwin. Camden's own comment in the *Britannia* chimes interestingly with Burton's mention of Lucian's *Icaromenippus* above: "*Nubrigensis* ... hath told as pretty and formall a tale of this place, as is that fable called

---

1   Burton, *Anatomy*, 3.1.2.2. (2.52); for William of Newburgh see Appendix C.

2   Camden, *Britain*, 463; e.g., Godwin, *The Succession of the Bishops of England* (London, 1625), 546 (where it is noted that William was very short).

the TRVE NARRATION of *Lucian.*" Yet William's most obvious meaning—and as he was later interpreted by the Jesuit polymath Athanasius Kircher, and by the antiquary John Aubrey commenting on his friend Edmund Halley's hypothesis of a habitable earth-inside-the-earth[1]—is the possibility of subterranean civilisation. But both Lucian's *Icaromenippus* and *True History* feature space-flight and a lunar visitation, so in both Camden and Burton the Green Children are given a space-age interpretation: they have become extraterrestrials. The *amnis* which separates the *terra* of the Green Children from the *terra* shining in the distance is no longer a river, but interplanetary space.

The use of William of Newburgh has a final significance. William's critical attitude has long been celebrated, especially his attack on the credibility of Geoffrey of Monmouth, whom he branded in the Prologue to his own history as a *fabulator* and a weaver of laughable fictions.[2] By contrast, William is scrupulously careful to register doubt in his narrative, and nowhere more so than in his chapter on the Green Children. He opens his account thus:

> And indeed I hesitated for a long time over this matter even though it was reported by many people, as it seemed to me that it was ridiculous to believe a thing of no or of the most obscure reason. Yet I was overwhelmed by the weight of so many and such witnesses, so that I am compelled to believe and to marvel, because I am not able by any strength of mind to understand or to investigate this matter.

He also partitions the Green Children off from his following chapter on further marvels judged to be less remarkable, the kinds of phenomena that wicked angels caused (live toads discovered in the middle of rocks, banquets inside hills, and so forth). Throughout his chronicle William also recounts several stories about British zombies, which have been paralleled to Scandinavian accounts, and William had Norwegian con-

---

1 Athanasius Kircher, *Mundus Subterraneus*, 2 vols. (Amsterdam: J.J. van Waesberge, 1678), 2.120-22; Aubrey cited from Bodleian Library, MS Aubrey 1, fol. 88v; N. Kollerstrom, "The Hollow World of Edmund Halley," *Journal for the History of Astronomy* 23 (1992): 185-92.

2 Antonia Gransden, *Historical Writing in England c. 550-c. 1307* (London: Routledge, 1996 [1974]), 263-68; N.F. Partner, *Serious Entertainments: The Writing of History in Twelfth Century England* (Chicago: U of Chicago P, 1977), 51-113.

tacts.[1] But the Green Children baffled William: "the frailty of our intelligence is quite incapable of unearthing this," he confessed.

William's critical attitude was not universally appreciated, and despite his "thunderclap" against Geoffrey's Arthurian fictions, some sixteenth-century English antiquaries riposted by blasting William's unpatriotic scepticism.[2] John Bale included William in his bibliography of English writers under the name "Gulielmus Petyte" or "Parvus"—that is, William the Little, a sobriquet deriving from the report that, like Domingo Gonsales, he was a very short man. Bale also recorded that despite Polydore Vergil's praise of this *veridicus auctor* he was sharply criticised by John Leland because of his dispraise of Geoffrey. As we have seen, William Camden dismissed William's Green Children as a "tale," without mentioning William's hesitations. Given that a major concern of *The Man in the Moone* is the interplay between fiction and fact, and what kind of testimony we can trust, William's careful attention to testimony when assessing the story of the Green Children as well as his mixed fortunes in sixteenth-century England become pertinent. William's critical attitude as much as his content proves an important contribution to Godwin's fiction, which is all the more subtle for it.

We can therefore confidently date *The Man in the Moone* to the last decade of Godwin's life, and most probably to after 1628, the publication date of Burton's third edition. Yet this study of dating also allows us to glimpse Godwin at work. Godwin knew of the Green Children from his research as an antiquary. He will also have known that his friend William Camden had discussed and dismissed the tale, and that Camden's fleeting remark had associated the Green Children with tales of lunar as opposed to subterranean civilisation. Many years later Godwin sat down to compose his fiction. In terms of physics and astronomy, he brought to his work an enthusiasm for Gilbertian magnetism, an enthusiasm that perhaps did not require Gilbert's folio itself but may have rested either on Mark Ridley's *Short Treatise of Magnet-*

---

1   Bruce Dickins, "A Yorkshire Chronicler (William of Newburgh)," *Transactions of the Yorkshire Dialect Society* 5, part 35 (1934): 15-26, at 22-26. But Dickins notes that these anecdotes (unlike the account of the Green Children and the subsequent chapter on marvels) were cut from the 1567 Antwerp edition, probably the edition Godwin used.

2   T.D. Kendrick, *British Antiquity* (New York: Barnes & Noble; London: Methuen, 1970 [1950]), 13. See 87 and 136 for two examples of sixteenth-century slander.

icall Bodies and Motions (1613; see Appendix F), largely Gilbert in English, or recent geographical textbooks such as Nathanael [sic] Carpenter's Gilbertian *Geography Delineated* (1625), or on vague memory alone. Godwin recalled also perhaps Galileo's sensational *Sidereus Nuncius* (1610) or maybe just Kepler's *Dissertatio cum Nuncio Sidereo* (1610), the text in which Kepler had mooted the idea that the moon and other worlds were inhabited, a question Galileo had prudently avoided.[1] Godwin will have had on his desk, however, various collections of travellers' tales, possibly that of Hakluyt, probably that of Linschoten, certainly Purchas, collections that supplied detail for Domingo's voyages among the islands off the coast of Africa as well as his experiences in China. But what drove him to write was the invitation to do so that he found in Burton. And when he came across the reference to the Green Children, he realised that he could make good fictional capital on Camden's old remark. Indeed, Godwin must have gone back to William's text itself in order to refresh his memory on some other details concerning the Green Children—their clothing, and their reverence of "Martinus," for instance—and to integrate them into his lunar fiction. It seems, then, that the origins of English science fiction are potentially to be sought in conversations between two Christ Church antiquaries, and the subsequent reading of one of them in a popular literary encyclopaedia of melancholy compiled by a younger Student [sic] of their old college. *The Man in the Moone*, then, is not quite as removed from Godwin's university days and his subsequent antiquarian work as it may at first seem.

Genres

The Man in the Moon

We cannot tell if *The Man in the Moone* is an authorial title, but the accompanying subtitle and illustration of a man in an intricate flying-contraption, with the moon above him, would signal to a contemporary reader at once that the title does not herald what it otherwise might easily have done: that this was to be a tale of the "Mon in þe mone" of the Middle English lyric, bearing thorns in his fork; or alternatively a dipsomaniacal farce, as the

---

1 Galileo Galilei, *Sidereus Nuncius, or the Sidereal Messenger*, ed. and trans. Albert Van Helden (Chicago: U of Chicago P, 1989); Johannes Kepler, *Kepler's Conversation with the Starry Messenger*, ed. and trans. Edward Rosen (New York: Johnson Reprint Corporation, 1965).

man in the moon was also the god of drunkards, and the name of at least three London taverns.[1] Nor are we are dealing with a work such as John Lyly's *Endimion, The Man in the Moon* (first acted in 1588, printed in 1591), a play of pagan deities uninterested in observational astronomy, and opening on some conventional allusions to Aristotelian cosmology. Lyly followed this up in 1597 with *The Woman in the Moone*, a similar mixture of pastoral and astronomical personification, opening with Nature herself declaring, "*Nature* descends from farre aboue the spheeres/To frolick heere in fayre *Vtopia*."[2] We move slightly closer to real astronomical interest with Michael Drayton's "The Man in the Moone" (1606), a poem in rhyming couplets in which, although the main text allegorises the moon into a maiden who wanders among men, "huntreslike" or as a "sheperdesse," the attendant shoulder-notes occasionally strip back the allegory to an astronomical base. Thus the moon's inconstancy is really "due to its varying situation with respect to the sun," whereby "it takes on varying appearances."[3] But the astronomical interest in Drayton's poem is incidental.

A more pertinent analogue is Ben Jonson's *News from the New World Discover'd in the Moone*, a masque first presented before King James on Twelfth Night, 1620. Jonson was fascinated by the new lore of the "Trunk":

Fact[or] ... but to your News Gentlemen, whence come they?
1 *Her*[ald] From the Moon, ours Sir.
Fact[or] From the Moon! which way? by Sea? or by Land?
1 *Her*[ald] By Moon-shine, a nearer way I take it.
Print[er] Oh by a Trunk! I know it, a thing no bigger than a Flute-case; A Neighbour of mine, a Spectacle-maker, has drawn the Moon through it at the bore of a Whistle, and made it as

1 Timothy Harley, *Moon Lore* (Wakefield: EP Publishing Limited, 1973 [1885]), esp. 5-52; Robert J. Menner, "The Man in the Moon and Hedging," *JEGP* 48 (1949): 1-14; Raymond Urban, "Why Caliban Worships the Man in the Moon," *Shakespeare Quarterly* 27 (1976): 203-05; Ewen A. Whitaker, *Mapping and Naming the Moon* (Cambridge: Cambridge UP, 1999), ch. 1; David Cressy, "Early Modern Space Travel and the English Man in the Moon," *American Historical Review* 111 (2006): 961-82.

2 John Lyly, *Endimion, The Man in the Moone* (London: for the widow Broome, 1591); *The Woman in the Moone* (London: William Jones, 1597), sg. A2r.

3 Michael Drayton, *Poems Lyrick and Pastorall* (London: N.L. and I. Flasket, [1606]), sgs. H1r-I1v, here sg. H2r (*Pro vario ad solem aspectu varias induit figuras*). This is a revision of the 1595 "Endymion and Phoebe."

great as a Drum-head twenty times, and brought it within the length of this Room to me, I know not how often.[1]

This short masque also ends with an antimasque of "Volatees," or feathered, Lucianesque lunar inhabitants:

And when they ha' tasted the Springs of Pleasure enough, and bill'd, and kist, and are ready to come away; the She's only lay certain Eggs (for they are never with Child there,) and of those Eggs are disclosed a Race of Creatures like Men, but are indeed a sort of Fowl, in part covered with Feathers (they call 'em *Volatees*,) that hop from Island to Island ....[2]

This incidence of semi-fowl (compare Godwin's Gansas), island-hopping (Godwin's Lunars fly from place to place by means of fans), and also the idea elsewhere in Jonson's short masque of a "lunatique language" based on music (Godwin's Lunars likewise communicate in melodies) suggests Jonson's influence upon Godwin's fiction. The difficulty is that Jonson's masque was not published in Godwin's lifetime, and so either Godwin's physical presence at one of the many performances of this masque, or his access to a manuscript, must be supposed.[3]

Picaresque

The obvious generic precedent for Godwin's fiction, however, as we turn over its opening pages, is picaresque. This is how it struck one of its very earliest readers: "I thanke you for the Man in the

---

1 Ben Jonson, "News from the New World Discover'd in the Moon" in *The Works* (London: H. Herringman *et al.*, 1692), 610-13, here 611. For Jonson's debt to Lucian, see the commentary in C.H. Herford and Percy Simpson, eds., *Ben Jonson* (Oxford: Clarendon P, 1954), 10.596-604; Douglas Duncan, *Ben Jonson and the Lucianic Tradition* (Cambridge: Cambridge UP, 1979). On "Trunk," the term *telescopium* and hence the English *telescope* only gradually caught on in the seventeenth century, and was first used consistently in the *Sphaera Mundi* (1620) of Joseph Blancanus. The *OED*'s earliest citation is from 1619, and terms such as *optic glass, perspective, perspective glass, trunk, trunke-spectacle, trunk glass, perspicillium, conspicillium, mathematician's perspicil, occhiale, specillium,* and *penicillium* were simultaneously current (Grant McColley, "Joseph Blancanus and the adoption of our word 'Telescope,'" *Isis* 28 [1938]: 364-65).
2 Jonson, *Works*, 612.
3 Paul R. Sellin, "The Performances of Ben Jonson's 'Newes from the New World Discover'd in the Moone,'" *English Studies* 61 (1980): 491-97.

Moune," wrote Lady Brilliana Harley in 1638; "I had h[e]ard of the booke, but not seene it; by as much as I have looke vpon, I find it is some kine to Donqueshot [i.e. Don Quixote]."[1] The first Spanish "picaresque" novella, *Lazarillo de Tormes*, had appeared in 1554 in Burgos, Alcalá, and Antwerp and was soon translated into other European vernaculars, including English (1568, reprinted 1596, 1624). The picaresque, therefore, was readily available in England and in English throughout Godwin's life and had already exerted an influence on Elizabethan prose fiction. *Lazarillo*, a short text similar in length to *The Man in the Moone*, had featured the first literary appearance of the *picaro*, the wandering rascal who uses his wits to survive and to seek respectability. Lázaro, indeed, starts out from Domingo Gonsales' university town of Salamanca and journeys from city to city, changing masters as occasion suits or forces him, not hesitating to maim or delude as he goes. *Lazarillo* opens similarly to *The Man in the Moone*, with a statement of genealogy also involving a Gonsales: "Your worship shall vnderstand before all things that my name is *Lazaro de Tormes* son of *Thome Gonsales* & *Antona Petes* natiue of *Tessiares*, a village neere Salamanka." Gonsales himself, hopping from location to location, and abandoning one master for the Ducal court as soon as his fortunes allow, reminds one of Lázaro quitting one job "perceiuing my selfe then in apparrell like an honest man," and moving on to a more classy post.[2]

Nonetheless, these similarities prove to be short lived. For a start, Gonsales is carefully placed among real contemporaries engaged in the gruelling wars of independence in the Low Countries. (Godwin here probably borrowed his detail from the London-based Dutch historian Emmanuel Van Meteren's annalistic work; Godwin himself would write English history in this vein.) Next, Gonsales, despite his fortunes, is a real nobleman, and he never lets the reader forget it. And although he is occasionally callous—he shoots a captive dead in battle and claims his goods as spoils—Gonsales is not really a rascal, and certainly not consistently so. Three times he laments being parted from his wife and children. Nor is he notably deceitful; much of *The Man in the Moone* rests upon Gonsales' insistence on his own eye-

---

1 Thomas Taylor Lewis, ed., *Letters of the Lady Brilliana Harley* (London: Camden Society, 1854), no. 14; reference noted by Janssen, *Francis Godwins "The Man in the Moone"*, 85, 126-27.
2 [?Diego Hurtado de Mendoza], *The Plesant Historie of Lazarillo de Tormes a Spaniarde*, trans. David Rouland (London: printed by Abel Jeffes, 1596), sgs. [A3]v, [G4]v.

witness reliability and transparency of conduct, at least toward the reader. *The Man in the Moone* does not sustain picaresque, then, but it sounds enough quasi-picaresque notes in its opening stages to evoke such a generic context, and thus to encourage the reader to register its departure from that context, just as Gonsales departs from Europe. Indeed, as has been argued, *The Man in the Moone* is thus more generically sophisticated than one of its most famed progeny, Cyrano's *Histoire Comique*, which reinstated and embraced picaresque, thereby upsetting Godwin's delicate counterpoint and his sense of generic transformation.[1]

Travel

The Man in the Moone leaves the picaresque genre behind, then, and next moves into the territory of the traveller's narrative, before its lunar and Chinese utopias, as Gonsales becomes a trader, a cast-away, and then a cosmonaut. Godwin's use of travel writing needs no apology: the blending of travel narrative with fantastic voyage and the depiction of an ideal state had received classic treatment in Thomas More's *Utopia* (1516), which had mixed together the fantasy of Lucian and the philosophy of Plato with the new voyages of discovery, notably the *Four Voyages* of Amerigo Vespucci (undertaken between 1497 and 1504). Travel writing itself had to negotiate its own internal interplay between fact and fiction in order to establish its credentials as a species of scientific discourse, and this was in turn exploited by some writers of prose fiction for the purposes of forgery.[2]

Gonsales' voyages back from the east, where he has spent his mid-forties making his fortune in trade, follow the conventional sea-route around the Cape of Good Hope and on to the Pacific islands off the west coast of Africa, initially established by the

---

1 Robert Philmus, "Murder most Fowl: Butler's Edition of Francis Godwin," *Science Fiction Studies* 23 (1996): 260-69, at 260; Marie-Christine Pioffet, "Godwin et Cyrano: deux conceptions du voyage," *Canadian Review of Comparative Literature* 25.1/2 (1998): 144-57. Sustained picaresque is assumed by Thomas A. Copeland, "Francis Godwin's 'The Man in the Moone': A Picaresque Satire," *Extrapolation* 16 (1975): 156-63.

2 Joan-Pau Rubiés, "Travel Writing as a Genre: Facts, Fictions and the Invention of a Scientific Discourse in Early Modern Europe," *Journeys* 1 (1996): 5-35; Daniel Carey, "Henry Neville's Isle of Pines: Travel, Forgery, and the Problem of Genre," *Angelaki* 1 (1993): 23-39.

Portuguese as stopping-off points on their long voyages to and from the east. These islands were also open to the English by the later sixteenth century, and English readers would have been aware of the route and particularly of the crucial role that St. Helena played in it, an essential refuelling stop. Knowledge of Thomas Cavendish's 1566-68 circumnavigation was a point of national pride, and readers of Hakluyt's collections would perhaps find themselves soon looking for Thomas Pretty's account in the *Principal Navigations*. There they could read of Cavendish setting ashore at St Helena, and how he and his fellow crew visited the church there, hung with its unfamiliar Catholic tapestries, and adorned with images of the Virgin Mary.[1] Hakluyt's redactions were published from 1598, the same year in which the English translation of Jan Huygen van Linschoten's *Discours of Voyages into the Easte and West Indies* appeared: "Part navigation treatise, part geography, and part commercial espionage manual, this extraordinarily important book described Portuguese vulnerabilities in the Indonesian archipelago."[2] It also described the routes to and from the East, and Linschoten's recollections of the West African islands corroborated in many particulars what Cavendish and others had reported. By the time Linschoten visited St. Helena (in 1589, about a decade before Gonsales' incarceration), almost a century of colonial occupation had left some striking traces: Linschoten records, for example, that since 1510, visitors had carved their names into the fig trees. The subsequent growth of the fig trees expanded these signatures, so that the oldest names now bulged out from the trees, "euery letter being of the bignesse of a spanne."[3]

Finally, Gonsales' crash-landing in China in the last dozen or so pages of the work returns Gonsales to the world of men, but to what was regarded as one of the most remote and fascinating lands in it. China was dimly known to the Western reader through medieval accounts, but it had suddenly sprung into literary prominence with the receipt in the West of the letters and geographical works of the Jesuit China Mission. St. Francis Xavier had died on the island of Shangchuan in the year of Gonsales' birth, 1552; but he was succeeded a generation later by the

---

1 Hakluyt, *Principal Navigations*, 2.823.
2 Robert Markley, *The Far East and the English Imagination 1600-1730* (Cambridge: Cambridge UP, 2006), 33.
3 Linschoten, *Discours of Voyages into the Easte and West Indies*, 174.

famous Matteo Ricci, also born in 1552.[1] Ricci was the most celebrated of the Jesuits in China, but as Gonsales mentions meeting only the (genuine) Jesuit missionaries Pantoja and Pasio, as noted in the section on dating above this suggests that Godwin was more influenced by the diversity of Purchas's sheaf of reports on China than by any single account. What these reports revealed was an alien political structure, privileging not an aristocracy but a highly scholarly bureaucracy; and a geography of vast extent, served by regional spoken languages that were rumoured to function tonally, and a constant national written "real character," in which words stood for things.[2] Although Western commentators did not therefore regard China as a utopia in the positive sense—it was protested that the Chinese emphasis on rhetorical scholarship made them backwards in divinity and natural philosophy; and their language must be hugely difficult to master[3]—dreamers after language reform and a society that valued its intellectuals long looked to China for comfort and inspiration. This was to culminate in an outlandish hypothesis that would have charmed Godwin: in 1669 the architect John Webb published his *Historical Essay Endeavouring a Probability that the Language of the Empire of China is the Primitive Language*, a work which proposed that both China's language and political structure bore traces of the original Adamic wisdom.[4] Now Godwin's lunar inhabitants do seem rather Edenic in their effortless virtue; and his Chinese are certainly as civilised as they were rumoured to be. But—to turn to the last generic label we might be tempted to attach to Godwin—Godwin's text considered as a whole is not so much a utopia as a tripartite narrative that engages with three distinct, potentially

1   Three pertinent studies are William Appleton, *A Cycle of Cathay* (New York: Columbia UP, 1951); David E. Mungello, *Curious Land: Jesuit Accommodation and the Origins of Sinology* (Stuttgart: F. Steiner Verlag Wiesbadem, 1985); Liam Matthew Brockey, *Journey to the East: The Jesuit Mission to China 1579-1724* (Cambridge, MA, and London: Belknap, 2007). There is a modern translation of Trigault: Louis J. Gallacher, *China in the Sixteenth Century: The Journals of Matteo Ricci 1583-1610* (New York: Random House, 1953).

2   See the discussion below (pp. 44-46) for some comments on the Chinese languages as they relate to Godwin's imagined lunar speech.

3   The most influential such complaints were made by José Acosta, *The Naturall and Morall Historie of the East and West Indies* (London: Edward Blount and William Apsley, 1604), 440-44 (book 6, chapters 5-6).

4   Rachel Ramsey, "China and the Ideal of Order in John Webb's *An Historical Essay*," *Journal of the History of Ideas* 62 (2001): 483-503.

utopian zones, but none quite subduing the restless narrative drive of the wandering Spaniard. St. Helena the earthly paradise, the lunar Christian utopia, and the pagan Chinese metropolis are all left behind by the "great discoverer," whose text ends with him seeking, but perhaps never quite reaching, his home.

Chronology

The Man in the Moone is carefully situated in its contemporary setting, and this care extends to chronological specificity.[1] Gonsales is born in 1552 and goes to fight in the Low Countries in 1568, when he must therefore have been about sixteen. He arrives in Antwerp in 1569 and pursues his northern adventures until 1573, when he returns to Spain, now about 21, where, having come of age, he settles down to family life and to the business of trading. His flight to Lisbon is in 1596, after some 23 years of domestic peace, by which time he is 44 (1-9). All the historical events alluded to or participated in throughout these years mesh into his biography without flaw.

The chronology of Gonsales' trading mission is less specific but no less plausible: if Gonsales fled Lisbon after the skirmish off the Isle of Pines (11/21 March 1596),[2] then he sailed to the East Indies in the later part of that year. He sickened on his return voyage, stayed on St. Helena alone for a year, and then lived for a month with the crews of the passing boats. Hence their casting-off from St. Helena on Thursday 21 June 1599 (32)—an accurate date in the Julian calendar—suggests that he spent the latter half of 1596 and most of 1597-98 travelling to and trading with the Indies.

More precise are the dates to do with the actual moon voyage. Two months after setting out from St Helena on 21 June 1599 the fleet falls into trouble, "towards the Autumn" when birds migrate (45). This suggests that Gonsales flew to the moon sometime in late August, which is just about plausible, since Tuesday 11 September is named as his landing day, when the moon was two days old and in the twentieth degree of Libra (66). This too is both an accurate date in the Julian calendar and a fairly accu-

---

1 Godwin makes no ambiguous mention of dates between 1 January and 25 March inclusive, so the problem of dating New Year does not arise.

2 Don Bernaldino Delgadillo de Avellaneda dated the battle to 11 March, and he was presumably reckoning on the Gregorian calendar (Henry Savile, *A Libell of Spanish Lies found at the Sack of Cale* [London: John Windet, 1596], 10).

rate astronomical observation.[1] The flight itself is also full of chronological specificity: the vertical flight immediately after take-off lasts for one hour before weightlessness ensues; the devils pester Gonsales on his first day in space and say they'll be back on Thursday; the journey itself, mostly at a speed of about 50 leagues per hour, lasts eleven days, with the final approach and landing taking place on the twelfth day of the voyage.[2] Gonsales also mentions his means of keeping time—by monitoring the earth's diurnal rotation (46-67). This is a device akin to Galileo's suggestion that the moons of Jupiter might be used as a celestial clock.[3]

Gonsales passes his time on the moon in various locations, and he is again relatively precise about time. After his initial few

---

1 Rough data could be calculated from popular general almanacs; see, e.g., Arthur Hopton, *A Concordancy of Yeares* (London: Company of Stationers, 1612). A more precise route would be to retrieve an almanac prepared specifically for 1599, e.g., Gabriel Frende, *An Almanacke and Prognostication for this Yeere of Our Lord Jesus Christ MDXCIX* (London: Richard Watkins and James Roberts, 1599), which gives the moon and the constellation degree (18 of Libra). But Godwin's use of exactly 20 suggests that he is working on the common averaging system of *decans*, whereby each sign is divided into three *decans* of 10 degrees each, the twelve signs thus completing 360°.

2 Gonsales' twelve-day flight (46-67) at fifty leagues an hour (in his edition McColley approximates this to 175 miles an hour) produces, so McColley states, a rough Earth-Moon distance of 50,000 miles (actually 54,000 on McColley's reckoning). But the more standard early-modern approximation was 200,000 miles, as McColley notes, so Godwin is in error here. Of the three types of league listed in common contemporary vernacular geography textbooks (e.g., Nathanael Carpenter's *Geographie Delineated*), the "Old" (12 furlongs), the "Newer" (16 furlongs), and the "Common" (24 furlongs), the resultant figures all fall short of 50,000. Now in Godwin, an approximately twelve-day journey at 50 leagues an hour produces a distance of roughly 14,000 leagues, disregarding the initial take-off and landing. Adopting the Common league, and remembering that a mile contains 8 furlongs, we multiply the distance in leagues by three to obtain the total distance in English miles, which amounts to 43,200. Even were we to propose that Godwin was cleverly operating on either of the Spanish leagues current in the period (the *legua legal* equals c. 4.2 modern kilometres or 2.6 miles; the *legua comùn* c. 6.6 km or 4.1 miles), we still fall similarly short. Lucian's *Icaromenippus* (*Certaine Select Dialogues* [Oxford: William Turner, 1634], 9) had claimed 3,000 furlongs to the moon, i.e., around a mere 375 miles; Godwin was closer to the astronomers than the wits.

3 Michael Sharratt, *Galileo: Decisive Innovator* (Cambridge: Cambridge UP, 1996), 132-33.

days' adventures, Gonsales reports that the lunar day (i.e., the first quarter of the moon) began to break "about the middle of *September*" (91), a time when all of slight stature must slumber through the terrestrial fortnight of the lunar day. So when Gonsales awakes, it is the end of September or the beginning of October 1599. He then spends "within two months" (95) learning the lunar language. Seven months pass before his meeting with Irdonozur, with whom he stays for a quarter of a moon (97), and then he spends some further time basking in the honour of having been given his set of special stones. We are now at some period around or after mid-May 1600, or mid-July 1600, if Gonsales' language lessons are not included in his seven-month space before meeting Irdonozur.

It is at this point that Godwin's text becomes inconsistent. Having earlier named 11 September 1599 as his day of landing on the moon, Godwin now states that it was actually the twenty-first of that month, having ascended El Pico on the ninth previous (110).[1] The date of arriving at Irdonozur's court is then retrospectively given as Friday 12 May (of 1600), returning back on the seventheenth to Pylonas' palace, where Godwin remained until March 1601. The May date requires us to include the two language-learning months within the seven named earlier (97), which is no problem, but the divergence between 11 and 21 September is more difficult. First, a shift of ten days suggests a switch in Gonsales' reckoning from the Julian to the Gregorian calendar, a calendrical reform imposed by Pope Gregory XIII in 1582 (not adopted in England until 1752), which deleted ten days from the calendar in order to harmonise the civil calendar with the lunisolar cycles behind which it was ever more erroneously lagging.[2] Thus in 1572, 4 October was followed by 15 October in most nations under papal influence. Godwin's specifications that it was a *Friday* on 12 May 1600, and a *Thursday* on 29 March 1601 are likewise accurate dates in the Gregorian but not the Julian calendar (110, 113). A sole inconsistency might be dismissed as a slip, but to slip consistently suggests a more organised reason.

So Gonsales eventually leaves the moon on a Gregorian Thursday 29 March 1601, three days after awakening from the lunar day hibernation; his return trip takes a mere nine days

---

1 In her note on this date in her edition, Amartin-Serin suggests that Godwin chose 21 September as the contemporary date for the autumnal equinox (it currently takes place on the 22 or 23 of September).

2 Almanacs such as that of Frende's cited above contained two columns, one with Julian and the other with Gregorian reckonings.

(113-14). Upon his landing and capture in China, he spends "many months" in the care of the Mandarin (121), without mentioning any more definite temporal markers. *The Man in the Moone*, therefore, closes some time in 1602 or later; Gonsales is by this point around 50 years old, having left Lisbon six years previously. The year 1602 is also the date attached to the long letter on China that Diego Pantoja, the "*Pantoia*" of Gonsales' acquaintance, sent back to Europe; this was translated and printed in Purchas, and forms a prominent source for Godwin's coda on China.

How are we to explain the one major problem, the calendrical shift? In his edition McColley suggested that Godwin was belatedly bowing to the chronology of his Catholic sources. This may be so, but it poses the question of textual integrity. Gonsales is a Spaniard, so he ought to have been working on Gregorian time throughout. If Godwin realised this late in the work, he had no reason to leave his earlier dates unrevised. Rather, the fact that two consistent systems are at work in discrete portions of the text reveals a faultline, on one side of which the material is calendrically revised, and on the other, not. This in turn hints at the state of the MS from which the printed text was prepared. Godwin realised quite late on in his draft that the nationality of his protagonist meant that he ought to be working on the Gregorian calendar, and so switched over. He then finished off in Gregorian, intending to revise the opening sections in which his—albeit precise—Julian dates had occurred. But he did not revise; and no-one involved in printing the text after Godwin's death noticed the inconsistency. The current text is thus technically unfinished, though the details of this inconsistency serve to underline Godwin's interest in the verisimilitude provided by exact mensuration.

Natural Philosophy

Domingo's voyage to the moon and what he finds there intersect with two overlapping but not identical discussions in Godwin's time: the relation between astronomy and natural philosophy, specifically celestial physics; and the notion of the plurality of worlds and of alien life.

Traditionally, natural philosophy had included the physics of the heavens, describing the regions above the moon. In the ideal divisions of academic labour, natural philosophy was distinct from and superior to astronomy, the latter offering only a mathematical modelling of the apparent movements of the heavenly bodies.

Such modelling did not necessarily describe the physical structure of the heavens. Thus, Aristotelian physics maintained that supralunary nature was structured as a set of geocentric spheres, each carrying either a planet or the "fixed" stars. This zone was changeless in its repetitions, and its motions were circular. It was made out of *æther*, or the quintessence, a corporeal but unearthly stuff. For some medieval commentators, this could mean that the spheres were strictly non-solid ("solid," as "liquid," is only predicable of sublunary stuff), but by Godwin's time it was commonly assumed that such spheres, if they existed at all, could only be meaningfully discussed as solids. Hence the famous conclusion of Tycho Brahe, whose system dictated an intersection of the orbits of Mars and the Sun, that no celestial orbs could exist at all.[1] Matter below the moon, in contrast, possessed rectilinear motion, and it ideally separated out into layers containing the four elements of fire (highest), air, water, and earth (lowest). If Ptolemaic astronomy required epicycles and similar devices to make its sums work, either these could have no physical correlates, or they had to assume a complicated mechanism of transparent shells and spheres. The material reality or otherwise of epicycles and eccentrics was much discussed in the sixteenth century, although the physical compromises generated were not entirely satisfactory. The Ptolemaic use of an equant point, for instance, in which the revolution of a given heavenly body was referred to a point other than the centre of the earth, was not compatible with the Aristotelian ideal of a system of uniformly rotating, homocentric orbs. Few, indeed, doubted the existence of such "large-scale" concentric orbs; it was the status of the smaller epicycles and eccentrics which prompted agnosticism or scepticism.[2]

---

1 On medieval astronomy, see Edward Grant, *Physical Sciences in the Middle Ages* (Cambridge: Cambridge UP, 1977). On the spheres, see Nicholas Jardine, "The Significance of the Copernican Orbs," *Journal for the History of Astronomy* 13 (1982): 168-94, esp. 170-74; Edward Grant, "Celestial Orbs in the Latin Middle Ages," *Isis* 78 (1987): 152-73.

2 Two useful general accounts are F.R. Johnson, *Astronomical Thought in Renaissance England: A Study of the English Scientific Writings from 1500 to 1645* (New York: Octagon Books, 1968 [1937]); John L. Russell, "The Copernican System in Great Britain," in Jerzy Dobrzycki, ed., *Reception of Copernicus' Heliocentric Theory* (Dordrecht: D. Reidel, 1972), 189-239. See, more generally, Edward Grant, *Planets, Stars, and Orbs: The Medieval Cosmos, 1200-1687* (Cambridge: Cambridge UP, 1994), and the relevant chapters in René Taton and Curtis Wilson, eds., *Planetary Astronomy from the Renaissance to the Rise of Astrophysics* (Cambridge: Cambridge UP, 1989).

Copernicus' *De Revolutionibus* (1543) had appeared prefaced by an epistle written by the Lutheran theologian Andreas Osiander (without Copernicus' permission; he died upon publication), which suggested that Copernicus' theories belonged to the realm of astronomy and therefore made no physical claims. And indeed many academic astronomers adopted some of the mathematical improvements afforded by the heliocentric model, without thereby necessarily assenting to its physical truth—those kinds of truths, they could argue, were not their business.[1] In England, for instance, Thomas Blundeville, endorsing the instrumental inter-pretation of Copernicus, wrote that Copernicus "by helpe of [the deliberately] false supposition" of a moving earth "hath made truer demonstrations of the motions and revolutions of the celes-tiall Spheares, then euer were made before."[2]

The separation of astronomy and physics, however, had always been somewhat problematic, and operated in theory more than in practice. Osiander's preface, by emphasising the traditional sepa-ration, may indeed have been intended to protect Copernicus from attack, and when Copernicus was faulted by the Dominican theologian-astronomer Giovanni Maria Tolosani (1470/71-1549), it was on the grounds that, although a separate discipline, astron-omy depended on physics, and their conclusions could not be dis-continuous.[3] Copernicus himself clearly thought that he was also making a physical claim, and examples from the recension of copies of the *De Revolutionibus* descending from his pupil Rheti-cus have angry red crayoning through Osiander's preface.[4] In Domingo Gonsales' own university of Salamanca, where the stu-dents from an early date could vote to be lectured on *De Revolu-tionibus*, the Jesuit theologian Diego de Zuñiga (1536-97) notori-

---

1 Robert S. Westman, "The Melanchthon Circle, Rheticus, and the Wit-tenberg Interpretation of the Copernican Theory," *Isis* 88 (1975): 164-93; "The Astronomer's Role in the Sixteenth Century: A Preliminary Study," *History of Science* 18 (1980): 105-47.

2 Thomas Blundeville, *M. Blundevile his Exercises* (London: John Windet, 1594), fp. 181r.

3 Robert S. Westman, "The Copernicans and the Churches," in David C. Lindberg and Ronald L. Numbers, eds., *God and Nature: Historical Essays on the Encounter between Christianity and Science* (Berkeley: U of California P, 1986), 76-113, esp. 87-89. Tolosani's work remained in manuscript, however, and Copernicus was not formally placed on the Index until 1616.

4 Owen Gingerich, *The Book Nobody Read: In Pursuit of the Revolutions of Nicolaus Copernicus* (London: William Heinemann, 2004), 62-63.

ously adopted the Copernican system in his commentary on Job (first published in 1584, but dating from some time in the 1570s) to expound Job 9:6 on God shaking the earth. Zuñiga thus treated Copernicanism not as an instrumental model but as a full physical theory, one supported by scripture.[1] In England, Thomas Digges (1546-95) expounded in the vernacular both the truth of Copernican mathematics and the attendant physical hypothesis of the earth's motion, the sun maintaining a central position in the universe. In his famous illustration, Digges portrayed the stars as scattered beyond the orbit of the outermost planet, extending to the edges of the pages and, in reality, beyond—"fixed infinitely vp," the realm of the blessed.[2] This starry region may, as in the old cosmology, have possessed changeless perfection, but now it was of limitless extension, and not confined to the thickness of a sphere.

Digges by no means represented the common opinion, academic or otherwise, although the mathematics of Copernicus proved popular. The later sixteenth century had witnessed a hardening of theological lines between Catholics and Protestants, and the renewed emphasis in the latter camp on the literal word of the Bible was ill disposed to the physical conclusions that might arise from the new astronomy. Galileo the Catholic would indeed later argue for the physical truth of his astronomical models, as would the Protestant Kepler, but both men stopped short of the more extreme corollaries of Digges. Lutheran Tycho Brahe, the famous Danish nobleman-astronomer, posited a mitigated Copernicanism, in which the planets orbited the sun, but the sun orbited the earth. From a purely mathematical point of

1 Diego de Zuñiga, *In Iob Commentaria* (Rome: Franciscus Zannettus, 1591), 140-41; due to its condemnation, this section is deleted in many copies of Catholic provenance. Zuñiga later rejected the earth's motion, and the book was entered as *donec corrigatur* into the Index in 1616. For Zuñiga and the Copernicanism of Salamanca, see Juan Vernet, "Copernicus in Spain," *Studia Copernicana* 5 (1972): 271-91, esp. 275-77; Dobrzycki, ed., *The Reception of Copernicus' Heliocentric Theory*, 271-91. Zuñiga's commentary was in Oxford at least by the time of the first Bodleian catalogue (1605), and the relevant portion was later translated into English in Thomas Salusbury, *Mathematical Discourses and Demonstrations* (London, 1665), 468-70.

2 Thomas Digges, "A perfit description of the Caelestiall Orbes," appended to Leonard Digges, *A Prognostication Everlastinge* (London: Thomas Marsh, 1576), fol. 43r. The text following this plate comprises a translation of *De Revolutionibus*, 1.10, 7, 8 (the omitted chapter 9 is on "trepidation," the axial variation in the earth's movement).

view, such a system was hard to fault; and neither the (geocentric) Alphonsine tables nor Kepler's (heliocentric) Rudolphine revisions were without their inaccuracies. England generally favoured either the old cosmology or the Tychonic system, and William Gilbert's *De Magnete* (1600), although it embraced the diurnal rotation of the earth, was cautiously indecisive about the other motions that a physical understanding of Copernicus dictated: the annual and axial motions of the earth. This indecisiveness fed into the textbooks following Gilbert, notably Nathanael Carpenter's *Geographie Delineated* (1625).

What could Godwin know of all this? Fuller reported that Godwin was a "skilful *Mathematician*," and no doubt his university training had included some mathematical astronomy.[1] A pertinent Cambridge comparison is provided by Godwin's elder contemporary Gabriel Harvey, a man whose annotations to his books throughout the 1580s demonstrate that he drifted from Ptolemy to Copernicus over these years. Harvey, like Godwin, was an interested eclectic rather than a serious mathematical astronomer, but both men would have little trouble accessing cutting-edge speculation.[2] Returning to Oxford, if we examine the *quaestiones philosophicae* disputed at the Vesperies and Comitia during Godwin's student career, we do see a marked increase in theses with astronomical or cosmological consequences roughly coinciding with Godwin's period of studies and continuing into the next century. In 1576, in the Vesperies, it was debated whether the earth rests in the centre of the world; in 1581 the same forum heard a debate on whether there was matter in the heavens, and, at the Comitia a few days later, whether there were or could be many worlds. In 1583, whether there were more elements than four was discussed; in 1584, whether comets caused ill or good; in 1587, whether the moon caused the tides; in 1588, again, if there were many worlds; in 1608, whether the earth was magnetic in nature, a sure sign of Gilbert's influence; and in 1611, whether the moon was habitable—the year Kepler's *Somnium* started circulating in manuscript on the continent.[3] A

---

1 See the biographical section above.
2 Virginia F. Stern, *Gabriel Harvey: His Life, Marginalia and Library* (Oxford: Clarendon P, 1979), 165-68.
3 Theses quoted and translated from Andrew Clark, ed., *Register of the University of Oxford* (Oxford: Clarendon P, 1887), vol. 2, part 1, 170-77. An M.A. awarded early in 1584 (as was Godwin's) was likely to have debated the theses recorded for that year. The habit of recording whether the inceptor affirmed or denied the proposition was only

further excitement in Godwin's student days may have been the visit of Giordano Bruno to Oxford in 1583 in the train of Prince Albert Laski, where, despite his own self-flattering account of the visit, Bruno merely antagonised the Oxonians with his empty vaunting. As George Abbot, then at Balliol, remembered, Bruno

> ... stripping vp his sleeues like some Iugler, and telling vs much of *chentrum & chirculus & circumferenchia* (after the pronunciation of his Country language) ... vndertooke among very many other matters to set on foote the opinion of Copernicus, that the earth did goe round, and the heavens did stand still; whereas in truth it was his owne head which rather did run round, & his braines did not stand still.[1]

Nor should Abbot's apparently slighting reference to Copernicus be taken to demonstrate Oxonian backwardness on such matters: as Feingold says, 1580s' Oxford contained many men who knew more about Copernicus than Bruno did, and all Bruno did was annoy them.[2] Famously, in the 1570s Henry Savile of Merton College had presented the Ptolemaic and Copernican systems side-by-side in his lectures on Ptolemy. Finally, Godwin's choice of Salamanca as Gonsales' alma mater may suggest that he was aware, through unknown channels, of its early Copernicanism.

What of Godwin's astronomy in *The Man in the Moone*? First, Domingo's flight, unscorched, to the moon gives him occasion to ridicule the Aristotelian cosmology of realms of fire and so forth, and his journey *through* space requires that it is not solid in any

---

started in 1592, though this is not too important as the inceptor, regardless of which side he argued, was answered by a senior disputant. B.A. and M.A. students alike were supposed to "frequent the schools," so if Godwin was a diligent student—there is no indication he was not—he should have been present at many of these debates. For the English reception of Kepler, see especially Wilbur Applebaum, "Kepler in England: The Reception of Keplerian Astronomy in England, 1599-1687" (Ph.D. diss., SUNY Buffalo, 1969); Adam Jared Apt, "The Reception of Kepler's Astronomy in England: 1596-1650" (D. Phil. thesis, Oxford, 1982).

1 George Abbot, *The Reasons Which Doctour Hill hath brought, for the Upholding of Papistry* (Oxford: Simon Waterson, 1604), 88.

2 Mordechai Feingold, "Giordano Bruno in England, Revisited," *Huntington Library Quarterly* 67 (2004): 329-46. One might also note that another notorious foreigner and heretic in Oxford at this time, Antonio del Corro, was *censor theologicus* at Christ Church (1578-86) throughout Godwin's time there.

sense, and can mix with or at least receive sublunary matter. But Domingo says nothing of a movement of axial orientation (something Digges too omitted in his partial translations of Copernicus), nor of the earth's path through space. To this extent, Godwin need have read no further than Gilbert, his major immediate physical influence. We must also, of course, avoid reading back into Godwin's cosmology a Newtonian understanding of celestial motions and the force ("gravity," a word not used by Godwin) powering them. *The Man in the Moone* was an important document for the popularising of *certain* astronomical ideas, and we know that Godwin inspired John Wilkins to write what were possibly the first textbooks of popular astronomy on the Copernican model. But Godwin is not a full Copernican, because he does not discuss the annual or axial motions of the earth, and it was magnetism, not gravity, which attracted him. To this extent, Godwin fits into the academic tendency identified by Feingold of accepting the diurnal motion of the earth, and thereafter maintaining either an open or a closed mind on the other two Copernican motions.[1] It is therefore unfair to say that Godwin's tale "contains little in the way of serious scientific speculation ... explicitly eluding the Copernican question"; there was nothing unscientific or unserious about such silence, which was shared by most commentators. And it is likewise unhistorical to claim that Godwin "*mislabels*" gravity "as a force something like magnetism."[2]

More original are Godwin's extraterrestrials. It is true that there is literary precedent for aliens—Lucian's *True History*, where the moon is populated by bald homosexuals, being the foremost example. Lucian's tale however scarcely rests upon a serious astronomical basis.[3] Conversely, what makes Godwin's

---

1 Mordechai Feingold, *The Mathematician's Apprenticeship: Science, Universities and Society 1560-1640* (Cambridge: Cambridge UP, 1984).

2 Mary Baine Campbell, "Impossible Voyages: Seventeenth-Century Space Travel and the Impulse of Ethnology," *Literature and History* 6.2 (1997): 1-17, at 3; Aaron Parrett, *The Translunar Narrative in the Western Tradition* (Aldershot: Ashgate, 2004), 54 (my italics). Compare the contemporary terminology of Mark Ridley's *A Short Treatise of Magneticall Bodies and Motions* (London: Nicholas Okes, 1613), extract in Appendix F below), 13: "Thus we proue that the Earth is placed and firmed by her Magneticall vertue, and not by her grauity and waight."

3 An interesting contrast is provided by Kepler, who thought otherwise of the *True History*, adducing Lucian's preface, which hints at a more serious purpose to his work. See James S. Romm, "Lucian and Plutarch as Sources for Kepler's *Somnium*," *Classical and Modern Literature* 9

extraterrestrials important is that they occur in a universe that is also operating on some of the physics suggested by the new astronomy. Alien life to Lucian may have been a joke, but it was a very serious matter, however lightly Godwin handles it, to the early modern age.[1] The reason for this was that the physics of supralunary changelessness had been yoked to a theologically driven anthropocentrism in which man had to be the exclusive centre of the universe, because he had been granted an exclusive saviour, who had died once, and once for all.[2] The possibility of alien life was thus a theological embarrassment, because it raised intractable questions about how efficacious the sacrifice of Christ was (did he save Martians too?), and forced one to make a decision about whether alien nations were fallen or not. That Bishop Godwin puts on his moon such effortlessly superior beings is therefore no small problem: their personal tranquillity and social utopianism lead one to doubt that they suffer from the same moral deficiencies as earthlings, and if they do not, then what is their place in a Christian universe? Are they fallen beings? And if not, then what is Christ to them?

Godwin senses these problems. His Lunarians, as soon as Domingo meets them, reveal themselves to be Christians, although their lack of reaction to the name of Mary suggests that they have not fallen into the errors of the Catholic Church, despite some otherwise rather Catholic-looking institutions on the moon. In a sense, the problem therefore remains unresolved, as Godwin introduces his aliens into the economy of a Christian universe but does not explain exactly what their role is in that economy. Indeed, the apparent sinlessness of the Lunars rather begs the question. The problem was daringly excised by Godwin's French translator Jean Baudoin, who, as we shall see, omitted the Christian sections altogether. Finally, Kepler's *Somnium*, the only comparable lunar voyage of Godwin's age,

---

(1988-89): 97-107; Anthony Grafton, *Commerce with the Classics: Ancient Books and Renaissance Readers* (Ann Arbor: U of Michigan P, 1997), 185-224, at 195-96.

1 Grant McColley, "The Seventeenth-Century Doctrine of a Plurality of Worlds," *Annals of Science* 1 (1936): 285-430; Stephen J. Dick, *Plurality of Worlds* (Cambridge: Cambridge UP, 1982), passim.

2 For a paradigmatic example, see Philip Melanchthon, *Initia Doctrinæ Physicæ* (Wittenberg, 1581) in Appendix D, where Melanchthon adds a theological appendix to his purely physical refutation. A convenient contemporary list of people who believed the moon was inhabited, with a final denunciation, can be found in Jean-Baptista Riccioli, *Almagestum Novum* (Bologna, 1651), 187-88.

imagines the creatures of the moon to be short-lived, thoroughly alien beasts, serpentine in nature, screeching before the lunar sunrise and dying in a day—truly alien life-forms. Next to Kepler's beings, Godwin's cheery anthropomorphoids feel distinctly human.[1]

Godwin's decision to locate his aliens on the moon taps into both the literary tradition of Lucian and the philosophical tradition extending back as far as the Pythagoreans, who had conjectured that the moon was another world, made of earthly matter, and hence habitable.[2] As we saw, precisely this question of habit-

---

1 Although Godwin may easily have read Kepler's *Dissertatio cum Nuncio Sidereo*, it is exceptionally unlikely that he had any access to or knowledge of the *Somnium*, which does not appear to have been known in England during Godwin's lifetime. For the latter, see Johannes Kepler, *Somnium, seu opus posthumum de astronomia lunari* (Sagan/Frankfurt: the heirs of Kepler, 1634); there is an excellent English translation and commentary by Edward Rosen, *Kepler's Somnium: The Dream, or Posthumous Work on Lunar Astronomy* (Madison: U of Wisconsin P, 1967; repr. New York: Dover, 2003). The possibility of this work being known in England prior to its publication is discussed by Rosen in Kepler, *Somnium*, Appendix E; and Poole, "Origins."

2 Particularly close to Godwin is (Pseudo-)Plutarch in "The Opinions of Philosophers": "The PYTHAGOREANS affirme, that the Moone appeereth terrestriall, for that she is inhabited round about, like as the earth wherein we are, and peopled as it were with the greatest living creatures, and the fairest plants; and those creatures within her, be fifteene times stronger and more puissant than those with us, and the same yeeld forth no excrements, and the day there, is in that proportion so much longer" (*The Philosophie, commonlie called, the Morals*, trans. Philemon Holland [London: Arnold Hatfield, 1603], 825). Diogenes Laertius reported of Anaxagoras that "he declared that there were dwellings on the moon, and moreover hills and ravines" (2.8); and Cicero in the *Academica* noted that "Xenophanes says that the moon is inhabited, and is a land of many cities and mountains" (2.39.123). Athenaeus in the *Deipnosophistae* related the curious anecdote, "But Neocles of Croton was mistaken in saying that the egg from which Helen sprang fell from the moon; for, though the moon-women lay eggs, their offspring are fifteen times larger than we are, as Herodorus of Heracleia records" (2.57). Aelian in *On Animals* reported the old myth that the Nemean Lion fell from the moon (12.7). Macrobius, *Commentary on the Dream of Cicero* (trans. with an introduction and notes by William Harris Stahl [New York: Columbia UP, 1990 [1952]), commented, "Natural philosophers called the moon the ethereal earth and its inhabitants lunar people, but their reasons for doing so here are too numerous for us to take up here" (11.7 [p. 131]).

ability was asked in Oxford in 1611, if to be denied—surely a sign of the almost instantaneous effect of Galileo's and Kepler's publications of 1610. That the moon usurped the other planets in such speculations is unsurprising given its dominance of the night sky, but the scientific connection between the earth and moon had been pressed by Gilbert in both his published and unpublished works. The advent of the telescope reasserted this connection, as even low-powered lenses, particularly at half-moon, can reveal the lunar craters in stunning detail. As Sir William Lower wrote to Thomas Hariot in early February 1610, he had turned Hariot's "perspective Cylinder" to the moon, which appeared to him "like the Descriptions of Coasts in the dutch bookes of voyages"—the same "dutch bookes" used by Godwin for the opening sections of his fiction.[1] The seventeenth century also saw the rise of selenography, or the cartography of the moon, starting with Gilbert's rudimentary map (it qualifies as such by virtue of being mounted on an 8 x 8 square grid), and developing into the 1645 map of Langrenus (Michiel van Langren, 1600-75); some 168 of Langrenus' 325 lunar place-names have survived.[2]

Literary or humanistic traditions and practical astronomy were not absolutely separate activities for early-modern astronomers.[3] Kepler, for instance, envisaged a work on the moon which resembled more a mixture of satire and utopianism than a formal astronomical treatise:

> Campanella wrote a *City of the Sun*. What about my writing a "City of the Moon"? Would it not be excellent to describe the cyclopic mores of our time in vivid colors, but in doing so—to be on the safe side—to leave this earth and go to the moon? More in his *Utopia* and Erasmus in his *Praise of Folly* ran into trouble and had to defend themselves. Therefore let us leave the vicissitudes of politics alone and let us remain in the pleasant, fresh green fields of philosophy.[4]

---

1 Quoted in John W. Shirley, *Thomas Hariot: A Biography* (Oxford: Clarendon P, 1983), 399.

2 Whitaker, *Mapping and Naming the Moon*, 3-68.

3 Anthony Grafton, "Humanism and Science in Rudolphine Prague: Kepler in Context," in *Defenders of the Text: The Traditions of Scholarship in an Age of Science 1450-1800* (Cambridge, MA: Harvard UP, 1991), 178-203; "Kepler as Reader," *Journal of the History of Ideas* 53 (1992): 561-72.

4 Letter to Matthias Bernegger, Linz, 4 December 1623, in Kepler, *Gesammelte Werke*, ed. Max Caspar, vol. 18 (Munich, 1959), 143; I have supplied the translation of Carola Baumgardt, *Johannes Kepler: Life and Letters* (London: Victor Gollancz, 1952), 155-56.

But, as Kepler says, this project was one he came to reject: the final *Somnium* is *not*, according to Kepler, a work indebted to utopianism, and his letter better predicts what Godwin would write; the bishop realised the project the astronomer abandoned.

Godwin would also have at hand the most famous collection of lunar speculation from antiquity, Plutarch's dialogue on the face in the moon—a dialogue, significantly, that would accompany the first publication of Kepler's *Somium*. This was a pointed gesture on Kepler's part, signalling literary debt rather than autobiography. Circulation of the *Somnium* manuscript had, after all, caused the prosecution of Kepler's mother on the charge of witchcraft.[1] Plutarch's dialogue usefully summarised most ancient commentary on the moon, and there Godwin could find ideas that were very similar to those being developed by Gilbert and others—notably the anti-Aristotelian thesis that there might be many different centres in the universe, and that the moon has its centre, and that it moves "by reason of a different soul or nature" than that operating in the earth—these thoroughly "Gilbertian" theses were therefore already available to any casual reader of Plutarch.[2] In some senses, then, the ancient and the modern astronomical traditions complemented rather than contested one another.

The Lunar Language

Godwin's lunar language relies heavily on contemporary reports of Chinese, a prolepsis of his later visit to China itself. Godwin was influenced by the reports of the tonal status of spoken Chinese, especially through Purchas's redaction of the Ricci-Trigault journals. He then made the connection between reports that spoken Chinese was a tonal language and that in its written form it functioned as a "real character," or a script in which words stood for things themselves, and were not mere notations of sounds.[3] As Francis Bacon summarized of the written language,

---

1 Kepler refers to the affair in the eighth note to the *Somnium* (38-41).
2 Plutarch, *De facie in orbem lunæ*, 926A.
3 On Godwin's lunar language and its sources, see Paul Cornelius, *Languages in Seventeenth- and Early-Eighteenth Century Imaginary Voyages* (Geneva: Librarie Droz, 1965), 45-48; H. Neville Davies, "Bishop Godwin's 'Lunatique Language,'" *Journal of the Warburg and Courtauld Institutes* 30 (1967): 296-316, esp. 310-11; Vivian Salmon, *The Works of Francis Lodwick* (London: Longman, 1972), 135-39, 147-49; James R.

And we vnderstand further, that it is the vse of *Chyna,* and the Kingdomes of the High *Leuant,* to write in *Characters reall,* which expresse neither *Letters, nor words in grosse,* but *Things* or *Nottons:* in so much as Countreys and Prouinces, which vnderstand not one anothers language, can neuerthelesse read one anothers Writings, because the *Characters* are accepted more generally, than the *Languages* doe extend; and therefore they haue a vast multitude of *Characters,* as many (I suppose[)], as Radicall words.[1]

These meditations prompted many of Godwin's contemporaries to posit the possibility of constructing an artificial language, Godwin's "great Mystery." This was exactly how John Wilkins interpreted this passage of Godwin: "The *utterance* of these Musicall tunes may serve for the universall *language,* and the *writing* of them for the universall *Character.*"[2] Yet interest in the possibilities of Chinese script had been voiced in England since the very first news of Chinese language reached the west, and given Godwin's own cryptographic interests, it is interesting to note that the first published English shorthand, Timothy Bright's *Characterie* (1588), had advertised itself as, among other things, a kind of superior Chinese.[3] Similar remarks—at once fascinated by Chinese, at once critical of its supposed cumbrousness and ambiguity—would be made for the next century, culminating in Robert Hooke's 1686 paper arguing that Chinese script represented the misunderstood remnants of an ancient and artificially imposed philosophical language.[4]

Knowlson, "A Note on Bishop Godwin's 'Man in the Moone': The East Indies Trade Route and a 'Language' of Musical Notes," *Modern Philology* 55 (1968): 357-61.

1 Francis Bacon, *Of the Proficience and Advancement of Learning* (London, 1605), 2.106-07; compare the account in Mendoza, *Historie of the Great and Mightie Kingdome of China* (London: Edward White, 1588), 101-05.

2 John Wilkins, *Mercury, or the Secret and Swift Messenger* (London: John Maynard and Timothy Wilkins, 1641), 144. See more generally Rhodri Lewis, *Language, Mind, and Nature: Artificial Languages in England from Bacon to Locke* (Cambridge: Cambridge UP, 2007).

3 Timothy Bright, *Characterie* (London: John Windet, 1588), sgs. A3v-A4r.

4 R[obert] H[ooke], "Some Observations, and Conjectures concerning the Chinese Characters," *Philosophical Transactions* 180 (1686): 63-78. Hooke's paper owes a good deal to the discussions of the Dutch scholar Jacobus Golius, as well as to John Wilkins's critical remarks on Chinese in his *Essay towards a Real Character, and a Philosophical Language* (London: Samuel Gellibrand and John Martyn, 1668), 450-52.

Godwin's lunar language is merely a musically notated cipher based on Latin, as Wilkins again first noted.[1] Such ciphers were common enough proposals in the cryptographical literature of the time.[2] In Godwin's version, a minim placed on the top line of the stave stands for "a"; a semibreve on the same line "b"; a minim on the space below "c"; a semibreve on that space "d"; and so forth down the stave, doubling i/j and v/w and omitting k and q. Thus "Glorie be to God alone" is (almost) accurately spelled out in Latin: G-l-o-r-i-a-D-e-o-S-o-l-i. The next sample (almost) spells G-o-n-s-a-l-e-s. Davies also notes that Wilkins's decipherment rationalises Godwin's own printed text, which is full of errors. Out of 21 characters musically represented, the 1638 edition misprints eight (Davies says six). These errors are: G and L of "gloria"; O and L of "soli"; G, N, L, E of "Gonsales." Of these errors, three derive from simple minim/semibreve confusions, two are near misses, where the adjacent note has been sounded instead, and the remaining three all involve "L," a curiously regular error. There is no doubt about the underlying order, however; such mistakes must arise from compositorial carelessness, unnoticed at the proof stage. The spacing of the notes also suggests that the compositor was no musician. Despite Wilkins's 1641 decipherment, the 1657 edition contained even more errors, and the continental translations likewise failed to understand the system. But then Gonsales too does say that he is "no perfect Musitian."

Godwin's Reception

Earlier Influence

Godwin's fiction was read exceptionally widely, and it prompted a range of reactions from readers, writers, and translators over the century following its publication, and beyond.[3] The earliest of these is arguably the work's own preface "To the Ingenious Reader," a preface probably but not certainly by Godwin himself. Here, the work is marked as formally fictional, "an essay of *Fancy*, where *Invention* is shewed with *Judgment*." Although the preface is largely comic in tone, concluding on the apparently mocking con-

---

1 Wilkins, *Mercury*, 141-44.

2 Salmon, *Works of Francis Lodwick*, 147-49.

3 Marjorie Hope Nicolson, *Voyages to the Moon* (New York: Macmillan, 1960 [1948]), provides much information on Godwin and especially his reception; she also supplies an eclectic catalogue of analogues and progeny (259-84). A useful recent survey is Cressy, "Early Modern Space Travel."

trast, the "*little* eye-witnesse, our *great* discoverer" (my italics), the connection with genuine natural philosophical discovery is ambiguously advertised throughout, and midget Gonsales does indeed turn out to discover great things. Nonetheless, it was unsurprisingly the picaresque dimension that stuck with most casual readers. We have seen earlier that Lady Brilliana Harley read the work in the year of its publication, finding it on first glance "some kine to Donqueshot." Indeed, for many early readers, the comic tone actually overpowered the work's natural philosophical interests. There are scores of jokes in all genres of the period mocking people by coupling "Domingo" or his "Gansas" (myriad spellings—"Gonsos," "Gansæs," "Ganzæs," etc.) with the suggestion that the target in question is merely a loony or a goose, an insinuation particularly mobile in polemic contexts—then as now, "goose" was slang for a fool.[1] The scientific populist (and himself later a bishop) John Wilkins was himself slurred in this way when his erstwhile but subsequently estranged collaborator George Dalgarno attacked Wilkins's support of Copernicus by likening him to "the knight errant w*ith* his Ganzæs," another glance at picaresque.[2] Godwin and Wilkins would be long associated in this way. Samuel Wesley in his *Maggots* of 1685 versified part of Lucian's *True History*, pointing out that Lucian's crew flew "without the help either of *Domingo*'s feathery, or others Christal or Brazen Chariot, or so much as the *French* Smith's wings"; and in his Pindaric "on Three Skipps of a Louse" he added,

> Two Bishops have wrote expressly of this new Plantation, and the way to sayl thither. One by making a Globe of Glass, or Brass lighter than the Atmosphere, which must therefore naturally ascend: The other by a way perhaps as practicable as the former, by harnessing a certain number of Fowl, called by the Spaniards [*Ganza's*] on which he makes *Signior Domingo* hoisted thither.[3]

---

1 William Poole, "Marvell's 'Ganza's': an emendation," *Notes and Queries* 53 (2006): 49-50. Indeed, so prevalent was the joke that "ganza" has its own entry in *The Oxford English Dictionary*.

2 George Dalgarno, "That there is both a diurnal and annual motion, either in the Heaven, or Earth, nothing can be more certain ..." (Oxford, Christ Church MS 162, fol. 102v, c. 1660-87).

3 *Maggots, or Poems on Several Subjects* (London: John Dunton, 1685), 121, 171, fonts reversed. Wesley's allusions are elucidated by the notes to Wilkins in Appendix H. But he was incorrect to ascribe the globe method to Wilkins: that was the actually very recent theory of the Italian Francesco Lana.

This association arose because Wilkins had been Godwin's first sympathetic reader. In the chapter on flight to the moon that he added to his 1640 expansion of *The Discovery of a World in the Moone* (1638), Wilkins concluded by remarking that, just as he was finishing his revisions, "I chanced upon a late fancy to this purpose under the fained name of *Domingo Gonsales*, written by a late reverend and learned Bishop."[1] Wilkins then offered a summary of Godwin's "very pleasant and well contrived" work in which he took seriously Godwin's claims that locusts and birds travelled periodically to the moon, and the possibility that humans might be able to hitch a lift with the latter. Wilkins next turned to Godwin's *Nuncius Inanimatus* in his 1641 crypto-graphic treatise *Mercury*, where he stated that *The Man in the Moone* and the *Nuncius Inanimatus* were written by the same person and that the former text could be used to unlock the secrets of the latter.[2] Finally, in 1648 Wilkins wrote a chapter on "the Art of Flying" in which he placed Godwin's Gansas along-side all the other ways humans have claimed to have been able to fly.[3] Hence in 1659 it was satirically suggested that Wilkins with his "winged Chariot" should be appointed as coachman to a pro-posed embassy "to the man in the Moone"; but Wilkins was instead to become one of the architects of the Royal Society of London "for the advancement of experimental philosophy," as Thomas Sprat subtitled his official history of the Society.[4] Wilkins's protégé, the great experimentalist Robert Hooke, was deeply interested in the problem of human flight too, and he owned a copy of Godwin's original fiction in its second edition, which included the *Nuncius Inanimatus*; Hooke was also inter-ested in telegraphy.[5] The Royal Society's more imaginative fellows would long be ribbed for their lunacy: in 1699 Thomas

---

1   *A Discourse concerning a New World, and Another Planet* (London: John Maynard, 1640), 240. On Wilkins and Godwin, see most recently Frédérique Aït-Touati, "La découverte d'un autre monde: fiction et théorie dans les oeuvres de John Wilkins et de Francis Godwin," *Etudes Epistémè* 7 (2005) <http://www.etudes-episteme.org/ee/articles.php ?lng=fr&pg=78>.

2   *Mercury*, 164-65.

3   This chapter is reproduced in Appendix H.

4   *Democritus Turned States-Man* (London: n.p., 1659), 3-4; Barbara Shapiro, *John Wilkins, 1614-1672: An Intellectual Biography* (Berkeley and Los Angeles: U of California P, 1969); Thomas Sprat, *The History of the Royal-Society of London* (London: John Martyn and James Allestry, 1667), 1.

5   *Bibliotheca Hookiana sive Catalogus Diversorum Librorum ... R. Hooke* (London, 1703), 48.

Baker was still mocking "the vanity of some few Men, who have been so *Planet-struck* as to dream of the possibility of a Voyage to the Moon, and to talk of making wings to fly thither, as they would of buying a pair of Boots to take a journey."[1] Wilkins was also probably the means through which Godwin's text caught the eye of Andreas Müller, a German sinologist who had lived and worked in England in the 1650s. Müller, better known for his supposed "Clavis" or key to Chinese, recalled Godwin's lunar language in the course of a scholarly work on the supposed Nestorian monument found in China. He translated the relevant section into German and pointed out that Godwin's lunar language was modelled on the tonality of spoken Chinese, although he failed to spot the cryptographic ploy behind Godwin's tones.[2]

And so it should not be forgotten that Godwin's story became an international phenomenon too. Perhaps most impressively, as early as 1645, before any translations had been published, the Flemish selenographer Langrenus had named one of the lunar craters on his celebrated map "Gansii" after the Gansas, the only such fictional referent in his selenography.[3] But Godwin's greatest impact was through translation. In his *Ephemerides* or journal for 1639, the intelligencer Samuel Hartlib noted that someone "was translating Gonzales as a pretty fiction that wil bee welcome to French and Italian wits." The person doing the translating appears by context somewhat surprisingly to be Sir William Boswell, the English Resident in Amsterdam, but we do not know what became of this effort.[4] There were six printings of a Dutch translation before 1700.[5] No contemporary Italian translation survives, but *The Man in the Moone* was translated into French by Jean Baudoin, and published in 1648 with subsequent editions in

---

1   Thomas Baker, *Reflections upon Learning* (London: A. Boswell, 1699), 84-85.
2   Cornelius, *Languages*, 55-57; Mungello, *Curious Land*, 198-200; on Müller see Donald Lach, "The Chinese Studies of Andreas Müller," *Journal of the American Oriental Society* 60 (1940): 564-75.
3   Whitaker, *Mapping and Naming the Moon*, 41, reproduces the map: "Gansii" is just to the bottom-right of the centre of van Langren's map. The modern equivalent is "Halley." John Wilkins had a crater named after him on the map too, as Wood noted (*Athenae Oxonienses*, 3.969).
4   *The Hartlib Papers*, 30/4/16B, transcribed from MS image. Hartlib writes "Boswel" in the margin against this entry.
5   Editions of 1645, 1651, 1663, 1670-71, 1695, 1700: see Cornelis W. Schoneveld, *Intertraffic of the Mind: Studies in Seventeenth-Century Anglo-Dutch Translation with a checklist of books translated from English into Dutch, 1600-1700* (Leiden: E.J. Brill, 1983), 199-200.

1666 and 1671. It is not obvious that Baudoin even knew who the original author was.[1] Baudoin himself was already well known for his translations of Francis Bacon and Philip Sidney, his work on Godwin coming toward the end of his long career.[2] Baudoin's translation is particularly important because it was also the base text for the German version (1659) that followed it, replicating unawares Baudoin's silent but systematic excision of Lunar Christianity, as noted below in the commentary.[3] It has been suggested that Baudoin's translation of Garcilaso de la Vega's history of the Incas can be read as a document of implicit deism: Vega's Incas "proceeded by the mere light of Nature, to the knowledge of the True Almighty God our Lord"; "but because they did not see him, they could not know him; and for that reason they erected not Temples to him, nor offered Sacrifice, howsoever they worshipped in their Hearts, and esteemed him for the unknown God."[4] Baudoin may just have thought that

---

1 See *The Man in the Moon/L'Homme dans la Lune*, notes et introduction de Annie Amartin-Serin (Nancy: Presses universitaires de Nancy, Collection "Textes Oubliés," 1984).

2 *L'Homme dans la Lune ou le voyage chimerique fait au Monde de la Lune: nouvellement découvert par Dominique Gonsales, advanturier espagnol, autremont dit le Courrier Volant. Mis en notre language, par I.B.D.* (Paris: chez François Piot et I. Guignard, 1648); H.W. Lawton, "Notes sur Jean Baudoin et sur ses traductions de l'anglais," *Revue de Littérature Comparée* 6 (1926): 673-81, at 677-79; Harold F. Kynaston-Snell, *Jean Baudoin et les "Essais" de Bacon en France jusq'au XVIIIe Siècle* (Paris: Jouve et Cie, 1939). Baudoin had been handed the English original by "D'Avisson" (i.e., William Davison (1593-1669), the Aberdeen-educated medic and chemist living in Paris, remembered chiefly as Thomas Hobbes's chemistry teacher), but admitted that he had also worked from a prior manuscript translation prepared by another Scotsman, "Thomas D'Anan" [sic] (sg. [av]v). "D'Anan" has defied identification. He may simply come from Annan, near Carlisle, as Black's *Surnames of Scotland* lists nothing close.

3 A bibliography of English, French, Dutch, and German editions of *The Man in the Moone*, with some secondary literature in German, is supplied by Thomas Bürger as an appendix to the Herzog August Bibliothek facsimile of the German translation (Wolfenbüttel: Herzog August Bibliothek, 1993), 145-59.

4 Geoffroy Atkinson, *The Extraordinary Voyage in French Literature Before 1700* (New York: Columbia UP, 1920), 67; Garcilaso de la Vega, *Le Commentaire Royal, ou l'Histoire des Yncas, Roys du Peru*, trans. Jean Baudoin (Paris: Augutin Courbé, 1633); English translation supplied from Vega, *The Royal Commentaries of Peru in Two Parts*, trans. Paul Rycaut (London: Richard Tonson, 1688), 28-29.

he was avoiding a conflict, but his revision of Godwin nevertheless turns his Lunars into beings comparable to Vega's Incas. For
countless continental readers of Godwin, then, the fiction by the
English bishop—if they even recognised its anglophone origin—
was based on a religious thesis that its original author had found
intolerable.

The other important continental phenomenon was the partial
cannibalisation of Godwin to form fresh works. Most celebrated
is Cyrano de Bergerac's *Comical History of the States and Empires
of the Worlds of the Moon and Sun* (1648), which was in turn to be
translated back into English. Cyrano's traveller to the heavens
meets Domingo himself on the moon, in this version degraded to
the status of pet monkey:

> I perceived amongst a troop of Monkeys and Apes who
> handed his Ruffe, Cloak, and Breeches, a little man entring,
> almost like to my self, for he went upon two leggs: as soon as
> he beheld me, he accosted me, with a *Criado de Vuestra Merced*;
> and I retorted his salute almost in the same terms.
>
> But alas! they no sooner saw us tattle together, but beleeved
> they had guest right; and it was impossible this conjecture
> should have a better success, for he of the Spectators that
> made the most favourable construction of us, protested, that
> our conversation was a grumbling, which our natural instant
> meeting together made us mutter. This little man told me, he
> was an *European*, native of *Old-Castile*, and that he had found
> a means by Birds to arrive at the Moon, where we then were;
> and being fallen into the Queens hands, she had taken him for
> an Ape; for as Fortune would have it, they cloath their Apes in
> that Countrey in Spanish cloathes; and finding him at his
> arrival in that habit, she doubted not but that he was of the
> same kind.[1]

There is no shortage of speculation on astronomy and physics
in Cyrano's work, but it has been argued that the continental
strain of the moon voyage represented by Cyrano is more rather
than less picaresque than Godwin's origin, which displays a
greater interest in the problems of establishing scientific trust.[2]

---

1   Cyrano de Bergerac, *Selenarchia, or the Government of the World in the
    Moon a Comical History*, trans. Thomas St Serf (London: Humphrey
    Robinson, 1659), sgs. F3v-F4r.
2   See "Genres" above on picaresque, especially the article by Pioffet cited
    there.

Cyrano was popular in England too, and he was translated for a second time, in 1687, by Archibald Lovell; in a parallel move, Bernard Le Bovier De Fontenelle's celebrated *Conversations on the Plurality of Worlds* made it into English in the period in no fewer than three separate translations, the first anonymous, but the last two by Aphra Behn and Joseph Glanvill (1687, 1688, 1695 respectively, and subsequent editions). Relevant translations into English of other continental works on aliens and the multiplicity of worlds included Pierre Borel's *A New Treatise Proving a Multiplicity of Worlds* (trans. 1658), and Christiaan Huygens's *The Celestial Worlds Discover'd* (trans. 1698).[1]

Back in England, *The Man in the Moone* was particularly popular as an ingredient of later, often extravagantly staged comic drama and opera: Aphra Behn, *The Emperor of the Moon: A Farce* (1687); Elkanah Settle, *The World in the Moon: An Opera* (1697); Thomas D'Urfey, *Wonders in the Sun, or the Kingdom of the Birds: A Comick Opera* (1706), really a sequel, starring Domingo and Diego. The generic subtitles to these plays show in what vein the lunar story was treated. Behn's play, for instance, features a Doctor who has turned lunatic through reading, significantly, Lucian, Godwin, and Wilkins. At the end of the play, not only Kepler and Galileo appear, but also "Iredonozur," i.e., Godwin's Irdonozur, Emperor of the Moon. But these men are not what they seem—they are merely friends dressed up to cure the Doctor of his madness. So the Doctor starts the farce convinced of the Moon's "people, their Government, Institutions, Laws, Manners, Religion and Constitution"; but he ends it disabused: "No Emperor of the Moon,—and no Moon World! ... there's nothing in Philosophy."[2]

Finally, *The Man in the Moone* also had a long and specifically English afterlife in the form of the version of it published by Nathaniel Crouch in 1686 in his *View of the English Acquisitions in Guinea, and the East Indies*.[3] Arriving at his discussion of St.

---

1 The opposite trajectory can be seen in the appearance of Wilkins in French: his 1640 tract was published in Rouen as *Le Monde dans la Lune* in 1655 and again in 1656, translated by Jean, Sieur de la Montagne.

2 Aphra Behn, *The Emperor of the Moon* (1687), in *The Works of Aphra Behn*, ed. Janet Todd (London: William Pickering, 1996), vol. 7 (1.92-97; 3.461-63, 656, 669); see also Nicolson, *Voyages to the Moon*, 89-93.

3 R.B. [Nathaniel Crouch], *A View of the English Acquisitions in Guinea, and the East Indies* (London: Nathaniel Crouch, 1686), 74-131. The English Short-Title Catalogue (ESTC) lists five editions between 1686

Helena, Crouch noted that this was the "Scene of that notable fancy," *The Man in the Moone*. He then recounted Wilkins's praise of the work as "pleasant and well contrived," as opposed to the merely improbable relations of Sir John Mandeville, and on those grounds resolved to reprint Godwin's fiction. He also portrayed this as a rescue mission, in case the original publication, now long since out of print, "be utterly lost." Crouch therefore reprinted right in the middle of one of his popular historical collections a lengthy fictional work, but one that he had significantly revised.[1] It was in this or in one of the continental forms that the fiction would be known in the eighteenth and nineteenth centuries.

Godwin's work continued to exert a waning influence throughout the eighteenth and early nineteenth centuries, but Edgar Allan Poe got to it in 1835;[2] and in tandem with Kepler's *Somnium* it was to make a triumphant late appearance as the inspiration behind H.G. Wells's homage to his seventeenth-century forbears, his significantly titled *The First Men in the Moon* (1901). Wells's publication came after the first modern editing of a version of Godwin's work, and just before the beginning of renewed critical attention to a text that Wells had implicitly saluted as the first work of English vernacular science fiction. Wells turned Godwin's weightlessness-inducing Ebelus-stone into "Cavorite," a substance that defies

---

and 1728. On the career of Crouch, who often wrote under the pseudonym of Robert Burton, see Robert Mayer, "Nathaniel Crouch, Bookseller and Historian: Popular Historiography and Cultural Power in Late Seventeenth-Century England," *Eighteenth-Century Studies* 27 (1993-94): 391-420.

1   One representative example of his revising habits is his adjustment of Godwin's "our *Galilæusses*, can by advantage of their spectacles gaze the Sunne into spots, & descry mountains in the *Moon*. But this, and more in the ensuing discourse I leave to thy candid censure" to "our *Virtuosi* can by their telescopes gaze the Sun into spots, and descry Mountains in the Moon, but this and much more must be left to the Criticks" (75). Gone also are the geographical engravings and the musical examples, but Crouch did manage to find the famous flying-contraption plate, which he employs.

2   Poe adopted the idea of lunar voyage undertaken by a midget in his "The Unparalleled Adventure of One Hans Pfaall" (1835, originally published in *The Southern Literary Messenger*, frequently reprinted): Poe's lunar balloonist Pfaall "could not have been more than two feet in height." Poe's notes subtly admit that his work is largely indebted to Godwin, but Poe assumed the fiction to be French in origin. This assumption was then replicated by Jules Verne in his 1865 *From the Earth to the Moon*.

gravity, named after its inventor Cavor, one of the two "first men in the moon"; but he darkened Godwin's fiction by interpreting Godwin's differently sized lunars as participants in (and mostly victims of) a ruthlessly hierarchical society, in which most existed in a condition of perpetual slavery. (Wells was not, however, the first Victorian writer to experiment with anti-gravity substances for the purposes of space travel.[1]) It is often as a writer of "science fiction" that Godwin has thus since been celebrated, and despite the anachronism of the term, it is surely defensible.[2] If the practice of science fiction is to make fictional interventions in contemporary scientific discussions, then Godwin's fascination with the debates over the plurality of worlds and the new magnetic philosophy qualifies him eminently as indeed the father of English science fiction. His work, however, was the progeny of a number of quite different genres, and it is true too that Godwin's own immediate generic progeny were similarly multiform.

The Modern Critical Tradition

The Man in the Moone, as appropriate to its picaresque origins, employs a somewhat wandering, episodic structure. It thereby contrasts sharply with the baroque, concentric narrations-within-narrations of *The Man in the Moone*'s continental analogue, Johannes Kepler's likewise posthumous *Somnium, seu opus post-*

---

1 See David Lake's comments in H.G. Wells, *The First Men in the Moon* (Oxford: Oxford UP, 1995), xvi-xvii; and Michael Hammerton, "Wells as Prophet," *Foundation* 45 (1989): 23-37, for the impossibility of such contrivances. Anti-gravity devices feature in "Chrysostom Trueman," *The History of a Voyage to the Moon* (London: Lockwood & Co., 1864), where "repellante" repels all but iron (45, 47); and Percy Grey, *Across the Zodiac*, 2 vols. (London: Trübner & Co., 1880), where "Apergy," "a repulsive force in the atomic sphere," is exploited (1.22).

2 Robert M. Philmus, *Into the Unknown: The Evolution of Science Fiction from Francis Godwin to H. G. Wells*, 2nd ed. (Berkeley: U of California P, 1983), 40-44; David Knight, "Science Fiction of the Seventeenth Century," *The Seventeenth Century* 1 (1986): 69-79; Adam Roberts, *The History of Science Fiction* (Basingstoke: Palgrave Macmillan, 2006), 38, 48-49. Many sf historians, it should be noted, are uneasy with this attitude: e.g., Robert E. Scholes and Eric S. Rabkin, *Science Fiction: History, Science, Vision* (Oxford: Oxford UP, 1977), 6; Parrett, *The Translunar Narrative*, 50-56. An influential theoretical essay on the genre is Darko Suvin, *Metamorphoses of Science Fiction: On the Poetics and History of a Literary Genre* (New Haven, CT: Yale UP, 1979), where Godwin wins the most fleeting of mentions (103).

humus de astronomia lunari (1634).[1] Kepler's multiple narrators rest on a seam of commentary that in its final version outweighs its tiny fictional load by a factor of eight to one, partially a result of four decades of transformative revision.[2] Godwin, in contrast, presents his unannotated fiction in a linear, paratactic fashion, employing one narrator, a haughty Spaniard who stands for everything the Englishman does not. Godwin dwells serially on the three geographical realms of Gonsales' western journeys (1-45), his lunar adventure (45-114), and his closing experiences in China (114-26). A comparison of these three realms is invited, and it is this that gives the work its literary coherence: the lunar civilisation anticipates the society of China, for instance, the orderly and peaceable nature of which in turn contrasts with the war-torn Europe of the opening pages.

Godwin also shifts his work serially through various generic affiliations: travel writing, natural philosophy, utopianism. Accordingly, it is these categories that have largely dictated the interests of modern critics of Godwin. (Needless to say, Godwin is also studied as an antiquary and historian, but this need not concern us here.) The early sustained commentary on Godwin in the 1930s of Nicolson and McColley privileged—though not to exclusion—Godwin's relation to the natural philosophy of his time, regarding *The Man in the Moone* primarily as a vehicle for the dissemination of the new astronomy, and hence as a barometer of the permeation of such knowledge from specialist to non-specialist zones. One generation on, such interests had sharpened rather than shifted, with Cornelius, Davies, and Knowlson investigating Godwin's interest in language and cryptography. The literary ancestry of *The Man in the Moone* was soon attracting attention, and discussion culminating in Jannsen's 1981 thesis dwelt upon generic issues, namely the relation of Godwin to previous English and continental traditions of prose fiction.[3] Such approaches defensibly if predictably associated *The Man in the Moone* with picaresque on the one side, and the rise of the novel on the other; it is routinely noted, for instance, that Daniel Defoe's *Robinson Crusoe* (1719) owes something to Gonsales and Diego on St. Helena, just as his *The Consolidator* (1705) cheerfully appropriates Gonsales' flight to

---

1   Roger Bozzetto, "Kepler's *Somnium*; or, Science Fiction's Missing Link," *Science Fiction Studies* 17 (1990).

2   See Kepler, *Somnium*, ed. Rosen, xvii-xxiii, on the compositional genetics of the work.

3   See also Paul Salzman, *English Prose Fiction 1558-1700: A Critical History* (Oxford: Clarendon P, 1985), 219.

the moon and his final sojourn in China. Yet Godwin's precise status in histories of both prose fiction and science fiction is likely to remain controversial due to the generically complex, polyvalent nature of his work.[1] More expansively, *The Man in the Moone*'s obvious relevance to colonial and ethnological discourses has since received attention, and it is good to see that Godwin's fiction is now usually placed within an array of many other genres: fictional and natural philosophical texts, certainly, but also antiquarian, anatomistic, journalistic, and theological discourses too.[2] As a result, the perennial interest of historians of science in Godwin is now producing more complex approaches than merely treating Godwin as a vehicle for other people's innovations: as the rhetoric of scientific texts has become an obsession for historians of science, so the reciprocity of scientific and non-scientific genres has come under scrutiny. Indeed, it is in the larger fields of intellectual and cultural history that Godwin's text is now most commonly found grazing, and this seems the best pasture for it.

Publication History

The publication history of the first edition of *The Man in the Moone* is significant, as the registration of the work renders it technically a hoax, though it is difficult to say precisely whose hoax it was. Unlike the *Nuncius Inanimatus*, the posthumous *Man in the Moone* was entered into the Stationers' Register, and a license obtained (sg. I8r) from Mathew Clay, who typically licensed plays and poems, perhaps an indication of the work's perceived generic affiliations.[3] The Stationers' entry is dated the next day and entered by the same Clay for Joshua Kirton and Thomas Warren. The first surprise is that the work is described as "written in Spanish by DOMINGO GONSALES and translated into English by EDWARD MAHON gent[leman]."[4] But *The Man in the Moone* was neither written by Gonsales, nor in Spanish, nor

---

1 Poole, "Origins."

2 E.g., Campbell, "Impossible Voyages"; Richard Grove, *Green Imperialism: Colonial Expansion, Tropical Island Edens, and the Origins of Environmentalism 1600-1860* (Cambridge: Cambridge UP, 1995); Cressy, "Early Modern Space Travel."

3 W.W. Greg, *Licensers for the Press, &c. to 1640: A Biographical Index Based Mainly on Arber's Transcript of the Registers of the Company of Stationers* (Oxford: Oxford Bibliographical Society, 1962), n.pag. "Clay."

4 Edward Arber, *A Transcript of the Registers of the Company of Stationers of London 1554-1640 A.D.* (London: The Stationers' Company, 1875-77), 4.400.

translated from it by Edward Mahon! Mahon is presumably to be associated with the "E.M." who signed the epistle to *The Man in the Moone*, as well perhaps as the "ED. M. Ch." of some Latin verse appended to the *Nuncius Inanimatus*, as also to some commendatory verse before Godwin's 1616 *De Præsulibus*. No historical trace of him has been found, and it appears therefore that this is a piece of literary pseudonymy. Godwin was after all interested in cryptographical tricks—the initial letters of the subsections to his 1616 *Rerum Anglicarum*, for example, spell out the hidden phrase "Franciscvs Godwinvvs Landavensis episcopvs hos conscripsit" ("Francis Godwin Bishop of Llandaff wrote these things"), a flourish reminiscent of a medieval scribe.

But pseudonymy as a cover for whom? Mahon, it has been argued, is simply Godwin himself, signing his texts under the guise of a commentator upon and/or a translator of his otherwise absconded self.[1] (Why the precise name "Edward Mahon" has not been fathomed.) But it cannot have been Godwin who expanded E.M. into Edward Mahon for the Stationers' Register, as he was five years in the grave in 1638. An alternative interpretation arises from the verse prefixed to the *De Præsulibus*. The first poem opens, in a rather filial vein,

Bishop, son of a bishop father,
(And soon to be father to future bishops,
To whom is related such a learned son;) ...

It concludes by anticipating further honours for the Godwin line:

Let honours proceed for the father's children,
Through the long line of the good Stuart,
So that by the long line appointed by God,
This God-prized house by Stuart
Kings might be cherished for ever and ever.[2]

---

1 Wood, *Athenae Oxonienses*, 2.558 (who incorrectly interprets "Ch" as a reference to Christ Church, and Mahon as a member); Grant McColley, "The Pseudonyms of Bishop Godwin," *Philological Quarterly* 16 (1937): 78-80.

2 "Praesul, praesule filius Parente,/(Mox & praesulibus Parens futuris,/Cui tam contigit erudita Proles;) ..."; "Natos*que* ad patris euehant honores,/Longam per seriem boni STVARTAE,/Vt longa serie Deo dicata,/Haec DILECTA-DEO domus, STVARTIS/Adsit regibus vs*que* & vs*que* chara." A marginal note on the Old English etymology of Godwin as "Prized by God" is added.

These dreadful poems are followed by the signature "*C. D. Q.* EDW. Mahonides, *Aliàs* CHRISTOPHER," and are stylistically similar to the (likewise dreadful) poems appended to the *Nuncius*. The "Edward Mahon" pseudonym is therefore repeated but with the alias of "Christopher," presumably an expansion that can be applied to the "ED. M. Ch." of the *Nuncius* too.[1] Mahon was a pseudonym, then, but the person behind the pseudonym may have been not *Francis* Godwin but one of his sons. We know that Thomas Godwin helped his father with his telegraphic work (see the *Nuncius Inanimatus* in Appendix A). We know too that Morgan Godwin translated his father's *Rerum Anglicarum* and that he was later granted an audience with Oliver Cromwell to discuss his father's telegraphic secrets.[2] Is "Mahon" or "Christopher" one of these two sons?

There is a further possibility. The hoax of Mahon and his Spanish exemplar was perpetrated after Godwin's death and into the midst of Stationers' Hall. Was this subterfuge known to Kirton and Warren, one of whom held a manuscript, presumably sold to them by the Godwins? *The Man in the Moone* was printed by John Norton, an experienced printer, and sold by a partnership fresh to the bookselling world.[3] *The Man in the Moone* was possibly Kirton and Warren's maiden publication, and this may also explain the presence of the striking illustrations accompanying this flagship venture, as Kirton and Warren seldom afterwards employed illustrations in their productions, although in fact they simply lifted two of the three from an earlier work, Sir Thomas Herbert's *A Relation of Some Yeares Travail Begunne Anno 1626 into Afrique and the Greater Asia* (1634).[4] Indeed, the printing of these

---

1 The poem in the 1615 English translation of the *De Præsulibus* contains the same signature, but terminating "... aliàs CH:" "C.D.Q." is presumambly an abbreviation for *consecrat dedicatque* (or *dicatque*), "he consecrates and dedicates" (more often encountered reversed as "D.C.Q.").

2 This meeting is reported in *The Hartlib Papers* 29/5/33B.

3 For career information, see R.B. McKerrow, gen. ed., *A Dictionary of Printers and Booksellers in England, Scotland, Ireland, and of Foreign Printers of English Books 1557-1640* (London: The Bibliographical Society, 1910); H.R. Plomer, *Dictionary of the Booksellers and Printers who were at work in England, Scotland and Ireland from 1641 to 1667* (London: The Bibliographical Society, 1907).

4 Kirton and Warren's only other 1638 work was a quarto, William Barlow's *Summe and Substance*, the rights for which must have been purchased from John Bill, who had produced the 1625 edition. The engravings of St. Helena and the Azores were recycled from Sir Thomas Herbert, *A Relation of Some Yeares Travail Begunne Anno 1626 into Afrique*

illustrations was initially bungled, and had to be fixed twice.[1] Again, the work features musical notation, in standard "choral" or "Huguenot" typography, another eye-catching feature.[2] And if *The Man in the Moone* is a first work, then this makes its fraudulent entry in the Register that little bit more fascinating.

In his youth Kirton had been apprenticed on 3 November 1628 to John Bill, Godwin's usual printer for his antiquarian work. Now Francis Godwin's third son, Paul, was also bound to the same John Bill on the first of the following month; it was not uncommon for clerics' sons to follow this career path at the time.[3] Paul thus joined Bill's house just before the appearance of the *Nuncius*, and he may have been the catalyst for that publication. Kirton was freed by Bill and Richard Whitaker on 7 November 1636, a year after the same men had freed Paul.[4] Thus the bishop's son and the future publisher of *The Man in the Moone* worked alongside one another for around seven years. Surely this was the avenue by which Kirton got hold of the manuscript, and decided, with Warren, to publish it. Paul may therefore have tidied up his father's MS for publication, and he may also be the

---

and the Greater Asia (London: William Stansby and Jacob Bloome, 1634), 215, 225, although the flying-machine engraving must have been commissioned specially for the publication of Godwin. The details on the recycled plates reflect aspects of Herbert's narrative not repeated in Godwin, hence the marking of 'Fayall' on the Azores map, not mentioned by Godwin. These were presumably acquired through Stansby himself, who printed Godwin from 1616 to 1630, or through Bill again, who employed Stansby as printer for these editions. None of the plates themselves is signed, but William Marshall is a possible candidate.

1 The work exists in three states: with the first two plates erroneously switched, with one plate corrected (resulting in a repetition accompanied by a pasted-in singleton), and with both plates corrected. See the textual notes.

2 D.W. Krummel, *English Music Printing 1553-1700* (London: The Bibliographical Society, 1975), 5.

3 Cyprian Blagden, "The Stationers' Company in the Civil War Period," *The Library*, 5th series, 13 (1958): 1-17, comments (2) that in the 1630s an average of seven clerical families a year were sending sons into the book trade.

4 Robin Myers, ed., *Records of the Worshipful Company of Stationers 1554-1920* (Cambridge: Chadwyck-Healey, 1985), Apprentice Register (1605-66), fol. 103r and Register of Freemen (1605-1703), fol. 42v (microform reels 34, 38); D.F. McKenzie, *Stationers Company Apprentices 1605-1640* (Charlottesville, Virginia: The Bibliographical Society of the University of Virginia, 1961), 10, 135.

author of the Mahonidean verse. But, finally, it is possible too that Paul had simply picked up a manuscript from his father's study, complete with the E.M. epistle, and had taken it at face value, as had Kirton and Warren. (He would still, however, need to explain the "E.M." initials to Kirton.) As the discussion of the work's chronology above suggests, the work as we have it is calendrically inconsistent in a fashion which suggests textual deficiency of a kind produced by an incomplete revision of an otherwise fair manuscript. So the work in its surviving state was penned in or after 1628, left unpublished by Godwin, acquired by his son Paul, and sold to his fellow apprentice Kirton. Wittingly or unwittingly, Paul Godwin and Joshua Kirton carried the fraud of a Spanish original and a gentleman translator into the guardian of publishers' rights in the period, the Stationers' Register.

Francis Godwin and his Contemporaries: A Brief Chronology

1552	Birth of Matteo Ricci, as well as Domingo Gonsales
1562	Birth of Francis Godwin
1582-98	Ricci works his way from Macao to Beijing
1588	Mendoza's account of China translated into English
1591	Sir John Harington, *Orlando Furioso* in English
1598	J.H. van Linschoten, *Discourse of Voyages into the East and West Indies* in English
1598-1600	Richard Hakluyt, *The Principal Navigations*
1600	William Gilbert, *De Magnete*
1601	Francis Godwin, *A Catalogue of the Bishops of England*; as a reward, Godwin becomes Bishop of Llandaff in the same year
1608	Sir John Harington, *A Supplie or Addicion to the Catalogue of Bishops*
1610	Galileo Galilei, *Sidereus Nuncius*
1610	Johannes Kepler, *Dissertatio cum Nuncio Sidereo*
1613	Mark Ridley, *A Short Treatise of Magneticall Bodies and Motions*
1615	Nicholas Trigault, *De Expeditione Christiana apud Sinas*
1616	Francis Godwin, *Rerum Anglicarum ... Annales*
1617	Godwin becomes Bishop of Hereford
1621	Robert Burton, *The Anatomy of Melancholy*
1625	Samuel Purchas, *Purchas his Pilgrimes*
1626	Samuel Purchas, *Purchas his Pilgrimage*
1627	Francis Bacon, *Sylva Sylvarum* and *The New Atlantis*
1629	Francis Godwin, *Nuncius Inanimatus*
1630	Death of Kepler
1630	George Hakewill publishes Godwin's estimates of old Roman coinage values
1633	Death of Godwin
1634	Francis Hickes, *Certaine Select Dialogues of Lucian*
1634	Johannes Kepler, *Somnium*
1638	Francis Godwin, *The Man in the Moone*
1638	John Wilkins, *The Discovery of a World in the Moone*

1640	John Wilkins, *A Discourse Concerning a New World and Another Planet*
1641	John Wilkins, *Mercury, or the Secret and Swift Messenger*
1642	Death of Galileo
1645	Langrenus, Map of the Moon with "Gansii" crater
1645	Translation of *The Man in the Moone* into Dutch
1648	John Wilkins, *Mathematicall Magick*
1648	Translation of *The Man in the Moone* into French
1659	Translation of *The Man in the Moone* into German

A Note on the Text

The first edition of *The Man in the Moone* (1638) is scarce. In some copies, the first two illustrations are reversed, or the flying-machine inadvertently repeated twice. Nor is the second edition (1657) common. Evidently it was a work that was not only read, but read to pieces. The second edition is textually unremarkable, recomposed from a copy of the first edition, which it follows scrupulously in format.[1] (One interesting variant shows that the second compositor was a decent Latinist, as he was supposed to be.[2]) There are no surviving MSS of the work. The following text is accordingly based directly on the 1638 edition, taken from the Ashmolean copy (Ashm. 940 (1)), bound significantly with Wilkins's 1638 *Discovery of a World in the Moone* (Ashm. 940 (2)) in the Bodleian Library, and collated against the British Library copy (C.56.c.2).[3] Editorial interventions are enclosed in square brackets and recorded in the textual notes, which also include the significant 1657 variants; these have been obtained from Anthony Wood's copy (Wood 632), also in the Bodleian.[4] Textual notes are identified by superscript Roman numerals and are located immediately following the text (p. 123). Signatures (for the preface) and page numbers (for the main text) are placed between square

---

1   The second compositor's interventions are almost all orthographical: he typically suppresses final "e"; often replaces "i" by "y"; changes older forms such as "yeeld" to "yield" consistently; and is more liberal with the ampersand.

2   He changes *contabundo* to *cunctabundo*, a licit alternative spelling. However, since he reproduces the un-Spanish "Therrando," plausibly an error in reading for "Fernando," he may be ignorant of Spanish itself (see textual notes on both words), as was therefore his predecessor.

3   My proof-text thus comes from the original Ashmolean Museum, presumably from its working academic library of Natural History and Philosophy, as opposed to its Chemical Library, all transferred to the Bodleian in 1860 (R.T. Gunter, "The Ashmole Printed Books," *Bodleian Quarterly Record* 6 [1930]: 193-95).

4   Wood attributed the work on its title-page to "Franc. Godwyn Bishop of Heref." But a strip pasted over his earlier guess shows that initially he was taken in: back-illumination reveals "Domingo Go[n]zales the author. Translated by E.M. The 1 edit. came out in Lond. 1638." It cost him 1*s* 3*d*, and is bound with Cyrano's moon voyage in the translation of Thomas St. Serf: *Selenarchia, or the Government of the World in the Moon* (London: Humphrey Robinson, 1659).

brackets. Exactly one sixth of these bisect words in the original text; in these cases, the bracketed pagination follows rather than interrupts the word in question. Catch-words are likewise suppressed. For consistency, the like practices are followed in the Appendices.

THE MAN IN THE MOONE:
OR
A DISCOURSE OF A
VOYAGE THITHER
BY
DOMINGO GONSALES
THE SPEEDY MESSENGER

[A3r]
To the Ingenious Reader.

THOU hast here an essay of *Fancy*, where *Invention* is shewed with *Judgment*. It was not the *Authors* intention (I presume) to discourse thee into a beleife of each particular circumstance. [A3v] Tis fit thou allow him a liberty of conceite; where thou takest to thy selfe a liberty of judgment. In substance thou hast here a new discovery of a new *world*, which perchance may finde little better entertainment in thy opinion, than that of *Columbus* at first, in the esteeme of all men. Yet his than[1] but poore espiall of *America*, betray'd unto knowledge soe much as [A4r] hath since encrease into a vaste plantation. And the then unknowne, to be now of as large extent as all other the knowne *world*.

That there should be *Antipodes* was once thought as great a *Paradox* as now that the *Moon* should bee habitable.[2] But the knowledge of this may seeme more properly reserv'd for this our discovering age: In which our *Galilæusses*, [A4v] can by advantage of their spectacles[3] gaze the Sunne into spots, & descry moun-

---

Note on the notes: if a proper name is unglossed, it may be taken as fictitious. Glosses for early-modern words are taken, unless otherwise noted, from the *Oxford English Dictionary*. In the notes to the text itself, when a number occurs on its own without "p.", it refers to a page number of Godwin's original text, as indicated in square brackets within the text, and not to the page number of this edition. When it appears with a "p.", it refers to material elsewhere in this edition before and after the text proper, and may therefore be found using the numbers at the bottom of the printed pages.

1 I.e., then.
2 Most notoriously by Lactantius, *Divinae Institutiones* 3.24; and Augustine, *De Civitate Dei* 16.9. This classic failure of the ancients had become a literary *topos* of both natural philosophical and travel writing by Godwin's time: e.g., Copernicus, *De Revolutionibus*, Dedication to Pope Paul III; Acosta, *Naturall and Morall Historie of the East and West Indies*, 1-4; Wilkins, *Discovery of a World in the Moone* (London: Michael Sparke and Edward Forrest, 1638), 6-12. It was imitated directly from Godwin at the opening of the anonymous late-seventeenth-century *The Lunarian*: "As the opinions of ye Antipodes was thought ridiculous to our Ancestours ..." (British Library, Add. MS 11812, fol. 5r). See further Valerie I.J. Flint, "Monsters and the Antipodes in the Early Middle Ages and Enlightenment," *Viator* 15 (1984): 65-80.
3 spectacles] telescopes

taines in the *Moon*.[1] But this, and more in the ensuing discourse
I leave to thy candid censure, & the faithfull relation of the little
eye-witnesse,[2] our great discoverer,[i]

E.M.[3]

---

1 References ultimately to Galileo Galilei's (1564-1642) *Starry Messenger*
  (1610), and perhaps to his *Letters on Sunspots* (1613). See Galileo
  Galilei, *Sidereus Nuncius*, 87-113, for an excellent discussion of the
  immediate reception of Galileo. See further William R. Shea, "Galileo,
  Scheiner, and the Interpretation of Sunspots," *Isis* 61 (1970): 498-519.
  This, the first of many parallels to Burton's "Digression of Ayre" in his
  Anatomy of Melancholy, signals the basic vernacular resource for much of
  Godwin's astronomical knowledge (see Appendix G). The major English
  literary exploitation of the idea that telescopes deceive is Samuel
  Butler's later burlesque on the Royal Society, "The Elephant in the
  Moon."
2 So commences the interplay between sight and hearing that runs
  through the work: the reader merely hears, but Gonsales sees. The *locus
  classicus* is Plautus, *Truculentus*, 490: "qui audiunt audita dicunt, qui
  vident plane sciunt" ("they who hear, [merely] tell what they hear; they
  who see, understand clearly").
3 On the identity of E.M., see the Publication History (pp. 57-58), above.

[1]
THE MAN IN THE MOONE.

IT is well enough and sufficiently knowne to all the countries of *Andaluzia*, that I *Domingo Gonsales*, was borne of Noble parentage, and that in the renowned City of *Sivill*, to wit in the yeare 1552.[1] my Fathers name being *Therrando*[ii] *Gonsales*, (that was neere kinsman by the mothers side unto *Don* [2] *Pedro Sanchez* that worthy Count of *Almenara*,) and as for my Mother, she was the daughter of the Reverend and famous Lawyer, *Otho Perez de Sallaveda*, Governour of *Barcellona*, and *Corrigidor*[2] *of Biscaia*: being the youngest of 17 Children they had, I was put to schoole, and intended by them unto the Church. But our Lord purposing to use my service in matters of farre other nature and quality, inspired me with spending sometime in the warres. It was at the time that *Don Fernando*,[iii] the Noble and thrice renowned Duke *D'Alva*,[3] was sent into the Low Countries, *viz*. the yeare of Grace 1568. I then following the current of my foresaid desire, leaving the Vniversitie of *Salamanca*,[4] (whither my Parents had sent me) without giving knowledge unto any of my dearest friends, got mee through *France*, unto *Antwerp*, where in the [3] moneth of *Iune* 1569, I arrived in something poore estate. For having sold my

---

1 *Domingo Gonsales*] Two stock Spanish names, probably without any specific allusion. But his father's name, Therrando, is a made-up Spanish name, Spanish not possessing "th"; perhaps the compositor misread "Fernando" (see the n. 2 to the Note on the Text, above, and textual note ii, below).

2 *Corrigidor*] chief magistrate (Spanish, properly *corregidor*)

3 Duke Fernando Alvarez de Toledo, third Duke of Alva (1507-82), sent to the Netherlands by Philip II of Spain to crush Protestantism. He was of course despised by the English. Godwin's source for contextual detail here was probably Emmanuel van Meteren, *Historia Belgica* ([Antwerp]: [n.p.], c. 1600), 63-88, where he would have found information on Alva, the *Gueux*, Cossé, and Mansfeld below; "*Mounsieur Tavier*" appears to be fictional, but see p. 70 n. 4 below. See also the Edward Grimestone/ William Crosse vernacular compilation from Pierre Le Petit/Emmanuel van Meteren, *A Generall Historie of the Netherlands* (London: Adam Islip, 1627 [previous editions of 1608, 1609]), 306-71. For a modern account, see Jonathan I. Israel, *The Dutch Republic: Its Rise, Greatness, and Fall 1477-1806* (Oxford: Clarendon P, 1998), ch. 8.

4 Salamanca was by the sixteenth century one of the largest universities in Europe, famed foremost for legal study, but later also for its ultramontane opposition to the conciliarism of Paris.

Bookes and Bedding, with such other stuffe as I had, which happily yeelded me some 30 duckats and borrowed of my Fathers friends some 20 more, I bought mee a little nagge with which I travailed more thriftily than young Gentlemen are wont ordinarily to doe: Vntill at last arriving within a league of *Antwerp*, certaine of the cursed *Geuses*[1] set upon mee, and bereaved me of Horse, monie, and all: Whereupon I was faine (through want and necessitie,) to enter into the service of Marshal *Cossey*[2] a French Nobleman, whom I served truly in honourable place, although mine enemies gave it out to my disgrace that I was his horse-keepers boy. But for that matter I shall referre my selfe unto the report of the Count *Mansfield*,[3] *Mounsieur Tavier*,[4] [4] and other men of knowne worth and estimation; who have often testified unto many of good credit yet living, the very truth in that behalfe, which indeed is this, that *Mounsieur Cossey*,[iv] who about that time had been sent Embassador unto the Duke *D'Alva*; Governour of the Low Countries, he I say, understanding the Nobility of my birth, and my late misfortune; thinking it would bee no small honour to him, to have a Spanyard of that qualitie about him, furnished mee with horse, armour, and whatsoever I wanted, using my service in nothing so much (after once I had learned the French tongue)[5] as writing his Letters, because my hand indeed was then very faire. In the time of warre, if upon necessitie I now and then dressed mine own Horse, it ought not to be cast in my teeth, seeing I hold it the part of a Gentleman, [5] for setting forward the service of his Prince, to submit himselfe unto the vilest office. The first expedition I was in, was against the Prince of *Orange*,[6] at what time the Marshall my

---

1 *Geuses*] the *Gueux* or "Beggars," a sixteenth-century Dutch revolutionary movement, who signed a petition known as the Compromise of the Nobility, in resistance to the Spanish heresy laws. The movement generated a violent popular wing. See van Meteren, *Historia Belgica*, 69. Van Meteren comments that the Beggars tended to despoil their victims not only of their property, but also of their noses and ears.

2 Artus de Cossé-Brissac, Comte de Secondigny, Marshal of France (1512-82). See van Meteren, *Historia Belgica*, 71.

3 Pierre-Ernest, Comte de Mansfeld (1547-1604). See van Meteren, *Historia Belgica*, 67.

4 Probably a garbled reference to Gaspard de Saulx Tavannes (1509-73), Marshal of France.

5 By the end of the work, Gonsales will have acquired French, Lunar, and a Chinese dialect, to add to his Spanish, Dutch, and Italian.

6 William, Count of Nassau (1533-84), the hero of the struggle from the conventional English point of view.

friend aforesaid, met him making a roade into *France*, and putting him to flight, chased him even unto the walls of *Cambray*.[1] It was my good hap at that time to defeat a horseman of the enemy, by killing his Horse with my pistoll, which falling upon his leg, so as he could not stirre, hee yeelded himselfe to my mercie; but I knowing mine owne weaknesse of bodie, and seeing him a lustie tall fellow, thought it my surest way to dispatch him, which having done, I rifled him of a chaine, monie, and other things to the value of 200 ducats: no sooner was that money in my purse, but I began to resume the remembrance of my nobilitie, and [6] giving unto *Mounsieur Cossey*^v the *Besa Los Manos*,[2] I got my selfe imediately unto the Dukes court, where were divers of my kindred, that (now they saw my purse full of good Crownes) were ready enough to take knowledge of mee; by their meanes I was received into pay, and in processe of time obtained a good degree of favour with the Duke, who sometimes would jeast a little more broadly at my personage than I could well brook. For although I must acknowledge my stature to be so little, as no man there is living I thinke lesse, yet in asmuch as it was the work of God, and not mine, hee ought not to have made that a meanes to dishonour a Gentleman with all. And those things which have happened unto mee, may bee an example, that great and wonderfull things may be performed by most unlikely bodies, if [7] the mind be good, and the blessing of our Lord doe second and follow the endeavours of the same. Well, howsoever the Dukes merriments went against my stomacke, I framed my selfe the best I could to dissemble my discontent, and by such my patience accommodating my selfe also unto some other his humors [sic], so wan his favour, as at his departure home into *Spaine*, (whither I attended him) the Year 1573[3] by his favour and some other accidents, (I will say nothing of my owne industry, wherein I was not wanting to my selfe) I was able to carry home in my purse the value of 3000 Crownes. At my returne home my Parents, that were marvellously displeased with my departure, received mee with great joy; and the rather, for that they saw I brought with mee meanes to maintaine my selfe without their charge, [8] having a portion sufficient of mine owne, so that they

---

1 See van Meteren, *Historia Belgica*, 79: "On the order of Alva, Marshal Cossé, sent by the French king, from afar off ... with several divisions of cavalry and 2,000 foot-soldiers, pursued Orange into France."

2 I.e., *Besar la mano* (Spanish), lit. to kiss the hand, i.e., to pay one's respects.

3 Accurate: Alva did return to Spain in this year.

needed not to defalke[1] any thing from my brethren or ·sisters for my setting up. But fearing I would spend it as lightly as I got it, they did never leave importuning mee, till I must needs marry the daughter of a *Portugais* a Merchant of *Lisbon*, a man of great wealth and dealings, called *Iohn Figueres*. Therein I satisfied their desire, and putting not onely my marriage money, but also a good part of mine owne Stock into the hands of my father in Law, or such as hee wished mee unto, I lived in good sort, even like a Gentleman, with great content for divers yeares. At last it fell out, that some disagreement happened between me and one *Pedro Delgades* a Gentleman of my kinne, the causes whereof are needlesse to be related, but so farre this dissention grew betweene us, [9] as when no mediation of friends could appease the same, into the field wee went together alone with our Rapiers, where my chance was to kill him, being a man of great strength, and tall stature. But what I wanted of him in strength, I supplied with courage, and my nimblenesse more then countervailed his stature. This fact[2] being committed in *Carmona*, I fled with all the speed I could to *Lisbone*, thinking to lurke with some friend of my Father in-lawes, till the matter might bee compounded, and a course taken for a sentence of Acquittall by consent of the prosecutors. This matter fell out in the Yeare 1596. even at that time that a certaine great Count of ours came home from the West-Indies, in triumphant manner, boasting and sending out his declarations in print, of a [10] great victory hee had obtained against the *English*, neere the *Isle of Pines*. Whereas the truth is, he got of the *English* nothing at all in that Voyage, but blowes and a great losse.[3]

Would to God that lying and Vanitie had beene all the faults he had; his covetousnesse was like to bee my utter undoing,

---

1 defalke] diminish
2 fact] crime
3 I.e., Don Bernaldino Delgadillo de Avellaneda and the skirmish off the Isla de Pinos (better known today as Isla de la Juventud), the main island lying south off the north-westerly end of Cuba. Godwin has in mind Savile, *A Libell of Spanish Lies*, which includes the Spanish text of the libel and a translation. The expedition, however, was also reported by Hakluyt, who likewise reproduced the libel (*Principal Navigations*, 3.583-98; *The Hakluyt Handbook*, 2 vols. [London: The Hakluyt Society, 1974], 449, 451). The expedition was remembered because Sir Francis Drake died on it. Godwin was to be followed much later by Charles Kingsley, who integrated the Savile account into his *Westward Ho!* (1855) to similar effect. Perhaps Henry Neville's *The Isle of Pines* (1668) also gestures to this reference in Godwin.

although since it hath proved a meanes of eternizing my name for ever with all Posteritie, (I verily hope) and to the unspeakable good of all mortall men, that in succeeding ages the world shall have, if at the leastwise it may please God that I doe returne safe home againe into my Countrie, to give perfect instructions how those admirable devices, and past all credit[1] of possibilitie, which I have light upon, may be imparted unto publique use. You shal [11] then see men to flie from place to place in the ayre; you shall be able, (without moving or travailing of any creature,) to send messages in an instant many Miles off, and receive answer againe immediately; you shall bee able to declare your minde presently unto your friend, being in some private and remote place of a populous Citie, with a number of such like things:[2] but that which far surpasseth all the rest, you shall have notice of a new World, of many most rare and incredible secrets of Nature, that all the Philosophers of former ages could never so much as dreame off. But I must be advised, how I be over-liberall, in publishing these wonderfull mysteries, till the Sages of our State have considered how farre the use of these things may stand with the Policy and good government of our [12] Countrey, as also with the Fathers of the Church, how the publication of them, may not prove prejudiciall to the affaires of the Catholique faith and Religion, which I am taught (by those wonders I have seen above any mortall man that hath lived in many ages past) with all my best endeavours to advance, without all respect of temporall good, and soe I hope I shall.[3]

But to goe forward with my narration, so it was that the bragging Captaine above named, made shew of great discontentment, for the death of the said *Delgades*, who was indeed some kinne unto him. Howbeit hee would have been intreated, so that I would have given him no lesse than 1000. Ducats (for his share) to have put up his Pipes,[4] and surceased all suite in his [13] Kins-

---

1   credit] belief
2   For Gonsales' telegraphic schemes, see the *Nuncius Inanimatus* in Appendix A, and the commentary there.
3   But I must be advised ... and soe I hope I shall.] An allusion to the Catholic practice of licensing. McColley's link to the renewed English licensing laws is unduly dramatic. This entire section was omitted by Baudoin in his French translation.
4   to have put up his Pipes] Proverbial for "to be silent, and desist from such and such a discourse" (M.P. Tilley, *A Dictionary of Proverbs in England in the Sixteenth and Seventeenth Centuries* [Ann Arbor: U of Michigan P, 1950], 345).

mans behalfe; I had by this time (besides a wife) two sonnes, whom I liked not to beggar by satisfying the desire of this covetous braggart and the rest, and therefore constrained of necessity to take another course, I put my selfe in a good Caricke that went for the East *Indies*, taking with me the worth of 2000. Ducats to traffique withall, being yet able to leave so much more for the estate of my wife and children, whatsoever might become of me, and the goods I carried with me. In the *Indies* I prospered exceeding well, bestowing my stocke in *Iewells*, namely, for the most part in *Diamonds*, *Emeraulds*, and great *Pearle*; of which I had such peniworths, as my stocke being safely returned into *Spaine*, (so I heard it was) must needs yeeld ten for one. But my selfe upon my way homeward [14] soone after we had doubled the East of *Buena Speranza*,[1] fell grievously sicke for many daies, making account by the same sicknesse to end my life, as undoubtedly I had done, had we not (even then as we did) recovered that same blessed *Isle* of S. *Hellens*, the only paradice, I thinke, that the earth yeeldeth, of the healthfullnesse of the Aire there, the fruitfullnesse of the soile, and the abundance of all manner of things necessary for sustaining the life of man, what should I speake, seeing there is scant a boy in all *Spaine*, that hath not heard of the same?[2] I cannot but wonder, that our King in his wisdome hath not thought fit to plant a Colony, and to fortifie in it, being a place so necessary for refreshing of all travaillers out of the *Indies*, so as it is hardly possible to make a Voyage thence, without touching there.

[16] It is situate in the Latitude[vi] of 16. degrees to the South, and is about 3. leagues in compasse, having no firme land or continent within 300. leagues, nay not so much as an *Island* within 100. leagues of the same, so that it may seeme a miracle of Nature, that out of so huge and tempestuous an Ocean, such a little peece of ground should arise and discover it selfe. Upon the

---

1   *Buena Speranza*] The Cape of Good Hope. This stretch of the narrative from here until the moon launch borrows heavily from contemporary accounts of the East Indies trade route: see Knowlson, "A Note on Bishop Godwin's 'Man in the Moone,'" for discussion.

2   Godwin derived his knowledge of the islands off the west of Africa primarily from Richard Hakluyt's redaction of Thomas Pretty's account of Thomas Cavendish's 1566-68 circumnavigation (*Principal Navigations*, 2.823-24), as well as perhaps from Linschoten (*Discours*, 171-75), also a major source for Purchas's chapters (Samuel Purchas, *Purchas His Pilgrimage* [London: Henry Fetherstone, 1626], 781-89). See Appendix E for an extract from Linschoten.

[15: St. Helena engraving]¹ ⁷ⁱⁱ

South side there is a very good harborough, and neere unto the same divers edifices built by the *Portingals* to entertaine passengers, amongst the which there is a pretty Chappell handsomly beautified with a Tower, having a faire Bell in the same. Neere unto this housing there is a pretty Brooke of excellent fresh water, divers faire walkes made by hand, and set along upon both sides, with fruit-Trees, especially Oranges, [17] Limmons, Pomgranats, Almonds, and the like, which beare Fruit all the yeare long, as do also the fig-Trees, Vines, Peare-Trees, (whereof there are divers sorts,) Palmitos,² Cocos, Olives, Plumms; also I have seene there such as wee call *Damaxælas*,³ but few; as for Apples I dare say there are none at all; of garden Hearbs there is good store, as of Parsely, Cole-worts, Rosemary, Mellons, Gourds, Lettice, and the like; Corne likewise growing of it selfe, incredible plenty, as *Wheate*, *Pease*, *Barley*, and almost all kinde of Pulse; but cheifly it aboundeth with *Cattell*, and *Fowle*, as *Goates*, *Swine*, *Sheepe*, and *Horses*, *Partridges*, wilde *Hens*, *Phesants*, *Pigeons*, and wild *Fowle*,

---

1 This engraving is recycled from Herbert, *A Relation of Some Yeares Travail*, 225, which may itself have been copied from the superior engraving in Linschoten, inserted between pages 172 and 173: "The true description, and situation of the Island St Helena on the East, North, and West sides, lying vnder 16. degrees on the Southsyde of the Equinoxiall line." The original engraver was Raygnald Elstrak. See the comments in the Publication History (pp. 58-59).

2 Palmitos] i.e., palmettos, any of the variety of fan palms

3 *Damaxælas*] presumably a (pseudo-)Spanish equivalent of damson, the fruit of *Prunus communis* or *domestica*

beyond all credit: especially there are to be seene about the Moneths of *February*, and *March*, huge flocks [18] of a certaine kinde of wilde *Swans* (of which I shall have cause heerafter to speake more) that like unto our *Cuckoes*, and *Nightingales*, at a certaine season of the yeare, doe vanish away, and are no more to be seene.[1]

On this blessed *Island* did they set mee ashore[2] with a *Negro* to attend me, where, praised bee God, I recovered my health, and continued there for the space of one whole yeare, solacing my selfe (for lacke of humane society) with *Birds*, and brute beasts, as for *Diego* (so was the *Blackmoore* called,)[3] he was constrained to live at the West end of the *Island* in a Cave. Because being always together, victuals would not have fallen out so plenty: if the Hunting or Fowling of the one had succeeded well, the other would finde means to invite him, [19] but if it were scant with both, we were faine both to bestirre our selves; marry that fell out very seldome, for that no creatures there doe any whit more feare a man, then they doe a *Goate* or a *Cow*; by reason thereof I found meanes easily to make tame divers sorts both of *Birds* and *Beasts*, which I did in short time, onely by muzzeling them, so as till they came either unto me, or else *Diego*, they could not feede. At first I tooke great pleasure in a kinde of *Partridges*, of which I made great use, as also of a tame *Fox* I had. For whensoever I had any occasion to conferre with *Diego*, I would take me one of them, being hungry, and tying a note about his necke, beat him from me, whereupon strait they would away to the Cave of *Diego*, and if they found him not there, still would they [20] beat up and downe all the West end of the *Island*, till they had hunted him out;

---

1   Both Hakluyt and Linschoten say that the Portuguese were responsible for introducing both the animals and the edible fruits to the island, which had previously lacked both, being "of it selfe ... verie ashie and drie" (Linschoten, *Discours*, 173). So despite its plentiful fish and favourable climate, St. Helena is to a significant extent a man-made, not a natural, paradise.

2   See Linschoten, *Discours*. Hakluyt's section on the Canaries reproduces the report of Thomas Nicols, an Englishman who remained there for seven years. Hakluyt recorded how one John Segar was left in 1591 on St. Helena to convalesce; picked up eighteen months later he was found "crazed in minde and halfe out of his wits." He died of distraction and lack of sleep eight days later (*Principal Navigations*, 2.108 [second pagination]; also Purchas, *Pilgrimage*, 781). Negro slaves were also recorded as being left behind to recuperate.

3   Diego] a common (Spanish) name, here awarded to a slave

yet this kinde of conveyance not being without some inconvenience needlesse heere to be recited; after a certaine space I perswaded *Diego* (who though hee were a fellow of good parts, was ever content to be ruled by me,) to remove his habitation unto a promontory or cape upon the North-West part of the *Island*, being, though a league off, yet within sight of my house and Chappell; and then, so long as the weather was faire, we could at all times by signalls, declare our minds each to other in an instant, either by night, or by day; which was a thing I tooke great pleasure in.

If in the night season I would signifie any thing to him, I used to set up a light in the Tower or [21] place where our bell hung: It is a pretty large roome, having a faire window well glased, and the walls within being plaistered, were exceeding white; by reason thereof, though the light were but small, it gave a great shew, as also it would have done much further off if need had beene. This light after I had let stand some halfe houre, I used to cover: and then if I saw any signall of light againe from my companion at the cape, I knew that he waited for my notice, which perceiving, by hiding and shewing my light, according to a certaine rule and agreement between us, I certified him at pleasure what I list: The like course I tooke in the day to advertise him of my pleasure, sometimes by smoake, sometimes by dust, sometimes by a more refined and more effectual way.

[22] But this Art containeth more mysteries then are to be set downe in few words: Hereafter I will perhaps afford a discourse for it of purpose, assuring my selfe that it may prove exceedingly profitable unto mankind, being rightly used and well imployed: for that which a messenger cannot performe in many dayes, this may dispatch in a peece of an houre.[1] Well, I notwithstanding after a while grew weary of it, as being too painfull[2] for me, and betooke me againe to my winged messengers.

Upon the Sea shore, especially about the mouth of our River, I found great store of a certain kinde of wild *Swan* (before mentioned) feeding almost altogether upon the prey, and (that which is somewhat strange,) partly of *Fish*, partly of *Birds*, having

---

1 A "discourse for it of purpose" was in fact published not by Gonsales but by Godwin: the *Nuncius Inanimatus* appeared in 1629 while *The Man in the Moone* remained in manuscript or under composition. Yet Gonsales landed in China in 1601, and for him 1629 was indeed a future date. On all these telegraphic schemes, see the *Nuncius Inanimatus* in Appendix A, and the notes there.

2 painfull] laborious

(which is also no lesse strange) [23] one foote with Clawes, talons, and pounces,[1] like an *Eagle*, and the other whole like a Swan or water fowle. These birds using to breed there in infinite numbers, I tooke some 30. or 40. young ones of them, and bred them up by hand partly for my recreation, partly also as having in my head some rudiments of that device, which afterward I put in practise. These being strong and able to continue a great flight, I taught them first to come at call affarre off, not using any noise but only the shew of a white Cloth. And surely in them I found it true that is delivered by Plutarch, how that *Animalia Carnivora*, they are *dociliora quam alterius cuiusvis generis*.[2] It were a wonder to tell what trickes I had taught them, by that time they were a quarter old; amongst other things I used them by little [24] and little to fly with burthens,[3] wherein I found them able above all credit, and brought them to that passe, as that a white sheet being displayed unto them by *Diego* upon the side of a hill, they would carry from me unto him, Bread, flesh, or any other thing I list to send, and upon the like call returne unto mee again.

Having prevailed thus farre, I began to cast in my head how I might doe to joyne a number of them together in bearing of some great burthen: which if I could bring to passe, I might enable a man to fly and be carried in the ayre, to some certaine place safe and without hurt.[4] In this cogitation having much laboured my wits, and made some triall, I found by experience, that if many were put to the bearing of one great burthen, by reason it was not possible [25] all of them should rise together just in one instant, the first that raised himselfe upon his wings finding himselfe

---

1 pounces] claws

2 *Animalia Carnivora*, they are *dociliora quam alterius cuiusvis generis*] "Carnivorous animals are more teachable than any other kind." If genuine, the quotation is presumably from one of the standard Renaissance Latin translations of Plutarch, who wrote originally in Greek. But a corresponding text in Greek has not been located, nor has the exact Latin edition Godwin might be using. The line sounds like it should come from one of Plutarch's consecutive essays in praise of the rationality of beasts and the desirability of vegetarianism: "Whether Land or Sea Animals are Cleverer"; "Beasts are Rational"; "On the Eating of Flesh" (*Moralia*, 959A-999B); so even if this is another false citation (as suggested by Janssen, *Man in the Moone*, 120), it at least sounds plausibly Plutarchian.

3 burthens] burdens

4 On flight, see the extract from Wilkins in Appendix H, and the commentary there.

stayed by a weight heavier than hee could move or stirre, would by and by give over, as also would the second, third, and all the rest. I devised (therefore) at last a meanes how each of them might rise carrying but his owne proportion of weight only, and it was thus.

I fastned about every one of my *Gansa's*[1] [viii] a little pulley of Corke, and putting a string through it of meetly[2] length, I fastened the one end thereof unto a blocke almost of eight Pound weight, unto the other end of the string I tied a poyse weighing some two Pound, which being done, and causing the signall to be erected, they presently rose all (being 4 in number,) and carried away my blocke unto the place [26] appointed.[3] This falling out according to my hope and desire, I made proofe afterwards, but using the help of 2. or 3. birds more, in a Lamb, whose happinesse I much envied, that he should be the first living creature to take possession of such a device.

At last after divers tryalls I was surprized with a great longing, to cause my selfe to be carried in the like sort. *Diego* my Moore was likewise possessed with the same desire, and but that otherwise I loved him well, and had need of his helpe, I should have taken that his ambitious affection[4] in very evill part: for I hold it farre more honour to have been the first flying man, then to bee another *Neptune* that first adventured to sayle upon the Sea.[5] Howbeit not seeming to take notice of the marke hee aymed [27] at, I onely told him (which also I take to be true) that all my *Gansa's* were not of sufficient strength to carry him, being a man,

---

1   This is the first time Godwin uses the term *Gansas*, coined from the Spanish *ganso*, or German/Dutch *Gans/gans*, a goose. But Philemon Holland had used the word previously in his translation of Pliny (1601), and perhaps Godwin was remembering it from there (*OED*, from Pliny, *Natural History*, 10.22). Linschoten mentioned that Ascension, the island adjacent to St. Helena, was populated by birds "of the bignesse of our Geese" (175). A *goose* was also slang, then as now, for a simpleton or fool.

2   meetly] fitting

3   It is not obvious how this technique assists the gansas. Each bird indeed now starts off bearing a smaller burden, but there will still come a point when the original block requires raising, and Godwin's contrivance merely increases the overall load.

4   affection] affectation

5   Casting lots for the three parts of the world, Jupiter won the skies, Pluto the underworld, and Neptune the seas and their islands (Natalis Comes, *Mythologiæ ... libri decem* [Geneva: Samuel Crispinus, 1612], 162-73).

[28: Gansas engraving][1]

---

1 This engraving is an original work, but note its deviation from the text:
   Gonsales says that he employed 25 birds, but the illustration shows only
   10. In the Bodleian copy, as in most, this illustration is also repeated as
   a frontispiece.

though of no great stature, yet twice my weight at least. So upon a time having provided all things necessary, I placed my selfe with all my trinckets, upon the top of a rocke at the Rivers mouth, and putting my selfe at full Sea upon an Engine (the description whereof ensueth) I caused *Diego* to advance his Signall: whereupon my Birds presently arose, 25 in number, and carried mee over lustily to the other rocke on the other side, being about a Quarter of a league.

[29] The reason why I chose that time and place, was that I thought somewhat might perchance fall out in this enterprize contrary to my expectation, in which case I assured my selfe the worst that could bee, was but to fall into the water, where being able to swim well, I hoped to receive little or no hurt in my fal. But when I was once over in safety, O how did my heart even swell with joy and admiration of mine owne invention! How often did I wish my selfe in the midst of *Spaine*, that speedily I might fill the world with the fame of my glory and renowne? Every hower wished I with great longing for the *Indian* Fleet to take mee home with them, but they stayed (by what mischance I know not[ix]) 3 Moneths beyond the accustomed time.

At last they came being in number [30] 3 Carickes sore weather-beaten, their people being for the most part sick and exceeding weak, so as they were constrained to refresh themselves in our Island one whole moneth.

The Captaine of our Admirall was called *Alphonso de Xima*, a Valiant man, wise, and desirous of renowne, and worthy better fortune then afterward befell him. Unto him I opened[1] the device of my *Gansa's*, well knowing how impossible it were otherwise to perswade him to take in so many Birds into the Ship, that would bee more troublesome (for the nicenesse[2] of provision to be made for them,) then so many men; Yet I adjured him by all manner of Oaths, and perswasions, to afford mee both true dealing, and secrecy. Of the last I doubted not much, as assuring my [31] selfe, he would not dare to impart the device to any other, before our King were acquainted with it. Of the first I feared much more, namely, lest Ambition, and the desire of drawing unto himselfe the honour of such an invention, should cause him to make mee away; yet I was forced to run the hazard, except I would adventure the losse of my Birds, the like whereof for my purpose were not to be had in all Christendome, nor any

---

1 opened] revealed
2 nicenesse] delicacy; difficulty

that I could be sure, would ever serve the turne. Well, that doubt in proofe[1] fell out to be causelesse: the man I thinke was honest of himselfe: but had he dealt treacherously with me, I had laid a plot for the discovery of him,[2] as he might easily judge I would, which peradventure somewhat moved him, yet God knowes how he might have used me, before [32] my arrivall in *Spaine*, if in the meane course wee had not beene intercepted, as you shall heare. Upon Thursday the 21. of *Iune*, to wit in the yeare, 1599.[3] wee set saile towards *Spaine*, I having allowed me a very convenient Cabin for my *Birds*, and stowage also for mine Engine, which the Captaine would have had me leave behinde me, and it is a mervaile[4] I had not, but my good fortune therein saved my life, and gave me that which I esteeme more than an hundred lives, if I had them: for thus it fell out, after 2. moneths saile, we encountred with a fleet of the *English*, some 10. leagues from the *Island* of *Tenerif*, one of the *Canaries*, which is famous through the World, for a Hill upon the same called *el Pico*,[5] that is to be discerned and kenned[6] upon the Sea no [33] lesse then 100. leagues off. We had aboord us 5. times the number of people that they had; we were well provided of munition, and our men in good health. Yet seeing them disposed to fight, and knowing what infinite riches wee carried with us, we thought it a wiser way to fly, if we might, then by encountring a company of dangerous fellowes to hazard not onely our owne lives, (which a man of valour in such a case esteemeth not) but the estates of many poore Merchants, who I am affraid were utterly undone by miscarriage of that businesse. Our fleete then consisted of 5. sayle, to wit, 3. Carickes, a Barke,

---

1 in proofe] in the event
2 We never learn what this plot was.
3 A real date in the Julian calendar: see the discussion of chronology in the Introduction (pp. 31-34). The voyage home follows a conventional sea route, although Godwin is drawing on Hakluyt, *Principal Navigations*, and Linschoten, *Discours*, 167-76.
4 mervaile] marvel
5 *el Pico*] El Pico was the early-modern equivalent of Everest: "In the Island of *Teneriffe* there is a hil called *Pico de Terraira*, which is thought to bee the highest hill that euer was found" (Linschoten, *Discours*, 176). Pico de Teyde or Tiede comprises most of Tenerife, the largest of the Canary Islands. It was thought to be between 9 and 70 miles high; Godwin's fifteen leagues "at least" (43) equals about fifty modern miles. Hakluyt thought it 45 miles high (*Principal Navigations*, 2.5 [second pagination]); Burton recorded estimates of 52 or 70 miles.
6 kenned] caught sight of; discerned by sight

and a Caravell,[1] that comming from the Isle of Saint *Thomas*, had (in an evill houre for him) overtaken us some few dayes before.[2]

The English had 3. Ships very [34] well appointed, and no sooner spied, but they began to play[xi] for us, and changing their course, as wee might well perceive, endeavoured straightway to bring us under their lee,[3] which they might well doe (as the wind stood) especially being light nimble vessells, and yare[4] of Sayle, as for the most part all the *English* shipping is, whereas ours was heavy, deepe laden, foule with the Sea:[5] our Captaine therefore resolved peradventure wisely enough (but I am sure neither valiantly, not fortunately) to flie, commanding us to disperse our selves: the Caravell by reason of too much hast fell foul upon one of the Carickes, and bruised her so, as one of the *English* that had undertaken her, easily fetcht her up and entred her: as for the caravell shee sanke immediately in the sight of us all. The [35] Barke (for ought I could perceive) no man making after her, escaped unpursued; and another of our carickes after some chase, was given over by the *English*, that making account to finde a booty good enough of us, and having us betweene them and their third companion, made upon us with might and main. Wherefore our Captaine that was aboord us, gave direction to runne aland upon the *Isle*, the Port whereof we could not recover, saying that hee hoped to save some of the goods, and some of our lives, and the rest he had rather should bee lost, than commit all to the mercy of the enemie. When I heard of that resolution, seeing the Sea to worke high, and knowing all the coast to bee full of blind Rockes, and Shoales, so as our Vessell might not possibly [36] come neere land, before it must needs be rent in a thousand peeces, I went unto the Captaine, shewing him the desperatenesse of the course hee intended, wishing him rather to trie the mercy of the enemie, then so to cast away himselfe, and so many brave men: but hee would not heare me by any means; whereupon discerning it to be high time to shift for my selfe,[6] first, I sought out my Box or little Casket of stones, and having put it into my sleeve, I then betooke me to my *Gansa's*, put them upon my Engine, and

1   A carrack is a large ship of burden, also fitted for warfare; a bark and a caravel are both small ships.
2   For similar sea-fights in this region, see Purchas, *Pilgrimes*, 1.124, 332 (second pagination).
3   lee] nautical: the sheltered side of the ship, so that the English would be blown toward their prey
4   yare] nautical: brisk or swift
5   foule with the Sea] nautical: having the bottom overgrown with seaweed, shellfish, etc.
6   shift for myselfe] look after myself

my selfe upon it, trusting (as indeed it happily fell out) that when the Shippe should split, my Birds, although they wanted their Signall, of themselves, and for safeguard of their owne lives (which nature hath taught every living creature to preserve [37] to their power) would make towards the Land; which fell out well (I thanke God,) according to mine expectation. The people of our Ship mervailed about what I went, none of them being acquainted with the use of my *Birds*, but the Captaine, for *Diego* was in the *Rosaria*, the Ship that fled away unpursued,[1] (as before I told you:) some halfe a league we were from the Land, when our Carick strake upon a Rocke, and split immediately: whereupon I let loose unto my *Birds* the raines,[2] having first placed my selfe upon the highest of the Decke: and with the shock they all arose, carrying mee fortunately unto the Land, whereof, whether I were well apaide[3] you need not doubt, but a pittifull sight it was unto me, to behold my friends and acquaintance in that miserable distresse [38] of whom (notwithstanding) many escaped better then they had any reason to hope for. For the *English* launching out their cockboates,[4] like men of more noble, and generous disposition then wee are pleased to esteeme them, taking compassion upon them, used all the diligence they could, to helpe such as had any meanes to save themselves from the furie of the waves and that even with their owne danger: amongst many, they tooke up our Captaine, who (as Father *Pacio*[5] could since tell me) having put himselfe into his Cock with 12. others, was induced to yeeld himselfe unto one Captaine *Rymundo*,[6] who

---

1 This is the last we hear of Diego, although he was to make an appearance in at least one of the sequels generated by Godwin's fiction, Thomas D'Urfey's *Wonders in the Sun, or the Kingdom of the Birds: A Comick Opera* (1706).

2 Imitating the Latin *immittere habenas*, to fling the reins loose, to give a horse its head, often used metaphorically.

3 apaide] satisfied, contented, pleased

4 cockboates] a cockboat is strictly the small boat that is often towed behind a coasting vessel or ship going up or down river, often just meaning a very small boat.

5 *Pacio*] a genuine Jesuit missionary, active in the Far East, Francesco Pasio. For his career, see Purchas, *Pilgrimes*, 3.321-22. That Pasio "could since tell" is prolepsis that Domingo will make it back to the society of men, although as the real Pasio died in the Orient, this does not confirm that Gonsales managed to return to Europe.

6 *Rymundo*] a Spanish mis-hearing for the real Captain George Raymond, who went down with his ship the *Penelope* (in 1591, so there is a slight anachronism here) after rounding the Cape of Good Hope.

carried him together with our Pilote along in their voyage with them, being bound for the East *Indies*; but their hard hap was by a breach[1] of the Sea neere [39] the cape of *Buona Esperanca*, to be swallowed of the mercilesse Waves, whose fury a little before they had so hardly escaped. The rest of them (as I likewise heard) and they were in all some 26. persons that they tooke into their ship, they set them a land soone after at *Cape Verde*.[2]

As for my selfe, being now a shore in a Country inhabited for the most part by *Spaniards*, I reckoned my selfe in safety. Howbeit I quickly found the reckoning, I so made, mine Host had not beene acquainted with all; for it was my chance to pitch upon that part of the Isle, where the hill, before mentioned, beginneth to rise. And it is inhabited by a Savage kinde of people,[3] that live upon the sides of that hill, the top whereof is alwayes covered with Snow, and held for the monstrous height and steepnesse not to [40] be accessible either for man or beast. Howbeit these Savages fearing the *Spaniards*, (betweene whom and them there is a kinde of continuall warre) hold themselves as neere the top of that hill as they can, where they have divers places of good strength, never comming downe into the fruitfull Valleys, but to prey upon what they can finde there. It was the chance of a company of them to espie mee within some howers space after my Landing: They thinking they had light upon a booty, made towards mee with all the speed they could, but not so privily as that I could not perceive their purpose before they came neere to me by halfe a Quarter of a League; seeing them come downe the side of a Hill with great speed directly towards mee, divers of them carrying Long Staves, besides other weapons, [41] which because of their distance from mee I might not discerne. I thought it high time to bestirre mee, and shift for my selfe, and by all meanes, to keepe my selfe out of the fingers of such slaves, who had they caught mee, for the hatred they beare to us *Spaniards*, had surely hewed me all to peeces.

The Country in that place was bare, without the coverture of

---

1 breach] surf made by the sea breaking over rocks
2 On Cape Verde, see Linschoten, *Discours*, 176.
3 Perhaps the Guanches, indigenous occupants of the Canaries, described by Hakluyt (*Principal Navigations*, 2.5 [second pagination]). Linschoten also reports how two "Caffares" of Mozambique, one "Iauer" [sic] with two women slaves jumped ship, hiding out in the mountains of St. Helena where they bred. These rebels were eventually captured and taken to Portugal, but only after many years' effort (*Discours*, 174).

any wood: But the mountaine before spoken of, beginning even there to lift up it selfe, I espied in the side of the same a white cliffe, which I trusted my *Ganza's* would take for a signall, and being put off; would make all that way, whereby I might quickly bee carried so farre, as those barbarous Cullions[1] should not be able to overtake mee, before I had recovered the dwelling of some *Spaniard*, or at least-wise might have [42] time to hide my selfe from them, till that in the night, by helpe of the starres, I might guide my selfe toward *Las Læguna*, the City of that Island,[2] which was about one league off, as I thinke. Wherefore with all the celeritie[3] that might be I put my selfe upon mine Engine, and let loose the raines unto my *Gansa's*, It was my good fortune that they tooke all one way, although not just that way I aymed at. But what then, O Reader?[xii] *Arrige aures*,[4] prepare thy selfe unto the hearing of the strangest Chance that ever happened to any mortall man, and that I know thou wilt not have the Grace to beleeve, till thou seest it seconded with Iteration of Experiments in the like, as many a one, I trust, thou mayest in short time; My *Gansa's*, like so many horses that had gotten the bitt betweene [43] their teeth, made (I say) not towards the cliffe I aymed at, although I used my wonted meanes to direct the Leader of the flocke that way, but with might and maine[5] tooke up towards the top of *El Pico*, and did never stay till they came there, a place where they say never man came before, being in all estimation at least 15 leagues in height perpendicularly upward, above the ordinary levell of the Land and Sea.

[45] What manner of place I found there, I should gladly relate unto you, but that I make hast to matters of farre greater Importance. There when I was set downe, I saw my poore *Gansa's*, fall to panting and blowing, gasping[xiii] for breath, as if they would all presently have died: wherefore I thought it not good to trouble them a while, forbearing to draw them in, (which they [were]

---

1   Cullions] lit. "bollocks," a newish curse in English at the time, from similar Spanish, French and Italian words
2   Former capital of Tenerife.
3   celeritie] swiftness
4   *Arrige aures*] Terence, *Andria*, 937: "prick up your ears." A stock example of *cacemphaton* (inappropriate or obscene twist to the sense) in the period; as Mosellanus commented, "for example, Terence's 'Arrige aures Pamphile', when 'arrectio' is more suitable to the genital member" (*Tabulæ de Schematibus et Tropis* [Antwerp: Martin Caesar, 1532], sg. B1r).
5   might and maine] utmost or greatest possible power or strength

[44: El Pico engraving][1]

never wont to indure without strugling) and little expecting that which followed.

It was now the season that these Birds were wont to take their flight away, as our Cuckoes and swallowes doe in *Spaine*, towards the Autumne.[2] They (as after I perceived) mindfull of their usuall voyage, even as I began to settle my selfe for the taking of them in, as it were with one consent, rose up, and having no other place higher to [46] make toward, to my unspeakable feare and amazement strooke bolt upright, and never did linne[3] towring upward, and still upward, for the space, as I might guesse, of one whole

---

1 This engraving once again derives from Herbert, *Relation*, 215, hence the redundant marking of "Fayall." See the comments in the Publication History (pp. 58-59).

2 On contemporary theories of bird migration, see Thomas P. Harrison, "Birds in the Moon," *Isis* 45 (1954): 323-30. The major exponent of the idea that birds might migrate to the moon was Charles Morton (1627-98), a Wadham man, who most probably derived his thesis from Godwin and John Wilkins, although he based his enquiry on an exegesis of Jeremiah 8:7 ("the stork in the heaven knoweth her appointed times"). The anonymous late-seventeenth-century *The Lunarian* presumably copied the idea of lunar migration directly from Godwin (British Library Add. MS 11812, fol. 7r). Compare John Ray, *Philosophical Letters* (London: William and John Innys, 1718), 198-99.

3 linne] to cease from, leave off, discontinue

hower; toward the end of which time, mee thought I might perceive them to labour lesse and lesse; till at length, O incredible thing, they forbare moving any thing at al! and yet remained unmoveable, as stedfastly, as if they had beene upon so many perches, the Lines slacked; neither I, nor the Engine moved at all, but abode still as having no manner of weight.

I found then by this Experience that which no Philosopher ever dreamed of, to wit, that those things which wee call heavie, do not sinke towards the Center of the Earth, as their naturall place, but as drawn by a secret property of the Globe of [47] the Earth, or rather some thing within the same, in like sort as the Loadstone draweth Iron, being within the compasse of the beames attractive.[1]

For though it bee true that there they could abide unmoved without the proppe or sustentation[2] of any corporall thing other then the ayre, as easily and quietly as a fish in the middle of the water, yet forcing themselves never so little, it is not possible to imagine with what swiftnesse and celeritie they were carried, and whether it were upward, downward, or sidelong, all was one. Truly I must confesse, the horror and amazement of that place was such, as if I had not been armed with a true *Spanish* courage and resolution, I must needs have died there with very feare.

But the next thing that did most [48] trouble me, was the swiftnesse of Motion, such as did even almost stop my breath; If I should liken it to an Arrow out of a Bow, or to a stone cast downe from the top of some high tower, it would come farre short, and short.

An other thing there was exceeding, and more then exceeding,[xiv] troublesome unto mee, and that was the Illusions of Devills and wicked spirits, who, the first day of my arrivall, came about mee in great numbers, carrying the shapes and likenesse of

---

1 Here, as throughout the astronomical section of *The Man in the Moone*, Godwin is indebted to William Gilbert's *De Magnete* (1600), which argued that the earth, like all other heavenly bodies, acted as a giant rotating magnet, with its own sphere of influence and centre, separate from the spheres and centres of the other heavenly and likewise rotating bodies. As such, all magnetic bodies have a sphere of influence more extensive than their material superficies, though not indefinitely so: hence Gonsales and the Gansas hover static above the earth (e.g., *De Magnete* 2.7, 5.11, 12). Unlike gravity, this force is not therefore universal. Gilbert treated magnetism as the soul of the earth, an animistic touch avoided by Godwin. See below, p. 149.

2 sustentation] support

men and women, wondring at mee like so many Birds about an Owle, and speaking divers kindes of Languages which I understood not, till at last I did light upon them that spake very good *Spanish*, some *Dutch*, and othersome[1] *Italian*, for all these Languages I understood.

And here I saw onely a touch of [49] the Sunnes absence for a little while once, ever after having him in my sight. Now to yeeld you satisfaction in the other, you shall understand that my *Gansa's*, although entangled in my lynes,[xv] might easily find means to sease upon divers kinds of *flyes* and *Birds*, as especially *Swallows*, and *Cuckoes*, whereof there were multitudes, as Motes in the sunne; although to say the truth I never saw them to feed any thing at all. As for my selfe, in truth I was much beholding unto those same, whether men or Divels I know not, that amongst divers speeches, which I will forbeare awhile to relate, told me, that if I would follow their directions, I should not onely bee brought safely to my home, but also be assured to have the command of all pleasures of that place, at all times.[2]

[50] To the which motions not daring to make a flat deniall, I prayed a time to thinke of it, and withall intreated them (though I felt no hunger at all, which may seeme strange) to helpe mee with some victualls, least in the meane while I should starve. They did so, readily enough, and brought me very good Flesh, and Fish, of divers sorts well dressed, but that it was exceeding fresh, and without any manner of relish of salt.

Wine also I tasted there of divers sorts, as good as any in *Spayne*, and Beere, no better in all *Antwerp*. They wished me then, while I had meanes to make my provision, telling me, that till the next Thursday they could not helpe me to any more, if happily then; at what time also they would find meanes to carry me backe, and set mee safe in [51] *Spayne* where I would wish to be, so that I would become one of their fraternity, and enter into such covenants and profession as they had made to their Master and Captaine, whom they would not name. I answered them gently for the time, telling them, I saw little reason to be very glad of such an offer, praying them to be mindfull of me as occasion served.

---

1 othersome] some others

2 Such tales of demonic luring are commonplace, of which perhaps the most famous are *The Historie of the Damnable Life, and Deserved Death of Doctor John Faustus* (London: Edward White, 1592 [earliest surviving edition]), and its adaptation for the theatre, Marlowe's *Dr. Faustus* (staged c. 1588-89, variant editions of 1604 and 1616).

So for that time I was ridd of them, having first furnished my Pocketts with as much Victuall as I could thrust in, amongst the which I fail[xvi] not to afford place for a little Botijo[1] of good Canary wine.

Now shall I declare unto you the quality of the place, in which I then was. The Clouds I perceived to be all under me, betweene mee and the earth. The starres, by reason it was alwaies day,[2] I saw at all times alike, [52] not shining bright, as upon the earth we are wont to see them in the night time; but of a whitish Colour, like that of the Moone in the day time with us: And such of them as were to be seene (which were not many) shewed[xvii] farre greater then with us, yea (as I should ghesse) no lesse then ten times so great. As for the Moone being then within two daies of the change, she appeared of a huge and fearfull quantitie.

This also is not to be forgotten, that no starres appeared but on that part of the Hemispheare that was next the Moone, and the neerer to her the bigger in Quantity they shewed. Againe I must tell you, that whether I lay quiet and rested, or else were carryed in the Ayre, I perceived my selfe still to be alwaies directly betweene the Moone [53] and the earth. Whereby it appeareth, not only that my *Gansa's* took none other way then directly toward the Moone, but also, that when we rested (as at first we did for many howers,) either we were insensibly carryed, (for I perceived no such motion) round about the Globe of the Earth, or else that (according to the late opinion of *Copernicus*,) the Earth is carried about, and turneth round perpetually, from *West* to the *East*, leaving unto the Planets onely that motion which Astronomers call natu-

---

1 Botijo] an earthenware jar (Spanish)
2 Godwin perpetuates the medieval assumption that it is light in space. In the late sixteenth century, Thomas Digges in his "A Perfit Description of the Caelestiall Orbes" (1576) realized that the darkness of night is not just a consequence of the earth's shadow, and that space was itself usually dark. He explained this by presuming that starlight was too feeble to fill the whole sky with light. Kepler in his *Conversation with the Starry Messenger* also discussed the issue, concluding that the universe did not contain enough stars to make the heavens perpetually bright, and that in consequence the universe must be finite. But brightly lit space would survive as late as Milton's *Paradise Lost* (1674 [1667], e.g., 3.540-57). For a history of the problem, discussing these examples, see Edward Harrison, *Darkness at Night: A Riddle of the Universe* (Cambridge, MA: Harvard UP, 1987).

rall,[1] and is not[2] upon the Poles of the Equinoctiall, commonly termed the Poles of the World, but upon those of the Zodiake;[3] concerning which question, I will speake more hereafter, when I shall have leysure to call to my remembrance the *Astronomy* that I learned being a young man at *Salamanca*, [54] but have now almost forgotten.[4]

The ayre in that place I found quiet without any motion of wind, and exceeding temperate, neither hot nor cold, as where neither the Sunne-beames had any subject to reflect upon, neither was yet either the earth or water so neere as to affect the ayre with their naturall quality of coldnesse. As for that imagination of the Philosophers, attributing heat together with moystnesse unto the ayre, I never esteemed it otherwise then a fancy.[5]

---

1 Natural motion in standard peripatetic thought is the internally prompted motion of an object, and is always uniform and self-similar, i.e., motion compounded of travel in a straight line or around a point (Johannes Magirus, *Physiologiæ Peripateticæ Libri Sex* [London: John Bill, 1619], 59).

2 Perhaps a past participle, for instance "founded," has dropped out here, between "is" and "not." The sense should be that the motion of the planets is not to be referred to the earth's axis, but to their zodiacal positions; their apparent diurnal rotation, along with the rest of the heavens, is an illusion created by the earth's daily spin.

3 Compare Mephastophilis' geocentric answer to Faustus in Marlowe's play: "All ioyntly moue from East to West in 24. houres vpon the poles of the world, but differ in their motion vpon the poles of the Zodiake" (*The Tragicall History of Doctor Faustus* [London: Thomas Bushell, 1604], sg. C3r). The "poles of the world" refer to the planetary axis, one end of which terminates very near to Polaris, the North Star; "the poles of the Zodiake" refer to the inclination of the earth's rotational axis to the plane of the sun's revolution around it in the geocentric model, equivalent to the earth's revolution around the sun in the heliocentric model.

4 In fact, Copernicanism was taught in Salamanca from a very early date; see the Introduction (pp. 36-37). The following section takes its cues largely from Burton's "Digression of Ayre" (see Appendix G, below), but the presence of other discussions is also plausible, notably Carpenter, *Geographie*, 1.71-97, on diurnal motion.

5 Peripatetic natural philosophy taught that the four elements of fire, air, water, and earth combined hot and cold with moist and dry to produce four different pairings. Air was indeed the element "moderately hot and very moist" (Magirus, *Physiologiæ Peripateticæ*, 171). Compare *The Historie of ... Doctor John Faustus*: "Knowest thou not that the earth is frozen cold and dry; the water running, cold and moist; the air flying, hot and moist; the fire consuming, hot and dry?" (ed. John Henry Jones as *The English Faust Book* [Cambridge: Cambridge UP, 1994], 114).

Lastly now it is to be remembered that after my departure from the earth, I never felt any appetite of hunger or thirst. Whether the purity of the Ayre our proper element not being infected with any Vapors of the Earth and water, might yeeld nature sufficient nutriment; or what [55] else might be the cause of it, I cannot tell but so I found it, although I perceived my selfe in perfect health of body, having the use of all my Limmes and senses; and strength both of body and minde, rather beyond and above, than any thing short of the pitch, or wonted vigor. Now let vs goe on: and on we shall go more then apace.

Not many howers after the departure of that divelish company from me, my *Gansa's* began to bestir themselues, still directing their course toward the Globe or body of the Moone: And they made their way with that incredible swiftnesse, as I thinke they gained not so little as Fifty Leagues in every hower.[1] In that passage I noted three things very remarkeable: one that the further we went, the lesser the Globe of the Earth appeared unto us; whereas [56] still on the contrary side the Moone[xviii] shewed her selfe more and more monstrously huge.[2]

Againe, the Earth (which ever I held in mine eye)[3] did as it were mask it selfe with a kind of brightnesse like another Moone; and even as in the Moone we discerned certaine spots or Clouds, as it were, so did I then in the earth. But whereas the forme of those spots in the Moone continue constantly one and the same; these by little and little did change every hower. The reason thereof I conceive to be this, that whereas the Earth according to her naturall motion, (for that such a motion she hath, I am now constrained to joyne in opinion with *Copernicus,*) turneth round upon her owne Axe[4] every 24. howers from the *West* unto the *East*: I should at the first see in the middle of the body [57] of this new starre a spot like unto a Peare that had a morsell bitten out upon the one side of him; after certaine howers, I should see that spot slide away to the *East* side. This no doubt was the maine of *Affricke*.[5]

---

1 The English common league is three miles.
2 According to Ptolemy, the actual ratios of diameters for the moon, earth, and sun were 1: 3.4: 18.8 (*Almagest*, v.16).
3 The "little eye-witnesse" (A4v) continually emphasises his own ocular presence: compare 58, 60, 66, 67, 72.
4 Axe] axis
5 Compare Ridley, *Short Treatise of Magneticall Bodies*, 15: "But how the Earth doth turne circularly we cannot well see it, with the sence of our eyes, vnlesse we had them placed in another globous body and starre, as

Then should I perceive a great shining brightnesse to occupy that roome, during the like time (which was[xix] undoubtedly none other than the great *Atlantick* Ocean). After that succeeded a spot almost of an Ovall form, even just such as we see *America* to have in our Mapps. Then another vast cleernesse representing the *West Ocean*; and lastly a medly of spots, like the Countries of the *East Indies*. So that it seemed unto me no other then a huge Mathematicall Globe, leasurely turned before me, wherein successively, all the Countries of our earthly world [58] within the compasse of 24 howers were represented to my sight.[1] And this was all the meanes I had now to number the dayes, and take reckoning of time.

Philosophers and *Mathematicians* I would should now confesse the wilfulnesse of their owne blindnesse.[2] They have made the world beleeve hitherto, that the Earth hath no motion. And to make that good they are fain to attribute unto all and every of the celestial bodies, two motions[xx] quite contrary each to other; whereof one is from the *East* to the *West*, to be performed in 24 howers; (that they imagine to be forced, *per raptum primi Mobilis*[3]) the other from the *West* to the *East* in severall proportions.

---

if they were in the Moone, where we might see the spots of the Earth to turne about, as well as now we see the spots in the Sunne, and *Iupiter* to moue circularly in their place" (15). Kepler's Subvolvans use the earth's diurnal rotation as a clock: "For even though it does not seem to have any motion in space, nevertheless, unlike our moon, it rotates in its place, and in turn displays a wonderful variety of spots, as these spots move constantly from east to west" (*Somnium*, 23).

1 The most celebrated English mathematical globes of the time were the 2-foot-diameter terrestrial and celestial globes made by Emery Molyneux (d. 1598) and elucidated by the Oxford mathematician and geographer Robert Hues (1553-1632) in his *Tractatus de globis et eorum usu* (1594), translated into English in the year *The Man in the Moone* was first published. Molyneux and Hues were friends of prominent geographers and explorers, including Hakluyt and Cavendish; Hues accompanied Cavendish on his first and attempted second circumnavigations, thereby anticipating Gonsales' sea-route.

2 Mimicking Gilbert's strident tones, Gonsales' confidence in the physical truth of the diurnal rotation of the earth is outspoken; compare the guarded Carpenter: "For mine owne part, I confesse not absolute subscription to this opinion; yet I could not conueniently leaue it out" (*Geographie*, 2.76).

3 *per raptum primi Mobilis*] "by the transport of the Primum Mobile" (Latin); the "Primum Mobile" is the outermost sphere of the geocentric universe, whose movement is communicated down through all the spheres below it.

O incredible thing, that those same huge bodies of the fixed stars in the highest orbe, whereof divers [59] are by themselves confessed to be more then one hundreth[xxi] times as bigge as the whole earth, should as so many nayles in a Cart Wheele, be whirled about in that short space, whereas it is many thousands of Yeares (no lesse, I trowe, they say, then 30 thousand) before that orbe do finish his Course from *West* to *East*, which they call the naturall motion.[1] Now whereas to every of these they yeeld their naturall course from *West* to *East*; therein they doe well. The *Moone* performeth it in 27 daies; the *Sunne*, *Venus*, and *Mercury* in a Yeare or thereabouts, *Mars* in three Yeare, *Jupiter* in twelve Yeares, and *Saturne* in 30.[2] [xxii] But to attribute unto these celestiall bodies contrary motions at once, was a very absurd conceit, and much more, to imagine that same Orbe, wherein the fixed stars are, (whose naturall course [60] taketh so many thousand of yeares) should every 24 howers be turned about. I will not go so farre as *Copernicus*, that maketh the Sunne the Center of the Earth, and unmoveable, neither will I define any thing one way or other. Only this I say, allow the Earth his motion (which these eyes of mine can testifie to be his due) and these absurdities are quite taken away, every one having his single and proper Motion onely.[3]

---

1 The *locus classicus* for this discussion is Ptolemy, *Almagest*, VII.3, where Ptolemy analyses the apparent rearward motion of the sphere of the fixed stars ("precession"; "precession of the equinoxes"). He settled on a precession of 1° every century, hence 36,000 years would see the recurrence of a given position ("the Great Year"; "the Platonic Year"). The matter was considerably complexified by Copernicus, *De Revolutionibus*, III.1-12, who asserted both that precession was caused by movement of the earth's axis, and that this itself varied over time. The modern estimate for a Great Year is about 10,000 years shorter than Ptolemy's.

2 These figures were more or less conventional, with certain variations. Godwin exactly follows Burton; see Appendix G.

3 Gonsales accepts the diurnal rotation of the earth, but withholds assent from heliocentrism, with its "unmoveable" sun. This was the position adopted by many English followers of Tycho Brahe and especially William Gilbert, and by Burton in the later editions of *The Anatomy of Melancholy*. A digest of contemporary opinion, perhaps standing behind both Burton and Godwin's accounts, is Carpenter, *Geographie*, 1.97-122. Nevertheless, Burton deduced from the single motion of the world that "*per consequens*, the rest of the planets are inhabited, as well as the moon"; this led him to argue from analogy for infinite heliocentrism, the theory that each star is a sun, and the centre of its own system. This is compatible with denying, as Domingo does, that *our* sun is the centre of

But where am I? At the first I promised an History, and I fall into disputes before I am aware. There is yet one accident more befell me worthy of especiall remembrance: that during the time of my stay I saw as it were a kind of cloud of a reddish colour growing toward me, which continually growing nearer and nearer, at last I perceived to [61] be nothing else but a huge swarme of Locusts.

He that readeth the discourses of learned men, concerning them, and namely that of *Iohn Leo*, in his description of *Affrike*, how that they are seene in the Ayre many dayes before they fall upon a countrey, adding unto that which they deliver, this experience of mine, will easily conclude, that they cannot come from any other place then the Globe of the Moone.[1] But give me leave now at last to passe on my journey quietly, without interruption for Eleven or Twelve daies, during all which time, I was carried directly toward the Globe or body of [xxiii] the Moone with such a violent whirling as cannot bee expressed.

For I cannot imagine that a bullet out of the mouth of a Cannon could [62] make way through the vaporous and muddie aire neere the earth with that celerity, which is most strange, considering that my *Gansa's* moved their wings but even now and then, and sometimes not at all in a Quarter of an hower together; only they held them stretched out, so passing on, as we see that *Eagles*, and *Kites* sometimes will doe for a little space, when (as one speakes, I remember) *contabundo*[xxiv] *volatu pene eodem loco*

---

the universe. Potentially Domingo is not going "so farre" as Copernicus, but further. See R.G. Barlow, "Infinite Worlds: Robert Burton's Cosmic Voyage," *Journal of the History of Ideas* 34 (1973): 291-302, at 297-98; Grant McColley, "The Theory of the Diurnal Rotation of the Earth," *Isis* 26 (1937): 392-402, and the discussion in the Introduction (pp. 34-40).

1 Gonsales apparently refers to Johannes Leo Africanus, *Africae Descriptio IX libri absoluta* (Antwerp, 1556), but it seems rather that Godwin just read Richard Pory's translation: "like a mightie thicke cloud they come raking along in the skie, and afterwards falling downe, they couer the face of the earth, deouring all things that they light vpon. Their coming towards any place is known two or three daies before by the yellownes of the sunne" (43), from "A description of places undescribed [sic] by Iohn Leo," prefaced to Johannes Leo Africanus, *A Geographical Historie of Africa*, trans. John Pory (London: George Bishop, 1600); compare 349 for Leo's remarks. Burton too mentions (the real) Leo's locusts (*Anatomy*, 2.2.3.1 [2.46]).

pendula circumtuentur;[1] and during the time of those pauses I beleeve they tooke their napps and times of sleeping; for other (as I might easily note) they had none.

Now for my selfe, I was so fast knit unto my Engin, as I durst commit my selfe to slumbring enough to serve my turne, which I tooke with as great ease (although I am loath to speake it, because [63] it may seeme incredible) as if I had beene in the best Bed of downe in all *Antwerp*.

After Eleven daies passage in this violent flight, I perceived that we began to approach neare unto another Earth, if I may so call it, being the Globe or very body of that starre which we call the Moone.

The first difference that I found betweene it and our earth, was, that it shewed it selfe in his naturall colours: ever after I was free from the attraction of the Earth; whereas with us, a thing removed from our eye but a league or two, begins to put on that lurid and deadly[2] colour of blew.

Then, I perceived also, that it was covered for the most part with a huge and mighty Sea, those parts only being drie Land, which shew [64] unto us here somewhat darker then the rest of her body (that I mean) which the Country people cal *el hombre della Luna*, the Man of the Moone.[3]

---

1 Adapted from Apuleius, *Florida*, 2, of an eagle: "inde cuncta despiciens ibidem pinnarum eminus indefessa remigio, ac paulisper contabundo volatu paene eodem loco pendula circumtuetur" (lit. "from afar off up there, with untired oarage of wings, looking down at the rest of things; and a while with lingering flight, hanging in almost the same place, casts about her gaze") (Apuleius, *Opera Omnia Quae Exstant* [Paris: Michael Sonnius, 1601], 404). Ironically for·"the little eye-witnesse, our great discoverer," Apuleius is here actually derogating the power of man's sight by comparing it to the superior gaze of the eagle; and rather embarrassingly for Gonsales, Apuleius argues that one man with ears is a better witness than ten with eyes. See also the Note on the Text (p. 63 n. 2).

2 lurid and deadly] pale and death-like

3 This is the reverse of the opinion of Plutarch, in *De facie in orbe lunae* ("To come now unto the face that appeareth therein: like as this earth upon which we walke, hath many sinuosities and vallies, even so as probable it is, that the said heavenly earth, lieth open with great deepe caves, and wide chinks or ruptures, and those conteining either water or obscure aire: to the bottome thereof the light of the Sunne is not able to pierce and reach, but there falleth, and sendeth to us hither a certeine divided reflexion" Plutarch, *The Philosophie*, 1174-75). Kepler initially argued in his 1604 *Astronomia pars optica* that the dark sections signalled

As for that part which shineth so clearly in our eyes; it is even another Ocean, yet besprinckled heere and there with *Islands*, which for the littlenesse, so farre off we cannot discern.

So that same splendor appearing unto us, and giving light unto our night, appeareth to be nothing else but the reflexion of the Sun beames returned unto us out of the water, as out of a glasse: How ill this agreeth with that which our *Philosophers* teach in the Schooles I am not ignorant.

But alas how many of their Errors hath time and experience refuted in this our age, with the recitall[xxv] [65] whereof I will not stand to trouble the reader.

Amongst many other of their vaine surmises, the time and order of my narration putteth me in mind of one, which now my experience found most untrue.

Who is there that hath not hitherto beleeved the uppermost Region of the Ayre to be extreame hot, as being next forsooth unto the naturall place of the Element of Fire.[1]

O Vanities, fansies, Dreames!

After the time I was once quite free from the attractive Beames of that tyrannous Loadstone the earth,[2] I found the Ayre of one and the self same temper, without Winds, without Raine, without Mists, without Clouds, neither hot nor cold, but continually after one and the same tenor, most pleasant, milde, [66] and comfortable, till my arrivall in that New World of the Moone.

---

the presence of water. But, following Galileo's *Sidereus Nuncius* (1610), he was obliged in his *Dissertatio cum nuncio sidereo* (1610) to accept that the lighter sections were liquid. In the *Somnium* (1634, posthumous), however, the spots again signal water (Dick, *Plurality of Worlds*, 71, 74-75, 81). William Gilbert's posthumous *De Mundo* identified the brighter patches with liquid (William Gilbert, *De Mundo nostro Sublunari Philosophia Nova* [Amsterdam: Ludovicus Elzevir, 1651], 173).

1 In Aristotelian cosmology, fire, the lightest of the four substances, tends to the highest position in the sublunar word, and hence the outermost sphere before the changeless realm of the heavens, encompassing the interior spheres of air, water, and lastly earth, is necessarily composed of fire. See Hieronymus de Sancto Marco, *Opusculum de Universali Mundi Machina ... editum ad mentem Aristotelis necnon aliorum philosophorum peritissimorum* (London: Richard Pynson, 1505), fps. 9v-10r, for a standard contemporary description, and Johnson, *Astronomical Thought in Renaissance England*, 66-92, for a discussion of the texts of pre-Copernican English astronomy.

2 A Gilbertian commonplace, e.g., "that great loadstone the earth" (*De Magnete* 3.12).

As for that Region of Fire our *Philosophers* talke of, I heard no newes of it; mine eyes have sufficiently informed me there can be no such thing.

The Earth by turning about had now shewed me all her parts twelve times when I finished my course: For when by my reckoning it seemed to be (as indeed it was) Tuesday the Eleventh day of *September*, (at what time the Moone being two daies old was in the Twentieth degree of *Libra*,)[1] my *Gansa's* staied their course as it were[xxvi] with one consent, and tooke their rest, for certaine howers; after which they tooke their flight, and within lesse then one hower, set me upon the top of a very high hill in that other [67] world, where immediately were presented unto mine eyes many most strange and unwonted[2] sights.

For first I observed, that although the Globe of the Earth shewed much bigger there than the Moone doth unto us, even to the full trebling[xxvii] of her diameter, yet all manner of things there were of largenesse and quantity, 10. 20. I thinke I may say 30 times more then ours.

Their trees at least three times so high as ours, and more than five times the breadth and thicknesse.

So their herbes, Beasts, and Birds; although to compare them with ours, I know not well how, because I found not any thing there, any *species* either of *Beast* or *Bird* that resembled ours any thing at all, except *Swallowes*, *Nightingales*, *Cuckooes*, *Woodcockes*, *Batts*, and some kindes [68] of wild *Fowle*, as also of such *Birds* as my *Gansa's*, all which, (as now I well perceived,) spend the time of their absence from us, even there in that world; neither do they vary any thing at all either in quantity or quality from those of ours heere, as being none other then the very same, and that not onely *specie, but numero*.[3]

But of these novelties, more hereafter in their due places.

No sooner was I set downe upon the ground, But I was surprised with a most ravenous hunger, and earnest desire of eating. Wherefore stepping unto the next tree, I fastened thereunto my engine, with my *Gansa's*, and in great haste fell to searching of my pockets for the Victuals I had reserved as aforesaid: but to my great amazement and discomfort, I found in stead of *Partridge*,

---

1 A precise astronomical observation. See the section on chronology in the Introduction (pp. 31-34). Libra, fittingly for Godwin, is the sign associated with mensuration (e.g., Manilius, *Astronomica*, 4.383).

2 unwonted] unusual

3 *specie ... numero*] "in species ... in number" (Latin)

[69] and *Capon* which I thought to have put there, a mingle mangle of drye leaves, of *Goats hayre, sheepe,* or *Goats-dung, Mosse,* and such like trash.

As for my *Canary Wine*, it was turned to a stinking and filthie kind of liquor like the Urine of some *Beast*.

O the illusions of wicked spirits, whose helpe if I had been faine only to rely upon, you see how I had been served.

Now while I stood musing and wondering at this strange *Metamorphosis*, I heard my *Gansa's* upon the sudden to make a great fluttering behind me. And looking back, I espied them to fall greedily upon a certaine shrub within the compasse of their lines, whose leaves they fed upon most earnestly; where heretofore, I had never seene them to eat [70] any manner of greene meate whatsoever. Whereupon stepping to the shrubb, I put a leafe of it between my teeth: I cannot expresse the pleasure I found in the tast thereof; such it was I am sure, as if I had not with great discretion moderated my appetite, I had surely surfetted[1] upon the same.[2]

In the mean time it fell out to be a baite[3] that well contented both my *Birds* and me at that time, when we had need, of some good refreshing.

Scarcely had I ended this banquett, when upon the sudden I saw my self environed with a kind of people most strange, both for their feature, demeanure, and apparell.[4]

Their stature was most divers but for the most part, twice the height of ours: their colour and [71] countenance most pleasing, and their habit such, as I know not how to expresse.[5]

---

1 surfetted] overeaten, gorged
2 This passage provided the prompt for H.G. Wells's *First Men in the Moon*, who do indeed surfeit upon the lunar food, which induces intoxicated fantasies of colonial conquest.
3 baite] food, refreshment; or a stoppage for such
4 The following description of the Lunars follows contemporary ethnographic practice within works of geography; the emphasis on clothing, though simultaneously indebted to William of Newburgh, is particularly suggestive. See Margaret T. Hodgen, *Early Anthropology in the Sixteenth and Seventeenth Centuries* (Philadeliphia: U of Pennyslvania P, 1964), esp. 176-77.
5 See Appendix C for William of Newburgh. His green children likewise wear clothing of an unknown material. This is the first of three direct allusions to William's account of the Green Children of Woolpit; see 83 and 105-06, below. Godwin was prompted here by Burton; see Appendix G.

For neither did I see any kind of *Cloth*, *Silke*, or other stuffe to resemble the matter of that whereof their Clothes were made; neither (which is most strange, of all other) can I devise how to describe the colour of them, being in a manner all clothed alike.

It was neither blacke, nor white, yellow, nor redd, greene nor blew, nor any colour composed of these.

But if you aske me what it was, then[xxviii] I must tell you, it was a colour never seen in our earthly world, and therefore neither to be described unto us by any, nor to be conceived of one that never saw it.

For as it were a hard matter to describe unto a man borne blind [72] the difference betweene blew and[xxix] Greene, so can I not bethinke my selfe of any meanes[xxx] how to decipher unto you this *Lunar* colour, having no affinitie with any other that ever I beheld with mine eyes.

Onely this I can say of it, that it was the most glorious and delightfull, that can possibly be imagined; neither in truth was there any one thing, that more delighted me, during my abode in that new world, than the beholding of that most pleasing and resplendent colour.

It remaineth now that I speake of the Demeanure of this people, who presenting themselues unto me upon the sudden and that in such extraordinary fashion as I have declared,[xxxi] being strucken with a great amasement, I crossed [73] my selfe, and cried out, *Iesus Maria*.

No sooner was the word *Iesus* out of my mouth, but young and old, fell all downe upon their knees, (at which I not a little rejoyced) holding up both their hands on high, and repeating all certaine words which I understood not.[1]

Then presently they all arising, one that was farre the tallest of them came unto me, and embraced me, with great kindnesse, and giving order (as I partly perceived) unto some of the rest to stay by my *Birds*, he tooke me by the hand, and leading me downe toward the foote of the hill, brought me to his dwelling, being more than halfe a league from the place where I first alighted.

It was such a building for beauty and hugenesse, as all our world [74] cannot shew any neere comparable to it.

---

1 Baudoin significantly revised this section. In his version, the Lunars appear, to Gonsales' great terror, but then prostrate themselves and utter some unknown words, either because they found him as astonishing as he found them frightening, or because they found him extraordinary enough to merit veneration. In other words, his Lunars are shown no Christian gestures, and return none.

Yet such I saw afterwards elsewhere, as this might seem but a Cottage in respect of them.

There was not a doore about the house, that was not 30 foote high, and twelve in breadth.

The roomes were between 40. and 50 foote in height, and so all other proportions answerable.

Neither could they well be much lesse, the Master inhabiting them, being full 28 [foote] high.[xxxii]

As for his corporature,[1] I suppose verily that if we had him here in this world to be weighed in the ballance, the poyse of his body would shew it selfe more ponderous then Five and Twenty, peradventure thirty of ours.

After I had rested my selfe with him the Value of one of our dayes; [75] he ledd me some Five leagues off, unto the *Palace* of the *Prince* of the Country.

The statelinesse of the building whereof I wil leave unto the second part of this worke,[2] as also many other particulars, which will minister more pleasure to the reader, then yet I may affoord him, being desirous in this first part to set down no more then what the processe of my story concerning my Iourney doth necessarily draw from me.

This *Prince* whose stature was much higher then the former, is called (as neere as I can by Letters declare it, for their sounds are not perfectly to be expressed by our Characters) *Pylonas*, which signifieth in their Language, *First*,[3] if perhaps it be not rather a denotation of his dignity and authority, as being the prime Man in all those parts.[4]

[76] In all those parts, I say. For there is one supreme *Monarch* amongst them, of stature yet much more huge then hee, com-

---

1 corporature] bodily form; physique
2 The joke about a planned second part which does not then materialise mimics the last sentence of Lucian's *True History*. But Godwin rather spoils it by telling it four times (75, 96, 102, 125), of which this is the first.
3 Though also similar to the Greek *pulôn*, gateway, from *pulê*, a gate, just as Pylonas is the means of access for Domingo to Irdonozur.
4 That the tallest rules in the ideal kingdom is an idea that extends back as far as Scylax, *Periplus*, on the Ethiopians: "These Ethiopians are the tallest race we know, with heights more than six feet, and in some cases seven and a half. They have long hair and beards and are the handsomest of mankind. They take as king the tallest among them" (cited in John Ferguson, *Utopias of the Classical World* [London: Thames and Hudson, 1975], 18). The statement is repeated by Herodotus, *The Histories*, 3.20.

manding over al that whole *Orbe* of that world, having under him 29 other Princes of exceeding great power, and every of them 24 others, whereof this *Pylonas* was one.[1]

The first ancestor of this great *Monarch* came out of the earth[2] (as they deliver) and by marriage with the inheretrice of that huge Monarchy, obtaining the government, left it unto his posteritie, who ever since have held the same, even for the space of 40 thousand daies or *Moones*, which amounteth unto 3077.Yeers.

And his name being *Irdonozur*, his heires, unto this day, doe all assume unto themselves that name, hee, they say, having continued there [77] well neere 400 *Moones*, and having begotten divers children, returned (by what meanes they declare not) unto the Earth againe: I doubt not but they may have their Fables, as well as we.

And because our Histories afford no mention of any earthly man to have ever beene in that world before my selfe, and much lesse to have returned thence again, I cannot but condemne that tradition for false and fabulous; yet this I must tell you, that learning seemeth to be in great estimation among them: And that they make semblance of detesting[xxxiii] all Lying and falshood, which is wont there to be severely punished.

Again, which may yeeld some countenance unto their historicall narrations,[xxxiv] many of them live wonderfull long, even beyond all credit, [78] to wit even unto the age as they professed unto mee of 30000 *Moones*, which amounteth unto 1000 Yeares

---

1 Thus the lunar princes number Irdonozur, 29 x 24 lesser princes, Hiruch, and Imozes the pope-like figure (see 90-91, below), totalling 699.

2 This idea appeared in reversed form in some travel accounts—that the exploring Europeans seemed as gods from the sky. As Antonio Pigafetta, the chronicler of Magellan, said of the race of giants they encountered while sailing for the Antarctic, "all which tyme they saw no man except that one daye by chaunce they espied a man of the stature of a giante, who came to the hauen daunsyng and syngynge, and shortly after seemed to cast dust ouer his heade ... When he sawe the capitayne with certeyne of his company abowte hym, he was greatly amased and made signes holdynge vppe his hande to heauen, signifyinge thereby that owre men came from thense. This giante was so bygge, that the heade of one of owr men of a meane stature, came but to his waiste"; when the other giants see the Europeans they also dance and point to the sky; the Europeans eventually capture two of them by tricking them with manacles fraudulently offered as presents. See Richard Eden, ed. and trans., *The Decades of the Newe Worlde or West India Conteynyng the Navigations and Conquestes of the Spanyardes* (London: William Powell, 1555), fps. 218v-219r.

and Upwards, (so that the ages of 3. or 4. men might well reach unto the time of the first *Irdonozur,*) and this is noted generally, that the taller people are of Stature, the more excellent they are for all indowments of mind, and the longer time they doe live.[1]

For whereas (that which before I partly intimated unto you) their stature is most divers, great numbers of them little exceeding ours; such seldome live above the age of a 1000 *moones,* which is answerable to 80. of our Yeares, and they account them most base creatures, even but a degree before bruite beasts, implying them accordingly in all the basest and most servile offices, tearming them by a word that signifieth [79] bastard-men, counterfetts, or Changelings; so those whom they account Genuine, naturall, and true *Lunars,* both in quantitie of bodie, and length of life, they have for the most part 30 times as much as wee, which proportion agreeth well with the quantitie of the day in both worlds, theirs containing almost 30 of ours.

Now when I shall declare unto you the manner of our travell unto the Palace of *Pylonas,* you will say you scarce ever heard any thing more strange and incredible.

Unto every one of us there was delivered at our first setting forth, two Fans of *Feathers,* not much unlike to those that our Ladies doe carrie in *Spaine,* to make a coole Ayre unto themselves in the heat of *Summer.* The use of which Fans before I declare unto you, I must let [80] you understand that the *Globe* of the *Moone* is not altogether destitute of an attractive Power: but it is so farre weaker than that of the earth,[2] as if a man doe but spring

---

1 This is Pythagorean in origin, but longevity is also a topos of the classical utopian/noble savage traditions. See Herodotus, *The Histories,* 3.22-23, where the Ethiopian king expresses contempt at the 80-year lifespan of the Persians; Ethiopians lived to 120 years on average. (They also, we might note, bind wrong-doers in chains of gold, the source of Thomas More's later Utopian practice, and later followed by lunar civilisation in Wells's *The First Men in the Moon.*) Stories of longevity were also reported of the dwellers of the African coastal islands earlier frequented by Gonsales. The occupants of St. Thomas, according to Purchas, "liue an hundred and ten yeeres: but few borne in Europe exceed fifty" (*Pilgrimage,* 781). These inhabitants, though, are both Portuguese and Negroid, indigenous and settled.

2 Thus the attractive power of the moon varies both with distance and with mass, although Godwin still adopts a "ceiling" interpretation of attraction—past a certain height the attraction disappears. This hypothesis again derives from Gilbert and is to be distinguished sharply from the notion of universal gravitation.

upward, with all his force, (as Dancers do when they shew their activity by capering) he shall be able to mount 50. or 60 foote high, and then he is quite beyond all attraction of the *Moones* earth, falling downe no more, so as by the helpe of these Fans, as with wings, they conveigh themselves in the Ayre in a short space (although not with that swiftnesse that Birds doe) even whither they list.[1]

In two howers space (as I could guesse) by the helpe of these fans, wee were carried through the Ayre those five Leagues, being about 60 persons. Being arrived at the Pallace of *Pylonas*, after our conductor [81] had gotten audience, (which was not presently) and had declared what manner of present he had brought; I was immediately called in unto him by his attendants: by the[xxxv] statelinesse of his Palace, and the reverence done unto him, I soone discerned his greatnesse, and therefore framed my selfe to win his favour the best I might. You may remember I told you of a certaine little *Box* or *Caskett* of *Iewels*, the remainder of those which being brought out of the *East Indies*, I sent from the *Isle*[xxxvi] of St. *Hellen* into *Spaine*.

These before I was carried in unto him I tooke out of[xxxvii] my pockett in a corner, and making choice of some of every sort, made them ready to be presented as I should think fit.

I found him sitting in a most [82] magnificent chaire of Estate, having his Wife or *Queene* upon one hand, and his eldest sonne on the other, which both were[xxxviii] attended, the one by a troope of Ladies, and the other of young men, and all along the side of the roome stood a great number of goodly personages, whereof scarce any one was lower of stature than *Pylonas*, whose age they say is now 21000 *moones*. At my first entrance falling downe upon my knees, I thought good to use unto him these words in the Latine tongue, *Propitius sit tibi Princeps Illustrissime*[xxxix] *Dominus noster Jesus Christus &c.*[2] As the people I first met withall, so they hearing the holy name of our *Saviour*, they all, I say, *King*, *Queene*, and all the rest fell downe upon their knees, pronouncing a word or two I understood not. They being risen [83] againe I proceeded thus, *& Maria Salvatoris Genitrix, Petrus & Paulus*

---

1 Compare Ben Jonson's lunar "Volatees" in the *News from the New World Discover'd in the Moon*, part-birds who "hop from Island to Island." Jonson's masque was acted in 1620, though not published until 1640 (*Works*, 612, and see the Introduction [pp. 25-26]).

2 *Propitius sit … &c.*] "May our most renowned prince and master Jesus Christ be favourable to you etc." (Latin)

&c.[1] and so reckoning up a number of Saints, to see if there were any one of them that they honoured as their patron, at last reckoning among others *St. Martinus*, they all bowed their bodies, and held up hands in signe of great reverence: the reason whereof I learned to bee, that *Martin* in their language signifieth God:[2] Then taking out my *Jewells*, prepared for that purpose, I presented unto the King or Prince (call him how you please) 7 stones of so many severall sorts, a *Diamond*, a *Rubie*, an *Emerauld*, a *Saphire*, a *Topaze*, a *Turquez*, and an *Opall*, which he accepted with great joy and admiration, as having not often seene any such before.[3]

Then I offered unto the Queene and Prince some other, and was about [84] to have bestowed a number of more, upon other there present, but *Pylonas* forbade them to accept, thinking (as afterwards I learned) that they were all I had, and being willing they should be reserved for *Irdonozur* his Soveraigne.

This done he imbraced me with great kindnesse, and began to inquire of me divers things by signes, which I likewise answered by signes as well as I could.

But not being able to give him content, he delivered me to a guard of a 100 of his Giants (so I may wel call them) commanding straightly,

First that I should want nothing that might be fit for me; Secondly that they should not suffer any of the dwarfe *Lunars* (if I may so tearme them) to come neere me;

Thirdly that I should with all [85] diligence be instructed in their Language.

And lastly, that by no meanes they should impart unto me, the knowledge of certaine things, particularly by him specified, marry what those particulars were, I might never by any meanes get knowledge.[4]

It may bee now you will desire to understand what were the things *Pylonas* inquired of mee.

---

1 *& Maria ... &c.*] "And Mary, Mother of the Saviour, Peter and Paul etc." (Latin)
2 The second borrowing from William of Newburgh's account of the Green Children (see p. 99 n. 5 above).
3 As before, in his version of this section, Baudoin revised out Christianity, Gonsales merely prostrating himself and offering his jewels. In the French translation, therefore, and in the other vernacular translations deriving from it, the Lunars are not Christians.
4 This emphasis on restrictions in knowledge recalls Francis Bacon's *New Atlantis*.

Why what but these? whence I came, how I arrived there, and by what means? what was my name? what my Errand, and such like?

To all which I answered the very truth as neere as I could.

Being dismissed, I was affoorded all manner of necessaries that my heart could wish, so as it seemed unto me I was in a very *Paradise*, [86] the pleasures whereof notwithstanding could not so overcome mee, as that the remembrance of my wife and Children, did not trouble mee much.

And therefore being willing to foster any small sparke of hope of my return, with great diligence I tooke order for the attendance of my *Birds*, (I mean my *Gansa's*) whom my selfe in person tended every day with great carefulnesse; All which notwithstanding had fallen out to little purpose, had not other mens care performed that which no indeavour of mine owne could.

For the time now approached, when of necessity all the people of^{xl} our stature, (and so my selfe among the rest) must needes sleepe for some 13. or 14. whole dayes together.[1]

[87] So it commeth to passe there by a secret power, and unresistable decree of nature, that when the day beginneth to appeare, and the Moone to bee enlightned by the *Sunne* beames, (which is at the first Quarter of the Moon) all such people as exceed not very much our stature inhabiting those parts, they fall into a dead sleepe, and are not possibly to be wakened till the *Sun* be sett, and withdrawne out of their sight, even as *Owles*, and *Batts*, with us cannot indure the light, so wee there at the first approach of the day, begin to be amazed with it, and fall immediately into a slumber, which groweth by little and little, into a dead sleepe, till this light depart from thence againe, which is not in 14. or 15 daies, to wit, untill the last quarter.

Mee thinkes now I heare some [88] man to demand what manner of light there is in that world during the absence of the *Sunne*, to resolve you for that point, you shall understand that there is a light of two sorts.

---

1 The notion of seasonal sleep Godwin may have derived from Burton's note on the Russians who sleep all winter; there is, however, a striking parallel with Kepler's *Somnium*, the lunar inhabitants of which, "in contrary fashion to us," sleep by day and live at night. Of course the duration of the lunar slumber is dictated by the lunar day, but perhaps Godwin might also have remembered with amusement that he himself had previously recalled in his *Annales* (1630 edition, 201-02) one William Foxley, a potmaker who fell asleep for 14 days and 15 nights in 1546, an inadvertent lunar day!

One of the *Sun* (which I might not endure to behold,) and another of the Earth: that of the Earth was now at the highest; for that when the Moone is at the Change, then is the Earth (unto them in the Moon) like a full Moone with us; and as the Moone increaseth with us; so the light of the Earth decreaseth with them: I then found the light there (though the Sunne were absent) equall unto that with us, in the day time, when the *Sun* is covered with clouds, but toward the quarter it little and little diminisheth, yet leaving still a competent[1] light, which is somewhat strange.

[89] But much stranger is that which was reported unto me there, how that in the other Hemisphere of the *Moone* (I mean contrary to that I happened upon,) where during halfe the Moone, they see not the sunne, and the Earth never appeareth unto them, they have notwithstanding a kinde of light (not unlike by their description to our Moon light) which it seemeth the propinquintie of the starres and other Planets (so much neerer unto them than us) affoordeth.

Now you shall understand that of the true Lunars there bee three degrees.

Some beyond the pitch of our stature a good deale, as perhaps 10 or 12 foote high, that can indure the day of the Moone, when the earth shineth but little, but not endure the beames of both; at such [90] time they must be content to bee laid asleepe.

Others there are of 20 foote high, or somewhat more, that in ordinary places indure all light both of earth & Sun. Marrie there is a certaine *Island*, the mysteries whereof none may know whose stature is not at least 27 foot high (I meane of the measure of the Standard of *Castile*)[2] If any other come a Land there in the Moones day time, they fall asleepe immediatly: This Island they call Gods *Island*, or *Insula Martini* in their language:[3] they say it hath a particular governour, who is (as they report) of age 65000 Moones, which amounteth to 5000 of our Yeares, his name is said to be *Hiruch*, and he commandeth after a sort over *Irdonozur* himselfe, especially in that *Island* out of which he never commeth.

---

1 competent] adequate

2 For Spanish mensuration in the period, see Roland Chardon, "The Elusive Spanish League: A Problem of Measurement in Sixteenth-Century New Spain," *The Hispanic American Historical Review* 60 (1980): 294-302. The Castilian foot was apparently 278.6 mm in the period, so 27 of Gonsales' Spanish feet equal over 75 modern metres, a huge height.

3 Underperformance by Godwin: this is just Latin for "Martin's Island," whereas the Lunar language, as we later learn, is based on music.

There is another repairing much [91] thither, they said is half his age and upwards, to wit, about 33 thousand Moones, or 26 hundreth of our Yeares, and hee commandeth in all things (throughout the whole Globe of the Moone) concerning matters of Religion, and the service of God, as absolutely as our holy Father the *Pope* doth in any part of *Italy*.[1] I would faine have seene this man, but I might not be suffered to come neere him: his name is *Imozes*.

Now give mee leave to settle my selfe to a long nights sleepe: My attendants take charge of my *Birds*, prepare my lodging, and signifie to mee by signes, how it must bee with mee. It was about the middle of *September*, where I perceived the Ayre to grow more cleare then ordinary, and with the increasing of the light, I began to [92] feele my selfe first dull, then heavy and willing to sleepe, although I had not lately been hindred from taking mine ease that way.

I delivered my selfe at last into the custody of this sister of Death, whose prisoner I was for almost a fortnight after; Awaking then, it is not to bee beleeved how fresh, how nimble, how vigorous, I found all the faculties both of my bodie and minde.

In good time, therefore, I setled my selfe immediately to the learning of the language which (a marvellous thing to consider) is one & the same throughout all the regions of the Moone, yet so much the lesse to bee wondred at, because I cannot thinke all the Earth of Moone to Amount to the fortieth part of our inhabited Earth; partly because the Globe of the Moone is much [93] lesse then that of the Earth, and partly because their Sea or Ocean covereth in estimation Three parts of[xli] Foure, (if not more) whereas the *superficies* of our land may bee judged Equivalent and comparable in Measure to that of our Seas.

The Difficulty of that language is not to bee conceived, and the reasons thereof are especially two:

First, because it hath no affinitie with any other that ever I heard.

Secondly, because it consisteth not so much of words and Letters, as of tunes and uncouth sounds, that no letters can expresse.

For you have few wordes but they signifie divers and severall things, and they are distinguished onely by their tunes that are as it were sung [94] in the utterance of them, yea many wordes there are consisting of tunes onely, so as if they list they will utter their

---

1 Baudoin does not translate the comparison to the Pope ("as ... *Italy*").

mindes by tunes without wordes: for Example, they have an ordinary salutation amongst them, signifying (*Verbatim*) Glorie be to God alone, which they expresse (as I take it, for I am no perfect Musitian) by this tune without any words at all.[1]

Yea the very names of Men they will expresse in the same sort.

When they were disposed to talke of mee before my face, [95] so as I should not perceive it; this was *Gonsales*.

By occasion hereof, I discerne meanes of framing a Language (and that easie soone to bee learned) as copious[2] as any other in the world, consisting of tunes onely, whereof my friends may know more at leasure if it please them.

This is a great Mystery, and worthier the searching after then at first sight you would imagine.

Now notwithstanding the difficulty of this language, within two months space I had atained unto such knowledge of the same, as I understood most questions to be demanded of mee, and what with signes, what with words, made reasonable [96] shift to utter my mind; which thing being certified unto *Pylonas*, hee sent for mee oftentimes, and would bee pleased to give mee knowledge of many things that my *Guardians* durst not declare unto mee.

Yet this I will say of them, that they never abused mee with any untruth that I could perceive, but if I asked a question that they liked not to resolve mee in, they would shake their heads, and with a Spanish shrugge[3] passe over to other talke.

---

1 See the Introduction (pp. 44-46): the lunar musical language is really a simple cipher, but Gonsales' description of it relies heavily on contemporary reports of Chinese.

2 copious] having a large vocabulary

3 Actually an English term for a voiceless gesture, "heaving up the shoulders" (John Wilkins, *An Essay towards a Real Character, and a Philosophical Language* [London: Samuel Gellibrand and John Martyn, 1668], 236).

After 7 moneths space it happened that the great *Irdonozur* making his progresse to a place some 200 leagues distant from the Palace of *Pylonas*, sent for mee.

The History of that Iourney, and the conference that passed between us shall bee related at large in my second booke. Onely thus much [97] thereof at this time, that hee would not admit me into his presence, but talked with me through a Window, where I might heare him, and he both heare and see mee at pleasure.[1] I offered him the remainder of my Iewells, which he accepted very thankfully; telling mee that hee would requite them with gifts of an other manner of value.

It was not above a Quarter of a Moone that I stayed there, before I was sent backe unto *Pylonas* again; and so much the sooner, because if we had stayed but a day or two longer, the Sunne would have overtaken us, before wee could have recovered our home.

The gifts he bestowed on me were such as a Man would forsake mountains of Gold for, and they were all stones, to wit 9 in number, and those of 3 sorts, whereof one [98] they call *Poleastis*, another *Machrus*, and third *Ebelus*, of each sort three.[2] The first are of the bignesse of an *Hazell-nutt*, very like unto jett, which among many other incredible vertues hath this property that being once heat in the Fire, they ever after retaine their heat

---

1   This recalls both the real historical difficulty of access to the Chinese emperor and also the Roman Catholic practice of Confession.

2   Godwin here draws on the "Books of Secrets" tradition concerning marvellous stones (see William Eamon, *Science and the Secrets of Nature: Books of Secrets in Medieval and Early Modern Culture* [Princeton: Princeton UP, 1994], esp. 71-72). This medieval tradition is best represented in Godwin's England by the many translations of *The Book of Secrets*, spuriously attributed to the great thirteenth-century theologian and natural philosopher Albertus Magnus, which went through several English editions in Godwin's lifetime. Pseudo-Albertus, for instance, writes of the "Ahaston" stone that it provides "a fyre continually vnable to be quenshed or put out" (*The Boke of Secrets of Albertus Magnus, of the Vertues of Herbes, Stones, and certayne Beastes* [(London): (John King), 1560], sg. Ciiiir-v). Giambattista della Porta, *Natural Magick* (London: Thomas Young and Samuel Speed, 1658), book 20, chapter 4, likewise discussed certain self-moving stones. Godwin may also have taken a hint from Gilbert, *De Magnete*, 2.38, on marvellous stones. Slightly later, Samuel Hartlib wrote in his *Ephemerides* for 1655 of a Machrus-like stone: he had heard of "an Italian <Receipt> to make Artificial Shining Stones, when they are wetted which is turned since into English" (*The Hartlib Papers*, 29/5/52B).

(though without any appearance) untill they be quenched with some kinde of liquor, whereby they receive no detriment at all, though they bee heat and quenched 10 thousand times.

And their heat is so vehement, as they will make red hot any mettall that shall come within a foot of them, and being put in a Chimney, will make a roome as warme, as if a great Fire were kindled in the same.

The *Machrus* (yet farre more precious then the other) is of the [99] colour of *Topaze*, so shining and resplendent, as (though not past the bignesse of a beane, yet) being placed in the midst of a large Church in the night time, it maketh it all as light, as if a 100 Lamps were hanged up round about it.[1]

Can you wish for properties in a stone of greater use than these. Yet[xlii] my *Ebelus* will affoord you that which I dare say will make you preferre him before these, yea and all the *Diamonds*, *Saphyres*, *Rubies*, and *Emeralds* that our world can yeeld, were they laid in a heap before you;

To say nothing of the colour, (the Lunar[2] whereof I made mention before, which notwithstanding is so incredibly beautifull, as a man should travell 1000 Leagues to behold it) the shape is somewhat flat of the breadth of a *Pistolett*,[3] and [100] twice the thicknesse. The one side of this which is somewhat more Orient of Colour then the other, being clapt to the bare skin of a man, in any part of his bodie, it taketh away from it all weight or ponderousnesse; whereas turning the other side it addeth force unto the attractive beames of the Earth, either in this world or that, and maketh the bodie to weigh halfe so much againe as it did before; do you marvell now why I should so overprize this stone?

---

1 Perhaps recalled by Margaret Cavendish in *The Blazing World* (1666). Her Empress induces religious awe in her subjects by means of a stone identical in properties to Godwin's Macrus, and by a different use of the Poleastis variant. With the first (obtained by dismantling a star), she constructs a chapel lined with "Star-stone," so that the whole chapel emits a "great light, yet ... without all heat." Another chapel she lines with "Fire-stone," thereby creating "an embleme of *Hell*," as the former was "an embleme of *Heaven*." Later, she uses a Poleastis relative, a sort of opposite stone, which, "being wetted, it would grow excessively hot, and break forth into a flaming-fire, until it became dry, and then it ceased from burning" (*A Description of a New World, Called the Blazing World* [London: A. Maxwell, 1666], 61-63).

2 the Lunar] i.e., the Lunar colour

3 *Pistolett*] a Spanish gold escudo, i.e., a coin

before you see mee on earth againe, you shall understand more of the value of this kinde and unvaluable[1] Iem.

I inquired then amongst them, whether they had not any kind of Iewell or other meanes to make a man invisible, which mee thought had beene a thing of great and extraordinary use.

[101] And I could tell that divers of our learned men had written many things to that purpose.[2]

They answered that if it were a thing faisable, yet they assured themselves that God would not suffer it to be revealed to us creatures subject to so many imperfections, being a thing so apt to be abused to ill purposes; and that was all I could get of them.

Now after it was known that *Irdonozur*, the great Monarch, had done me this honour, it is strange how much all men respected mee more then before: my Guardians which hitherto were very nice in relating any thing to mee, concerning the government of that world, now became somewhat more open, so as I could learne (partly of them and partly of *Pylonas*,) what I shall deliver unto you concerning that matter, [102] whereof I will onely give you a taste at this time: referring you unto a more ample discourse in my second part, which at my returne into *Spaine* you shall have at large; but not till then for causes heretofore related.

In a thousand yeares it is not found that there is either Whore-monger amongst them, whereof these reasons are to bee yeelded: There is no want of any thing necessary for the use of man.

Food groweth every where without labour, and that of all sorts to be desired.

For rayment, howsing, or any thing else that you may imagine possible for a man to want, or desire, it is provided by the command of Superiors, though not without labour, yet so little, as they doe nothing but as it were playing, and with pleasure.

[103] Againe their Females are all of an absolute beauty: and I know not how it commeth to passe by a secret disposition of nature there, that a man having once knowne a Woman, never desireth any other. As for murther[3] it was never heard of amongst

---

1 unvaluable] priceless
2 E.g., *The Boke of Secrets of Albertus Magnus*, sg. C1r-v: "If thou wilt be made inuisible, Take the stone, which is called Ophethalmius [i.e., opal], and wrappe it in the leafe of the Laurell, or Baye tree, it is called Lapis obtelmicus, whose colour is not named, so it is of many colours, and it is of such vertu, that it blindeth the sightes of them that stand about. Constantinus carying this in hys hande, was maid inuisyble by it."
3 murther] murder

them; neither is it a thing almost possible to bee committed: for there is no wound[xliii] to bee given which may not bee cured, they assured mee, (and I for my part doe beleeve it,) that although a mans head be cut off, yet if any time within the space of Three Moones it bee put together, and joyned to the Carkasse againe, with the appointment of the Iuyce of a certaine hearbe, there growing, it will be joyned together againe, so as the partie wounded shall become perfectly whole in a few houres.

[104] But the chief cause, is that through an excellent disposition of that nature[xliv] of people there, all, young and old doe hate all manner of vice, and doe live in such love, peace, and amitie, as it seemeth to bee another Paradise. True it is, that some are better disposed then other: but that they discerne immediately at the time of their birth.

And because it is an inviolable decree amongst them, never to put any one to death, perceiving by the stature, and some other notes they have, who are likely to bee of a wicked or imperfect disposition, they send them away (I know not by what meanes) into the Earth, and change them for other children, before they shall have either abilitie or opportunitie to doe amisse among them: But first (they say) they are faine to keepe them there [105] for a certaine space, till that the ayre of the Earth may alter their colour to be like unto ours.[1]

And their ordinary vent for them is a certaine high hill in the North of *America*, whose people I can easily beleeve to be wholly descended of them, partly in regard of their colour, partly also in regard of the continuall use of Tobacco which the *Lunars* use exceeding much, as living in a place abounding wonderfully with moysture, as also for the pleasure they take in it, and partly in some other respects too long now to be rehearsed.[2] Sometimes

---

1   See William of Newburgh in Appendix C: "Eventually, they gradually changed their colour due to the influence of our food, became like us, and also learned our language."

2   Thus Godwin takes the often-made connection between the discoveries of the New World and of the plurality of habitable worlds, and forges a literal link: the Native Americans *are* from the moon. See John Adams, "Outer Space and the New World in the Imagination of Eighteenth-Century Europeans," *Eighteenth-Century Life* 19 (1995): 70-83, esp. 72-73. That the man in the moon smoked tobacco was an old piece of moon-lore, presumably deriving from the smoke-like effect created when thin clouds pass over the moon's disc at night: see Harley, *Moon Lore*, 13-14. Not, therefore, a reference to James VI and I's much publicised dislike of smoking. Godwin may also be glancing at Plutarch, *Face in the Moon*, 938C.

they mistake their aime, and fall upon Christendome, *Asia* or *Affricke*, marry that is but seldome: I remember some yeares since, that I read certain stories tending to the confirmation of these things delivered by these *Lunars*, as especially [106] one Chapter of *Guil: Neubrigensis, de reb Angl:* it is towards the end of his first booke, but the chapter I cannot particularly resigne.[1]

Then see *Jnigo Mondejar* in his description of *Nueva Granata*, the second booke; as also *Ioseph Desia de Carana*, in his history of *Mexico*: if my memory faile mee not, you will find that in these, which will make my report much the more credible: But for testimonies I care not.[2]

May I once have the happinesse to return home in safety, I will yeeld such demonstrations, of all I deliver, as shall quickly make void all doubt of the truth hereof.

If you will aske mee further of the manner of government amongst the Lunars, and how Iustice is executed?

[107] Alas what need is there of Exemplary punishment, where there are no offences committed: they need there no Lawyers, for there is never any contention, the seeds thereof, if any begin to sprout, being presently by the wisedome of the next Superior puld up by the roots.

And as little need is there of Physitians; they never misdiet themselves, their Ayre is alwaies temperate and pure, neither is there any occasion at all of sicknes, as to me it seemed at least, for I could not heare that ever any of them were sicke.

But the time that nature hath assigned unto them being spent, without any paine at all they die, or rather (I should say) cease to live, as a candle to give light, when that which nourisheth it is consumed.

[108] I was once at the departure of one of them, which I wondred much to behold; for notwithstanding the happy life hee led, and multitude of friends and children hee should forsake, as soone as certainly hee understood and perceived his end to approach, hee prepared a great feast, and calling about him all

---

1 resigne] remember. This is the final, and this time explicit, reference to William of Newburgh's Green Children. See p. 99 n. 5 and p. 105 n. 2 above and the section on dating in the Introduction (pp. 20-24).

2 These books, however, are fictitious, as Godwin compensates for the initial oddity of a Spaniard referring to an English chronicler. There was a well-known Spanish family of the time boasting many men called Iñigo López de Mendoza, Marquis de Mondejar, and Godwin might have generated his spoof name from there. But "Carana" appears to be entirely fanciful.

those hee especially esteemed of, hee bids them be merry and rejoyce with him, for that the time was come he should now leave the counterfeit pleasures of that world, and bee made partaker of all true joyes and perfect happinesse.

I wondred not so much at his constancy, as the behaviour of those his friends: with us in the like case, all seeme to mourne, when often some of them doe but laugh in their sleeves, or as one sayes under a visard.

[109] They all on the other side, young and old, both seemingly, and in my conscience, sincerely did rejoyce thereat, so as if any dissembled, it was but their owne griefe conceived for their owne particular losse.[1]

Their bodies being dead putrifie not, and therefore are not buried, but kept in certaine roomes ordained for that purpose; so as most of them can shew their Ancestors bodies uncorrupt for many generations.[2]

There is never any raine, wind, or change of the Ayre, never either Summer, or Winter, but as it were a perpetuall Spring, yeelding all pleasure, all content, and that free from any annoyance at all.

O my Wife and Children, what wrong have you done mee to bereave mee of the happinesse of that place: but it maketh no matter, for by [110] this voyage am I sufficiently assured, that ere long the race of my mortall life being run, I shall attaine a greater happinesse elsewhere, and that everlasting.

It was the Ninth day of *September*[3] that I began to ascend from

---

1 This follows the Utopian reaction to a good death: "all that depart merely [i.e., "merrily"] and ful of good hoope, for them no man mournethe, but followethe the heerse with ioyfull synging, commending the soules to god with great affection": Thomas More, *Utopia*, trans. Ralph Robynson (1556), ed. J.H. Lupton (Oxford: Clarendon P, 1895), 277. It became a common motif: Foigny's Australians long for death, and when permitted to commit assisted suicide, do so with joy and ceremony: Gabriel du Foigny, *A New Discovery of Terra Incognita Australis* (London: John Dunton, 1693), 104-06; and Swift's Houyhnhnms die with no sorrow, behaving merely "as if they were going to some remote Part of the Country": Jonathan Swift, *Gulliver's Travels*, ed. Robert A. Greenberg (New York: W.W. Norton, 1970), 240 (Book 4, ch. 9). The idea has both Epicurean and Stoic antecedents.

2 Godwin is surely recalling plate XXII of Thomas Hariot's *A Brief and True Report of the New-Found Land of Virginia* (Frankfurt: Wechel, 1590), depicting "The Tombe of their Werowans or chieffe Lordes."

3 This is calendrically inconsistent. See the discussion of chronology in the Introduction (pp. 31-34).

El Pico; twelve dayes I was upon my Voyage, and arrived in that Region of the Moone, that they call *Simiri*, September the 21 following.

The 12 day of *May* being Friday, wee came unto the Court of the great *Irdonozur*, and returned backe the Seventeenth unto the Palace of *Pylonas*, there I continued till the moneth of *March*, in the yeare 1601. at what time I earnestly besought *Pylonas* (as I had often done before) to give mee leave to depart, (though with never so great hazard of my life) backe into the earth againe.

[111] Hee much disswaded mee, laying before mee the danger of the voyage, the misery of that place from whence I came, and the abundant happinesse of that I now was in; But the remembrance of my Wife and Children overweighed all these reasons, and to tell you the truth, I was so farre forth moved with a desire of that deserved glory, that I might purchase at my return, as me thought: I deserved not the name of a *Spanyard*, if I would not hazard 20 lives, rather than loose but a little possibility of the same. Wherefore I answered him, that my desire of seeing my Children was such, as I knew I could not live any longer, if I were once out of hope of the same. When then he desired one yeares stay longer, I told him it was manifest I must depart now or never: My *Birds* began to droope, for want of their wonted [112] migration, 3 of them were now dead, and if a few more failed, I was for ever destitute of all possibilitie of returning.

With much adoe at last hee condescended unto my request, having first acquainted the great *Irdonozur* with my desire, then perceiving by the often baying of my *Birds*, a great longing in them to take their flight; I trimmed up mine Engine, and took my leave of *Pylonas*, who (for all the courtesie hee had done mee) required of mee but one thing, which was faithfully to promise him, that if ever I had meanes thereunto, I should salute from him *Elizabeth*, whom he tearmed the great *Queene* of *England*, calling her the most glorious of all women living, and indeed hee would often question with mee of her, and therein delighted so much, as it seemed hee was never satisfied in talking[xlv] [113] of her;[1] hee also delivered unto mee a token or present for her of no small Value: Though I account her an enemy of Spayne, I may not faile of performing this promise as soone as I shall bee able so to doe: upon the 29 day of *March* being Thursday,[2] 3 dayes after my

---

1 Throughout the work, Godwin has been running an implicit pro-English campaign; compare 9-10, 38.

2 An accurate date in the Gregorian calendar.

awakeing from the last Moones light, I fastened my selfe to mine Engine, not forgetting to take with mee, besides the Iewels *Irdonozur* had given mee (with whose use and vertues *Pylonas* had acquainted mee at large) a small quantitie of Victual, wherefore afterward I had great use as shall bee declared.

An infinite multitude of people, (and amongst the rest *Pylonas* himselfe being present,) after I had given him the last *Beza los manos*, I let loose the raines unto my *Birds*, who with great greedinesse taking wing quickly [114] carried mee out of their sight, it fel out with me as in my first passage, I never felt either hunger or thirst, till I arrived in *China* upon a high mountaine, some 5 Leagues from the high and mighty City of *Pachin*.

This Voyage was performed in lesse than 9 dayes; I heard no newes by the way of these ayrie men, which I had seen in my ascending.

Nothing stayed my journey any whit at all: Whether it was the earnest desire of my *Birds*, to return to the Earth, where they had missed one season, or that the attraction of the Earth so much stronger then that of the Moone, furthered their labour; so it came to passe; although now I had 3 *Birds* wanting of those I carried forth with mee.

For the first 8 dayes my *Birds* flew before, and I with the Engine was as it were drawne by them.

[115] The Ninth day when I began to approach unto the Clouds, I perceived my selfe and mine Engine to sincke towards the Earth, and goe before them.

I was then horribly afraid, lest my *Birds* not being able to beare our weight, they being so few, should bee constrained to precipitate both mee and themselves headlong to the Earth: wherefore I thought it no lesse then needfull to make use of the *Ebelus*, (one of the stones bestowed upon me by *Irdonozur*,) which I clapped to my bare flesh within my hose: and it appeared manifestly thereupon unto mee that my *Birds* made their way with much greater ease then before, as being lightned of a great burthen; neither doe I thinke it possible for them to have let mee downe safely unto the Earth without that helpe.

[116] *China* is a Country so populous, as I thinke there is hardly a peece of ground to bee found (in the most barren parts of the same) though but thrice a mans length, which is not most carefully manured.[1] I being yet in the Ayre, some of the Country

---

1 The coda on China derives chiefly from the various accounts collected by Purchas (see *The Purchas Handbook*, 2 vols. [London: The (Continued)

people had espied mee, and came running unto mee by troopes, they seised upon mee, and would needs, by and by, carrie mee unto an Officer. I seeing no other remedy, yeelded my selfe unto them. But when I assayed[1] to goe, I found my selfe so light, that I had much adoe, one foote being upon the ground, to set downe the other, that was by reason of my *Ebelus*, so applyed, as it tooke quite away all weight and ponderousnesse from my body: Wherefore bethinking my selfe what was to be done, I fained a desire of performing the [117] necessitie of nature, which by signes being made knowen unto them (for they understood not a word of any Language I could speake) they permitted mee to go aside among a few bushes, assuring themselves that for mee to escape from them it was impossible; Being there I remembred the directions *Pylonas* had given mee, concerning the use of my stones, and first I tooke them all together, with a few Iewells yet remaining of those I had brought out of *India*, and knit them up in my handkerchiefe, all, except one the least and worst *Ebelus*.[2]

Him I found meanes to apply in such sort unto my body, as but the halfe of his side touched my skin, whereby it came to passe that my body then had but halfe the weight, that being done I drew towards these my Guardians, till seeing them [118] come somewhat neere together they could not crosse my way, I shewed them a faire paire of heeles.[3]

This I did to the end I might recover an opportunitie of finding my Stones, and Iewells, which I knew they would rob mee off, if I prevented them not.

Being thus lightned I bid them such a base,[4] as had they been all upon the backs of so many *Zebra's*, they could never have overtaken me: I directed my course unto a certaine thicke wood, into which I entred some quarter of a League, and then finding a

---

Hakluyt Society, 1997], 1.268-77 for an analysis and list). Among these we might mention the redactions of Gaspar da Cruz, Galeotto Perera, Diego de Pantoja, Matteo Ricci/Nicholas Trigault (*Purchas his Pilgrimes*, 3.166-209, 316-411). Godwin could also consult Mendoza, *Historie*; Linschoten, *Discours*, 37-44; Hakluyt, *Principal Navigations*, 2.68-80, 88-98; and Purchas, *Purchas His Pilgrimage*, 435-76.

1 assayed] attempted

2 But Gonsales earlier claims that he gave away the "remainder" of his earthly jewels to Irdonozur (97).

3 Proverbial for "to flee"; see Shakespeare, *1 Henry IV*, 2.4.47-48 (Arden edition), related to Tilley, *Proverbs*, H397.

4 bid them such a base] to challenge a chase at the game of "base," a catching game involving two sides.

pretty spring, (which I tooke for my marke,)^{xlvi} hard by it, I thrust my jewells into a little hole made by a Want,[1] or some such like creature.

Then I tooke out of my pocket my Victualls, (to which in all my Voyage I had not till then any desire) [119] and refreshed my selfe therewith, till such time as the people pursuing mee, had overtaken mee, into whose hands I quietly delivered my selfe.

They led mee unto a meane Officer, who (understanding that once I had escaped from them that first apprehended mee,) caused a certaine seat to be made of boords, into which they closed mee in such sort, as onely my head was at liberty, and then carried mee upon the shoulders of 4 slaves, (like some notorious malefactor)[2] before a man of great authority, whom^{xlvii} in their language as after I learned, they called a *Mandarine*,[3] abiding 2 dayes journey off, to wit one League distant from the great and famous City of *Pachin*, or *Paquin*, by the *Chinesse* called *Suntien*.[4]

Their language I could no way [120] understand; onely this I could discerne, that I was for something or other accused with a great deale of vehemence.

The substance of this accusation it seemes was, that I was a *Magician*, as witnessed my strange carriage in the ayre; that being a stranger, as appeared by my both language and habit, I contrary to the Lawes of *China*, entred into the Kingdome without warrant, and that probably with no good intent. The *Mandarine* heard them out, with a great deale of composed gravitie; and being a man of quicke apprehension, and withall studious of novelties, he answered them, that hee would take such order with mee, as the case required, and that my bold attempt should not want its deserved punishment. But having dismissed them he gave order to his Servants, that I [121] should be kept in some remote parts of his vast Palace, and bee strictly watched, but courteously used: This doe I conjecture, by what at the present I

---

1 Want] mole

2 Compare Gaspar da Cruz's description: "the other *Portugals* were carried in Coopes with their heads out fast by the neckes betweene the boards that they could not pull them in" (Purchas, *Pilgrimes*, 3.191).

3 *Mandarine*] deriving from the Portuguese term for a Chinese *guan* ("official"), and a recent English borrowing drawn into currency through the English translations of Mendoza, Linschoten, Acosta, and Purchas, whence Godwin derived it.

4 Compare Purchas, *Pilgrimes*, 3.402, on the name of Peking: "*Pequin*, *Paquin*, and *Puckin*; yea, by other language *Taybin*, and *Cambalu*, and *Suntien*, or *Citie of Heaven*."

found, and what after followed. For my accommodation was every way better, then I could expect; I lodged well, fared well, was attended well, and could not fault any thing, but my restraint. In this manner did I continue many moneths, afflicted with nothing so much as with the thought of my *Gansa's*; which I knew must be irrecoverably lost, as indeed they were. But in this time, by my own industry, and the forwardnesse of those that accompanied me, I was growne indifferent ready[1] in the ordinary language of that Province, (for almost every Province in *China*, hath its proper Language) whereat I discerned they tooke no small content.[xlviii] [122] I was at length to take the ayre, and brought into the spacious garden of that Palace, a place of excellent pleasure, and delight, as being planted with herbes and Flowers of admirable both sweetnes and beauty, and almost infinite variety of fruits both *European* and others, and al those composed with that rare curiositie, that I was ravished with the contemplation of such delightfull objects. But I had not here long recreated my selfe, yet the *Mandarine* entred the Garden, on that side where I was walking, and being advertised thereof by his servants, and wished to kneel down to him (as I after found it to be the usuall publique reverence to those great Officers) I did so, and humbly craved his favour towards a poore stranger, that arrived in those parts, not by his own destination, but by the secret disposall of the heavens: [123] Hee in a different language (which al the *Mandarines*, as I have since learned, do use)[2] and that like that of the Lunars did consist much of tunes,[3] but was by one of his servants interpreted to me. Hee, I say, wished mee to bee of good comfort, for that he intended no harme unto mee, and so passed on. The next day was I commanded to come before him, and so conducted into a sumptuous dining roome exquisitely painted and adorned. The *Mandarine* having commanded all to avoid the roome, vouchsafed conference with mee in the vulgar language; inquiring first the estate of my Country, the power of my Prince, the religion and manners of the people; wherein being

---

1 indifferent ready] tolerably proficient
2 Compare Purchas, *Pilgrimes*, 3.384: "Each Prouince hath also its owne [language], and all haue one common Tongue besides, which they call *Quonhoa*, or the Court Language."
3 Compare Purchas, *Pilgrimes*, 3.342-43: "... that speech consisting wholly of Monosyllables, the want of skill in those Accents had caused that they [the Europeans] neither did, nor were vnderstood." See the section on lunar language in the Introduction (pp. 44-46).

satisfied by mee, hee at last descended to the particulars of my education and studies, and what brought mee into this remote countrey:[1] Then did I at [124] large declare unto him the adventure of my life, only omitting here and there, what particulars I thought good, forbearing especially any mention of the stones given me by *Irdonozur*. The strangenes of my story did much amaze him. And finding in all my discourse nothing any way tending to Magique; (wherein he had hoped by my means to have gaind some knowledge) he began to admire the excellence of my wit, applauding me for the happiest man, that this world had ever produced: and wishing me to repose my selfe after my long narration, he for that time dismissed me. After this, the *Mandarine* took such delight in me, that no day passed, wherein he sent not for me. At length he advised me to apparell my selfe in the habit of the Country (which I willingly did) and gave mee not only the liberty of his house, but took mee [125] also abroad with him, when he went to *Paquin*, whereby I had the opportunitie by degrees to learn the disposition of the people, and the policie of the Country, which I shall reserve for my second part. Neither did I by this my attendance on him gaine only the knowledge of these things, but the possibility also of being restored to my native soyle, and to those deare pledges[2] which I value above the world, my Wife and children. For by often frequenting *Paquin*, I at length heard of some Fathers of the Society that were become famous for the extraordinary favour by the King vouchsafed them, to whom they had presented some *European* trifles, as Clockes, Watches, Dials, and the like, which with him passed for exquisite rarities.[3] To them by the *Mandarines* leave, I repaired, was welcomed by them, they much wondring [126] to see a Lay *Spaniard* xlix there, whither they had with so much difficulty obtained leave to arrive. There did I relate to Father *Pantoja*,[4] and

---

1   This recalls the Chinese Emperor's questioning of Pantoja and Ricci (Purchas, *Pilgrimes*, 3.356-57), and indeed the earlier questions of Pylonas within the fiction itself.

2   pledges] a legal term for persons who act as a surety for another; here metaphorically people Gonsales must not default on by abandoning them

3   The Jesuits had in fact only very recently been allowed into Peking.

4   *Pantoja*] Diego Pantoia or Pantoja, a genuine Jesuit missionary, and colleague of Matteo Ricci. His 1602 letter on China to Luis de Guzman is redacted by Purchas, *Pilgrimes*, 3.350-79, and is discussed by Amartin-Serin in her edition of Godwin (137-40). Pantoja is remembered as the Jesuit who introduced diacritics into the Romanised notation (Continued)

those others of the society these fore-related adventures, by whose directions I put them in writing, and sent this story of my fortunes to *Macao*, from thence to be conveighed for *Spaine*, as a forerunner of my returne.[1] And the *Mandarine* being very indulgent unto me, I came often unto the Fathers, with whom I consulted about many secrets; with them also[li] did I lay a foundation for my returne, the blessed houre whereof I doe with patience expect; that by inriching my Country with the knowledge of hidden mysteries, I may once reape the glory of my fortunate misfortunes.

FINIS.[lii]

---

of spoken Chinese, to help Europeans grasp the five tone variations in spoken Chinese. Again, this should remind us of the Lunar language.

TEXTUAL NOTES

i   THOU hast ... great discoverer] originally in reversed fonts.

ii   *Therrando*] sic. The name is impossible in Spanish, and was more likely "Fernando" in the original MS; the compositer has, I propose, made the plausible mistake of misreading majuscule "F" (written in secretary hand as the two-part graph "ff"; and in italic often with a pronounced upper-left-hand serif) as "Th," and has then gone on to mistake an "n" for an "r."

iii   *Fernando*] 1657. 1638: *Ferrando*

iv   *Cossey*] 1638: *Coßey*

v   *Cossey*] 1638: *Coßey*

vi   Latitude] 1638: Altitude, a muddling of the first two letters (not a typographical switch, though, which would have produced "lAtitude").

vii   In the Bodleian copy, the Gansas engraving has been printed onto sg. B8r, i.e., page [15], the verso of which is page 16 of the text. This was clearly an error, as the same engraving is then repeated in its proper place on sg. C6v, page [28], following page 27. The error was then corrected by pasting in the St. Helena engraving as a singleton between pages 14 and [15], thereby still preserving the otiose Gansas engraving, which could not be excised without the loss of the text on its verso. (The Bodleian copy therefore prints the Gansas three times.) But the British Library copy has the Gansas on sg. B8r, and St. Helena on sg. C6v. The Bibliothèque Nationale copy (Rés. p. V. 752 [6]) has St. Helena on sg. B8r, and sg. C6 has been entirely cut away (it must have sported the Gansas). This corrected ordering is also witnessed in the John Rylands (call number SC12770A), Harvard (call number STC 11943.5), and Folger (call number STC 11943) copies. In other words, there are three states here: an erroneous state of reversed plates (British Library, also Beineke Library Ih G549 63B); an erroneous state of two Gansas engravings, corrected in the Bodleian copy by the reprinting of gathering C, and one insertion of a singleton into the still defective gathering B; and finally a corrected printing of both gatherings B and C (Bibliothèque Nationale [though mutilated], Harvard, Folger). So there was confusion in the initial printing where the plates should go, followed by a partial, and then a full state of correction. The 1657 edition follows the BNF/Harvard/ Folger and *corrected* Bodleian state, omitting the erroneous Gansas plate, and this is the practice adopted here. See the entries in the *Short-Title Catalogue*, nos. 11943, 11943.5. "Variant 1" refers to the first erroneous state, "Variant 2" to the second erroneous state.

viii   Gansa's] 1638: Gans'as

ix   know not] 1638. 1657: do not know

x   *Tenerif*] 1638, 1657: *Tenerik*. Misprint for *Tenerif*, the preferred spelling of Hakluyt and others. The sorts in question are not near one another in the printer's tray, but final f/k in secretary hand can appear close.

xi   play] 1638, 1657. Possibly a variant spelling for ply.

xii   But what then, O Reader?] 1657: But what then? O Reader

xiii   gasping] 1638, 1657: gaping.

xiv   exceeding] 1638: exeeding

xv   lynes] 1657: line

xvi   fail] 1638. Perhaps a misprint for failed.

xvii shewed] 1657. 1638: I shewed

xviii Moone] 1638: MOONE

xix   (which was] 1638, 1657: (which (was

xx   celestial bodies, two motions] 1657: celestial bodies two motions,

xxi   hundreth] 1638, 1657

xxii 30] 1638: 3[.] (damaged); emended

xxiii of] 1638: of of

xxiv *contabundo*] 1638. 1657: *cunctabundo*. Both are licit forms.

xxv recitall] 1638: re-cital[catchword]/tall

xxvi were] 1657. 1638: was

xxvii trebling] 1638 the 't' failed to print-to-paper

xxviii was, then] 1657. 1638: was then;

xxix and] 1638: and and

xxx   meanes] 1657. 1638: meane

xxxi declared,] 1657. 1638: declared [comma perhaps failed to print-to-paper]

xxxii 28 [foote] high] 1638: 28 high. 1657: 28. high.

xxxiii detesting] 1638: "s" damaged; as a result McColley unnecessarily read "detecting." 1657: detesting

xxxiv narrations,] 1657. 1638: narrations)

xxxv attendants: by the] 1657. 1638: attendance: the

xxxvi the *Isle*] 1638: *Isle* 1657: the *Ile*

xxxvii out of] 1657. 1638: out

xxxviii both were] 1638. 1657: were both

xxxix Illustrissime] 1638: Illustrißime

xl   of] 1638: of of

xli   of] 1657. 1638: or

xlii   Yet] 1638, 1657: Yes

xliii wound] 1657. 1638: woun-

xliv nature] 1638. 1657: stature

xlv   talking] 1638: talk-ing[catchword]/king

xlvi marke,)] 1638: marke, (1657: marke)

xlvii whom] 1638: (whom

xlviii content.] 1638: con-tent. [catchword] tent [no full stop or paragraph break]

xlix Lay *Spaniard*] 1638: Lay a *Spaniard*

l   returne.] 1638: returne

li   secrets; with them also] 1638: secrets with them also. 1657: secrets with them; also

lii   The concluding paragraph of the text is symmetrically tapered.

Appendix A: Francis Godwin, Nuncius Inanimatus (1629)[1]

[While convalescing on St. Helena, Godwin's Gonsales experiments with various telegraphic systems. His contrivances were well known to contemporary readers of the sixteenth-century popular manuals of Giambattista della Porta, Blaise de Vigenère, or William Bourne (Godwin's own copy of Porta survives).[2] But Domingo also claims that he has perfected "a more refined and effectual way" than his overt mechanisms (22). "Hereafter," he declares, "I will perhaps afford a discourse for it." Something rather like Domingo's "discourse" did indeed appear in Latin in 1629, roughly the year when *The Man in the Moone* was completed, but in the future for fictional Gonsales, who made his promise in around 1602. Although the *Nuncius Inanimatus* (literally "Lifeless Messenger") was unsigned, it was swiftly attributed to Godwin by writers including John Wilkins, and published under the imprint "In Vtopia" by the major London stationer John Bill, Godwin's normal publisher and the boss of his son Paul. It is very scarce.[3] A passing reference to "Nuntius animatus" [sic] in the 1628 edition of Burton's *Anatomy of Melancholy* also suggests that Godwin's telegraphic tract was known or at least known of in manuscript prior to its printing.[4] We know, too, that in 1621 Godwin petitioned the

---

1 For a full discussion of this tract, its sources, and its analogues, see William Poole, "*Nuncius Inanimatus*: Telegraphy and Paradox in the Seventeenth Century: the Schemes of Francis Godwin and Henry Reynolds," *The Seventeenth Century* 21 (2006): 45-71.

2 Fire and dust signals were well known from Giambattista della Porta, *De Occultis Literarum Notis* (Montbéliard: Lazarus Zetsnerus, 1593), 39-43 (1.10) [Godwin's copy of this edition is in Cambridge University Library, N. 4. 85]; Blaise de Vigenère, *Traicté des Chiffres ou Secretes Manieres d'Escrire* (Paris: Abel L'Angelier, 1586), fps. 252v-253r; William Bourne, *Inventions and Devises* (London: Thomas Woodcock, 1590), 60-62.

3 Only four copies are currently in the public domain. Three of these display interestingly near-contemporary provenances: the Folger copy derives from William Brereton's library, bearing the note "Cost 16. pence at my Ld. Breretons auction London June 1697"; one of the two Bodleian copies belonged to John Selden; and the British Library copy was purchased from the Macclesfield Library. The *Nuncius* is a tiny book, just one sheet of duodecimo, bearing a striking device of a winged Mercury on its title-page; this is what confirms that Bill printed it (see R.B. McKerrow, *Printers' and Publishers' Devices 1485-1640* [London: The Bibliographical Society, 1913], no. 382, used in three Bill productions 1617-22).

4 Burton, *Anatomy*, 3.2.2.5 (3.133).

state in the names of both himself and his son Thomas with a similar proposal, dated 7 March 1620/21, reproduced here in full:

> I shall vndertake to certify [i.e., pass information] into any town or fortresse, never so streightly beseiged any errand needfull, and to receive an answer of the same vpon these condicions,
>
> 1. that I bee brought to some place, where I may see the saide fortres, and have liberty to performe there what is requisite in that case, as safety of person, and an howers tyme.
>
> 2. that I have in the saide fortres one that is not ignorant of this art, and is provided to receive and returne notice.
>
> 3. that my saide consort bee appointed certaine tymes, as such an hower in the morning, or such in the evening, or some such hower of the day, when to expect the notice.
>
> 4. that hee may be able to guesse at the place, from whence it is to bee had, either this, or that, of 6. 7. 8. or 10. places, within the compasse of eight miles.
>
> Fr[anciscus] Heref[ordensis]
Thom[as] Godwyn[1]

In other words, Godwin was serious about his telegraphy, a point worth pondering when we compare the fictional activities of Gonsales, the cagey Latin anonymous manifesto of 1629, and his own formal (but apparently unanswered) 1621 plea to the English government. The connection between *The Man and the Moone* and the *Nuncius Inanimatus* was perceptible enough to prompt the translation and printing of the latter as an appendix to the 1657 edition of *The Man in the Moone*, this time published solely by Kirton. This accurate and literal translation, reproduced below, was undertaken by Thomas Smith (1638-1710), the famous non-juring scholar and orientalist, who only acknowledged his translation almost half a century later in a private letter to his friend the antiquary Thomas Hearne.[2] Although Wilkins thought otherwise, it seems most likely that behind Godwin's deliberately obscure rhetoric, he was advocating a method of secret communication based on natural magic. Page numbers keyed to the

---

1 London, The National Archives, SP 14/120/17. I have silently expanded all contractions.

2 Wood, *Athenae Oxonienses*, 2.558. Smith acknowledged his translation in a 1705 letter to Thomas Hearne, cited by the latter in the preface to his *Duo Rerum Anglicarum Scriptores Veteres, viz. Thomas Otterbourne et Johannes Wethamstede* (Oxford: Sheldonian Theatre, 1732), LXXXIII-LXXXIV, in which Smith also states that he had assumed that the work was "designed onely in the way of wit and phansy"; and that both the Latin original and the English translation were now "irretrievable."

1657 text are enclosed in square brackets. Godwin supplied his own occasional marginal notes; these have been expanded and multiplied in the footnotes. Three insignificant typographical errors have been silently emended.]

Nuncius Inanimatus, or The Mysterious Messenger &c.

[1]
1. It cannot be imagined, that any one who hath but the lest knowledge in Philosophy, should be ignorant, that, nothing can be perceived by human understanding without the help of the exteriour Senses,[1] so that he that intends to communicate the secrets of his minde to one either absent or present, it is altogether necessary that he have an accesse by this way. [2]
2. And certainly to those that are present, we use no other means than that of Speech, which by the subserviency of the sense of Hearing, doth disclose one mans minde unto another, and as it were joyn them both together, unless peradventure sometimes another *Pallas* be found, who (as *Tacitus* relates of that freeman of *Claudius*) was wont to command his servants by no other way than by writing, or nodding with his head.[2]
3. They who would declare any thing to their freind that is absent, and yet will not trust to the fidelity of the Messenger, do present that unto their Eyes, which they cannot, or at least think not safe to do unto the Ears; to which end and purpose the indicting of Letters, being the interpreters of our minde, began to be in common use; which for the most part do faithfully perform that Arrant whereon they are sent, unless when the trechery or [3] negligence of those that carry them, or the impediments of the journey cause that these Demonstrations of our minde, come not to the place to which they are destinated.
4. There are many several remedies of these inconveniencies invented by the Antients, which not only seem to facilitate the way, and to point out fit Messengers not easily to be corrupted, but also they promise a kind of swiftness as is beyond the power of man, unless he like another *Perseus* can purchase I know not what winged *Pegasus* for the conveyance of himselfe and Letters.

---

1   Latin "ad intellectum humanum nihil nisi exteriorum sensuum adminiculo peruenire," a version of the Aristotelian commonplace "Nihil in intellectu quod prius non fuerit in sensu."
2   Probably a misremembering of Tacitus, *Annales*, 11.10: "[Cleopatra] nodding with her head in token that shee had, commandeth *Narcissus* [Freedman of Claudius] to be called for" (*The Annales of Cornelius Tacitus*, trans. Richard Greneway [London, 1598], 152); the original ("atque illa adnuente cieri Narcissum postulat") does not strike one as particularly cryptographic. Godwin's own incorrect reference is to book 13.

5. It will not repent me of my labour in reckoning up their Inventions of this sort, as I finde them recorded by the penns of Historians, that at the last when I have given, in some measure, a description of this my Nuncio, and have related what he promiseth, then it may be made known to the intelligent [4] Reader how far our inventions exceed and go beyond those of the Ancients.

6. *Cecinna* of *Volatera*, a Noble man of *Rome* (according to the testimonie of *Pliny*) bringing with him into the City, Swallows that had been taken, sent them with tidings of victory unto his freinds, painting them with the colour which betokens Victory: And *Fabius Pictor* also relates in his Annales, that when a Roman Garison was besieged by the *Ligurians*, that there was a Swallow, brought from her young ones to him, with a peice of thred tied unto one of her leggs, that he should signify by the knots what day he would come with more aid that they might make a Sally: And *Decimus Brutus*, at the siege of *Modena*, sent Letters that were tied at the feet of Pigeons into the Tents of the Consulls *Hirtius* and *Pansa*, who came to his releife against *Anthony*.[1] [5]

7. But that invention of the Ægiptian Mamalucks dwelling at *Alexandria* doth far exceed all these, of whom *Bernard* de *Bridenbach* Dean of *Mentz*, thus writeth;[2] Although, saith he, perchance it may seem incredible, yet nevertheless what I shall declare, really came to pass: *Amiraldus* had allwaies with him some tutored Pigeons, which were so taught, that wheresoever they flew, they would at length return to the Court of *Amiraldus*; Now those Pilots that are sent out to meet with Ships sayling to the Port of *Alexandria* to be their conduct, carry two or three Pigeons along with them to Sea, till they come even to the place where they make full search, where presently they draw up an Inventory containing those things that are necessary to be known, which they hang at the neck of one of the Pigeons, and so let it fly away, who by its continuall and restless motion, soon [6] arrives with the Schedule at the Table of *Amiraldus*, and shews who they are that are a comming: But if after the sending forth of the first Pigeon, any thing more is to be made known to *Amiraldus*, presently they send forth a second, and so a third, if there be any need: So that *Amiraldus* perfectly knowes who and what they are, a long time before ever the

---

1   These anecdotes, including the one from Fabius Pictor, are all recounted in Pliny's *Natural History*, book 10, chs. 24, 37.

2   Bernhard von Breydenbach, *Opusculum sanctarum peregrinationum ad sepulchrum Christi* (Mainz: Erhard Reuwich, 1486), entry for 28 October 1483. This beautiful incunable, the pilgrimage diary of the Dean of Mainz, is often considered the first printed travel book, replete with long folding-out maps, and many illustrations of peoples and scripts. Godwin cites it by date alone, as it was neither signatured nor paginated. Godwin's reference and Smith's translation, running to the end of the paragraph, are accurate.

Ships enter into the Harbour. It is also affirmed, that he hath other Doves, which he sends to the Sultan at *Cairo*, by which he signifies that some suddain and difficult busines hath hapned; Moreover if the Pilots sent out from *Amiraldus*, cannot finde out the conditions of the Ship, they declare this very thing to him by the Doves.

8. By these and the like means we finde sometimes a thing may be made known in a short space, but it is allwaies done by Birds who are the Carriers, whereas we promise to exhibit [7] an Inter-Nuncio, who is not a Bird, neither is he winged, no not so much as a living Creature, and yet notwithstanding by many degrees goes beyond any creature whatsoever, though never so swift in celerity of motion.

9. That invention of theirs cometh somewhat nigh to our purpose, who by fires that were kindled in the night, and by smoke in the day, which may be perceived in a short space of time, did declare their intents to their friends that were far distant. Thus did the Grecians when they were at *Chios*, to their Confederates who pitched their Tents at *Artemisium*, and *Mardonius* the Persian, from *Athens* even to *Asia*, as it is asserted by *Herodotus*.[1]

10. Yet they (as much as I perceive) could not shew by these signes every thing which was expedient, but onely that one thing, about which they had agreed before among themselves, [8] that *Athens* was taken in that moment of time, or that there was a marching down into the Enemies Quarters just then, when in those places they had either kindled a fire or raised a smoke.

11. For my part I think that to be a more ingenuous exploit of the *Tybereans*, related by *Suetonius*, who at the same time when this wicked Monster rioted in the Island of *Caprea*, and then chiefly when he endeavoured to curbe the haughty spirit of *Sejanus*, commanded signalls to be erected afar off (lest the Messengers should slack their speed) to be lifted up higher, that he might understand beforehand what was done; whose words seem to intimate thus much, that *Tyberius* devised this way, that he himself dwelling in the Island, might understand all things nedful to be known (by these Signes that were then lifted up) in the Continent or Main land.[2] [9]

12. In which particular, if I am not much mistaken, it is easily to be admired how it comes to pass, that this kind of art, thus declaring the very secrets of our minde without the help of any Messenger, to those

---

1 Herodotus, *Histories*, 7.183; 9.3.

2 Suetonius, *Tiberius*, §65, trans. as *The Historie of Twelve Caesars* (London, 1606), 117: "Yea & whiles his ships were readie rigged and prepared to what Legions soever he ment for to flie, hee stood looking ever and anon from the highest cliffe that was, toward the markes and signes, which he had appointed (least messengers might stay too long) for to be reared a great way of: thereby to have intelligence, as any occurrent (good or bad) fell out."

that are absent a great way from us, should alltogether decay in this our *Europe*; or at least should from that time to this never be used, as I finde in reading Classick Histories.

13. I say in this our *Europe*, for it is most certain, that even to this day it is in great perfection among the Cathayans, as appears by the testimony of *Augerius Busbequius*; to doubt of whose fidellity, would be allmost Piacular, unless he leaned on another mans credit; hear himself thus speaking.

14. *After the travell of many a month we came at last to the very straights and skirts of the Kingdom of* Cathay, *for a good part of the Dominions of the King of* Cathay *is Mediterranean,* [10] *encompassed with sleep and untractable Mountains, and dangerous Rocks, neither can any one enter into it but by the narrow passages thereof, which are kept by the Kings Garrison; there the Merchants are questioned what they bring, from whence they come, and how many there are of them; which being known, the Watchmen appointed by the King, shew it in the day time by smoke, in the night by fire to the next high hill, that in like manner to the next, and so one after another; so that in the space of a few houres, which a Messenger could not do in many daies, newes is brought to the King of* Cathay *of the arivall of those Merchants, who answers with the like swiftness and in the same manner, whether it stands with his good pleasure that all should be admitted, or that they should partly be excluded or deferred.*[1]

15. Our Ancestors were not ignorant that from high Hills of this kind (which we in *England* call Beacons) a thing might be made manifest, from [11] whom also we have derived this custome, that by their help we give notice of the invasion of a forein Enemy; But by this means onely, particularly to relate the exact number of Men and Beasts, Nation, Merchandize and things needfull to be known, seems to be a more abstruse and difficult work than (as I think) to be performed by the subtilty of a barbarous Nation alltogether ignorant of Philosophy, aswell Humane as Divine. And let this suffice to be spoken about Sight, which, not without just cause, the Prince of Orators stiles the sharpest of all the Senses.[2]

16. That now we may pass from the eys the ears, by reading hitherto I have not yet found any way either invented by the Ancients, or put in practise by any of our time, whereby a man that is a far distant may receive notice of any business by the benefit of this sense, unless by the speech of the Messenger that goes to each. [12]

17. Yet to this belongeth that which Mr. *Cambden* the Son of all Antiq-

---

1 A.G. Busbequius, *Itinera Constantinopolitanum et Amasianum* (Antwerp, 1581), letter 4, complete translation in Busbequius, *The Four Epistles ... concerning his Embassy into Turkey* (London: J. Taylor and J. Wyat, 1694), this extract pp. 304-05.
2 Cicero, *De Oratore*, 2.87.357.

uity (especially of our British) hath exposed to publick view in these words; The Inhabitants of the Picts Wall (which *Severus* built at the Northerne part of *England*) do report that there was a brazen Pipe put into the wall, with that rare artifice that it run through each Tower and Castell, (Pieces, whereof they now and then find) that if any one did but sound his voyce into it, let him be in what Tower soever, presently the sound went into the next, and so to the third, so that the sound passed through each of them, without any interruption, to signify where about they feared the assault of the enemy; *Xiphiline* in the life of *Severus* relates a wonder of the same kind in the Towers of *Constantinople*: but whereas saith he the Wall is now demolished, and the Pipe is not to be found, many here on every side hold their Lands of our Kings successively [13] in Cornage as the Lawyers phrase is, that by the sound of a Horne they should signifie to their neighbours the irruptions of an Enemie, which some think to be borrowed from the old Roman custome: thus far *Cambden* who in these words hath comprised all the inventions of the Ancients tending to this end.[1]

18. Perchance it will not be altogether impertinent, that after we have spoken somewhat about seeing and hearing, we should say a little about touching, by the help of which sense that any thing should be signified to them that are afar off, especially without a Messenger is not yet asserted of any one as I think, neither doth it seem credible, but for my part I dare say that it may be done, and that with ease, at the distance of a mile or perchance two, although I have not tryed the verity thereof by any experiment, and I list not to say whether it wil be worth our labour for the future. [14]

19. But that which concernes those senses (to wit, of seeing and hearing) I dare say and do confidently assert, that a man skilfull in this art may tell whatsoever he pleases or thinks, may conduce to his good, to another that is afar off if alike skilfull (if he be within a quarter of a mile) though besieged, or lying hid, or perchance detained in any place which is not directly knowne to him that sends the tydings, and if knowne, yet not to be gone to; Let nobody come near him, secure the body in a prison, let the hands be bound, hoodwink the face, but be not trouble some any other way, and he shall understand the words of his absent friends, if this liberty be not taken away from him, that he may be able to do those things which are wont sometimes to be done by Freemen, or may do them without fear or danger.

20. I say moreover, that if the place be known where a friend resides, to [15] whom our message should be brought, and if both enjoy a full liberty, the causes being before agreed upon, which conduce to the

---

1 I.e., Hadrian's Wall. See Camden, *Britain*, 794 [mispaginated "787"], including the anecdote from Xiphiline.

disposition of the meanes, any thing may be told to such a friend without any Messenger going between each, or any living creature, though he be a hundred, nay perchance a thousand miles off, and that in a short space of time, perchance an hour, or it may be somewhat less.

21. These things some whisperingly say are strange and wonderfull, but they are not so soone to be believed: but doth this seeme so wonderfull and uncredible. You have yet but this only in the *Genus* and *Species*, behold an individuall is presented to thy eyes, which thou wilt less believe. Tell unto this my *Nuncio* at *London* in as few words as may be, what you desire may be told to me dwelling at *Bristol*, *Wells*, or if you will rather at *Exeter*, for I do not much regard the length of the way, so it is but passable; I say tell him [16] at *London*, and that just about noone any one whole verse of the sacred Scripture, I will see that he shall perform our commands in the designed place (marke what I say) before the high noone of the same day.

22. Do not rashly pronounce this proposall impossible, for the course of the Sun makes the noone later by some minutes at *Bristol* than at *London*: this it is you may wonder at, that this Messenger should exceed the heavenly motion thereof in swiftness. This he will do, will do it I say, if there be need, or else I am the vainest person of all that know how either to speake or write.

23. What speak I of Towers, or Cities that are besieged? our inanimate *Nuncio*, not fearing any thing, will pass through whole troops of enemies; A trench digg'd almost as low as hell, or a wall though higher than those of *Babylon*, shall not hinder his journey, but he will faithfully performe the [17] message (so it be in as concise termes as may be) of him that sent him, though besieged, or whether he would have it told to him that is besieged, and that with such an incredible swiftnes, if he be to be found within 5. or 7. miles, though I doubt not but it may be done effectually within 20. miles.

24. You have here 3. promises of this my *Nuncio*, presented to your consideration, perchance it will be worth our while to shew how they differ among themselv's for perspicuities sake.

25. In the first I set forth the subtlety of deceiving: in the 2 *d*. the swiftness of its passage: in the 3 *d*. its unconquered power and strength in penetrating all things.

26. That in the first place will easily be performed without any cost or labour of any one, save him that sends, but it hath this inconvenience, that its frequent use will not be free from suspition.

27. That in the second place is very [18] often effected, without any help from others, and in some places almost without any charge, but for the most part it will do little or nothing without preparation, and that such that for each mile it will cost five pounds more or less, if it

be designed for perpetual use, and nothing can be done without the countenance and authority of the Magistrate, who can easily, if he please, hinder our Nuncios journey.

28. As concerning the third, truely it requireth no great charge, but it must be observed, that he that doth act, be setled in a place without danger, and that not too far distant, where he may resist his enemies force, untill he hath perfected his work, and here we must not deny, that the condition of him that sends in, than of him that sends out is the worst.

29. You seem to me, O Reader, to ask by what sense, a friend may perceive those things that are to be told, for the senses are the guard, Interpreters [19] and Messengers of the Understanding (so *Cicero*)[1] by which alone we come to understand: I answer somtimes by hearing, and sometimes by sight; You ask a reason how? you shall have it in few terms, and perchance not so clearly, but that you require examples.

30. If you desire to represent any thing to the eyes of your absent friend, I say absent, and at a great distance sooner than any sublunary body can come to the place that is separated by so long an intervall, (for I undertake that) we must see that the *Ideas* or visible forms be increased in quantity, multiplyed in number, and be varied according to the variety of the things, to be signified in quality, quantity, position or order.

31. There is none but knowes that nothing can be perceived by the eares without a sound, it is therefore necessary that he to whom any thing is to be declared by the mediation of hearing, should heare those sounds, and those must be distinguished according to the [20] number of the things to be heard, which because they are infinite, the variety of sounds that are to be echoed forth must be infinite also: nevertheless it will be sufficient, that they be distinguished either in the kind, or time, manner and number.

32. He that shall rightly understand (and by examples they are more clear than the Sun in its meridian splendor) how sounds of this nature are reported to a place far distant will never question the verity hereof.

33. And here lest any one should timerously suspect these things to be effected by unlawfull and condemned arts, in the presence of that God who is both the greatest and the best: I protest, and openly denounce, that this discipline contains in it nothing that is unlawfull, or that is contrary to the Laws either of God or man, and that many things are done by the help of Arithmetick, Geometry and Musick, the rest if not by usuall, yet by lawfull [21] means, and that at a very small cost, I had almost said none at all, for certainly many things may be performed in this kind without the least expence or loss that can be imagined.

---

1 Cicero, *Laws*, 1.9.26; *On the Nature of the Gods*, 2.56.140.

34. And seeing that it is so, I leave it to the judgment of those that are judicious to consider how much and how far these our inventions may be profitable to the Common-wealth for the future: if they are defective, let them dye, and as untimely birth let them not see the light, or if they chance to see the light, let them not enjoy a little, but forthwith let them vanish into nothing.

35. Yet I my self think the use of this art to be very great, as well in times of Peace as War, and I thought it my duty to bestow some pains in the delivery thereof, which I will not do so willingly, lest that when it shall be made known to many, we cannot use or practise these things in their due time.

FINIS.[1]

---

1 The English translation omits two short, riddling Latin epigrams supplied on the final verso of the Latin edition: "Lectori de Authore // Præstat pòl Scilo, Artifex peritus / Dæmon, Artifici: Artifex sed hicce / Et Motu prior, atque maior Arte, / Præstat credito, Dæmon vel ipso; / Præstat Dæmoni & anteuertit ipso. // Ed. M. Ch." [To the reader concerning the author // Indeed, Scilo, an expert artificer stands out / A demon for the artificer: but here the artificer / Is both earlier than motion, and greater than art, / He is manifest to the believer, or the demon is to him; / He is manifest to the demon, and anticipates him.] "Aliud eiusdem. // Dic quæso, si non duce Dæmone tanta, quis ergo? / Angelus hic bonus est? *Aggelos* est bonus, Hic." [Another of the same // Tell me, I ask, if not by the means of a demon guide, then who? / Is this angel good? This angel is good.] For discussion of "Ed. M. Ch." see the Publication History (pp. 57-58). If these verses are indeed by Morgan Godwin, it is perhaps relevant that he was lampooned at the time for his obscure preaching style by Clement Barksdale, *Nympha Libethris* (London: for F.A. in Worcester, 1651), 34: "Vis'n verum? mi Prælector doctissime, vestra / Lectura est Clero plurima, nulla poplo" (i.e., "You want the truth? My most learned lecturer, your / Talk means a great deal to the clergy, but it's nothing to the rest").

Appendix B: From Lucian of Samosata, The True History

[The ironist Lucian of Samosata (c. 125–c. 180), "that rational merry mad Droll *Lucian*,"[1] was an immensely popular author in the early-modern period, not least because Erasmus had placed him first among models of Greek prose style to be imitated by schoolboys.[2] In Godwin's England, Lucian influenced in particular Ben Jonson, whose own lunar masque rests heavily on Lucian's work.[3] One of Lucian's most popular works, the *Icaromenippus*, featured flight by means of birds' wings. But it is in Lucian's *True History* that the moon is properly explored. The translation excerpted below is that of Francis Hickes, published posthumously with notes by his son Thomas in 1634. This was the first published English translation.[4]]

[Untrue History:]
[108] ... this one thing I confidently pronounce for a truth, that I lie: and this I hope, may be an excuse for all the rest, when I confesse what I am faultie in: for I write of matters which I neither saw nor suffered, nor heard by report from others, which are in no beeing, nor possible ever to have a beginning: let no man therefore in any case give any credit to them.

[Voyage to the Moon:]
[111] On the morrow wee put to sea again, the winde serving us weakely, but about noone, when wee had lost sight of the Island, upon a suddaine a whirlewinde caught us, which turned our shippe round about, and lifted us up some three thousand furlongs into the aire, and suffered us not to settle againe into the sea, but wee hung above ground, and were carried aloft with a mightie wind which filled our sailes strongly. Thus for seven daies space and so many nights, were wee driven along in that manner, and on the eight[h] day, wee came in view of a great countrie in the aire, like to a shining Island, of a

---

1 Francesco Lana, trans. Robert Hooke, in *Philosophical Collections* 1 (1679): 24.

2 Desiderius Erasmus, *Literary and Educational Writings 2: De Copia and De Ratione Studii*, ed. Craig R. Thompson, *Collected Works of Erasmus*, 24 (Toronto: U of Toronto P, 1978), 661-91.

3 Duncan, *Ben Jonson and the Lucianic Tradition*.

4 *Certaine Select Dialogues of Lucian, together with his True History* (Oxford: William Turner, 1634). There is an excellent modern translation by Paul Turner, *Lucian: Satirical Sketches* (Bloomington and Indianapolis: Indiana UP, 1990).

round proportion, gloriously glittering with light, and approaching to it, we there arrived, and tooke land, and surveying the countrie, we found it to be both inhabited and husbanded: and as long as the day lasted we could see nothing there, but when night was come many other Islands appeared unto us, some greater and some lesse, all of the colour of fire, and another kind of earth underneath, in which were cities, & seas, & rivers, & woods, and mountains, which we conjectured to be the earth by us inhabited : and going further into the land, we were met withall & taken by those kind of people, which they call *Hippogypians*:[1] these *Hippogypians* are men riding upon monstrous vultures, which they use instead of horses: for the vultures there are exceeding great, every one with 3 heads apiece: you may imagine their greatnesse by this: for every feather in their wings was bigger & longer than the mast of a tall ship: their charge was to flie about the countrie, & all the strangers they found to bring them to the [112] King: and their fortune was then to seize upon us, and by them wee were presented to him: As soone as he saw us, he conjectured by our habit what country-men we were, and said, are not you strangers *Grecians*? which when wee affirmed, and how could you make way, said hee, thorow so much aire as to get hither? then wee delivered the whole discourse of our fortunes to him, whereupon hee began to tell us likewise of his owne adventures, how that hee also was a man, by name *Endymion*, and rapt up so long since from the earth, as he was asleep, and brought hither, where he was made King of the Countrie, and said it was that region: which to us below seemed to bee the Moone, but hee bad us be of good cheare, and feare no danger, for we should want nothing we stood in need of [...]

[Lunar Life:]

Now, what strange novelties worthy of note I observed during the time of my abode there, I will relate unto you. The first is, that they are not begotten of women but of mankinde: for they have no other marriage but as males: the name of women is utterly unknowne among them: untill they accomplish the age of five and twentie yeares, they are given in marriage to others: from that time forwards they take others in marriage to themselves: for as soone as the infant is conceived the legge begins to swell, and afterwards when the time of birth is come, they give it a lance and take it out dead: then they lay it abroad with open mouth towards the winde, and so it takes life: and I thinke thereof the *Grecians* call it the bellie of the legge, because therein they beare their

---

1 "A made word signifying hors-vultures, or vulture-horses, or vulture riders: and so are the rest that follow, names coined, and composed for his purpose" (Hickes).

children instead of a belly. I will tell you now of a thing more strange than this: there are a kinde of men among them called *Dendritans*, which are begotten in this manner: they cut out the right stone of a mans codd, and set it in their ground, from which springeth up a great tree of flesh, with branches and leaves, bearing a kinde of fruit much like to an acorne, but of a cubite in length, which [118] they gather when they are ripe, and cut men out of them: their privie members are to be set on, and taken off, as they have occasion: rich men have them made of Ivorie, poore men of wood, wherewith they performe the act of generation, and accompanie their spowses: when a man is come to his full age hee dieth not, but is dissolved like smoake and is turned into aire. One kinde of food is common to them all: for they kindle a fire and broyle frogges upon the coales, which are with them in infinite numbers flying in the aire, and whilst they are broyling, they sit round about them, as it were about a table, and lappe up the smoake that riseth from them, and feast themselves therewith, and this is all their feeding: for their drinke, they have aire beaten in a morter, which yeeldeth a kinds of moysture much like unto dew: they have no avoydance of excrements, either of urine or dung, neither have they any issue for that purpose, like unto us: their boyes admit copulation, not like unto ours, but in their hammes, a little above the calfe of the legge, for there they are open: they hold it a great ornament to be bald, for hairie persons are abhord with them, and yet among the Starres that are Comets, it is thought commendable, as some that have travelled those coasts reported unto us: such beards as they have, are growing a little above their knees: they have no nailes on their feete, for their whole foote is all but one toe: every one of them at the point of his rumpe, hath a long colewort growing out in stead of a tale, alwaies greene and flourishing, which though a man fall upon his backe, cannot be broken: the dropping of their noses is more sweete than honey: when they labour or exercise themselves, they annoint their bodie with milke, whereinto if a little of that honey chance to drop, it will be turned into cheese: they make very fat oile of their beanes, and of as delicate a savour as any sweet ointment: they have many vines in those parts, which yeeld them but water: for the grapes that hang upon the clusters [119] are like our hailestones: and I verily thinke, that when the vines there are shaken with a strong winde, there falls a storme of haile amongst us, by the breaking down of those kinde of berries: their bellies stand them instead of sachels, to put in their necessaries, which they may open and shut at their pleasure, for they have neither liver, nor any kind of entralls, onely they are rough and hairie within, so that when their young children are cold, they may be inclosed therein to keepe them warme: the rich men have garments of glasse, very soft and delicate, the poorer sort of brasse woven, whereof they have great plentie, which they inseame with water, to make it fit for the workman, as we do our wooll. If I should write what manner of eies they have, I doubt I should be taken for a liar, in publishing a matter so incredible: yet I cannot chuse but tell it: for they have eyes to take in and out as please themselves: and when a man is so disposed, hee may take them out and lay them by till hee have occasion to use them, and then put them in and see againe: many when they have lost their owne eies, borrow of others for the rich have many lying by them: their eares are all made of the leaves of plane-trees, excepting those that come of acornes, for they onely have them made of wood. I saw also another strange thing in the same court: a mightie great glasse, lying upon the top of a pit, of no great depth, whereinto, if any man descend, hee shall heare every thing that is spoken upon the earth: if hee but looke into the glasse, hee shall see all cities, and all nations as well as if hee were among them:[1] there had I the sight of all my friends, and the whole countrie about: whether they saw mee or not I cannot tell: but if they beleeve it not to be so, let them take the paines to goe thither themselves and they shall finde my words true: then we tooke our leaves of the king, and such as were neare him, and tooke shipping, and departed: at which time *Endymion* bestowed upon mee two mantles made of their glasse, & five of brasse, with a compleat armour of those shells of lupines, [120] all which I left behinde mee in the whale [...]

---

1 Compare the parallel contrivance in Lucian's *Icaromenippus* (*Certaine Select Dialogues*, 18-19; *Satirical Sketches*, 119-21).

Appendix C: From William of Newburgh, "On the Green Children" (1196-98)

[Godwin's Lunars deport unwanted offspring to the earth. Gonsales, for a moment donning the hat of a sixteenth-century English anti-quary, even references this practice (104-05) to an anecdote found in the twelfth-century Yorkshire chronicler William of Newburgh. William was a historian of the northern school in the tradition of the Venerable Bede, and celebrated as a chronicler who ridiculed the credulity of Geoffrey of Monmouth.[1] Godwin, as we saw in the Intro-duction (p. 20), was prompted to include the story by his reencounter with it in Burton's *Anatomy of Melancholy*, but he returned to the Latin text of William of Newburgh in order to flesh out his fiction. The fol-lowing extracts are translated directly from the first printed edition of William (Antwerp, 1567).[2] Godwin cited William of Newburgh in his 1601 *Catalogue*, so he will have used this edition. See the Introduction (pp. 20-23) for a discussion of William's fuller significance. The para-graphing is editorial.]

Book I, chapter 27.

Nor should a strange event, unheard of in all ages, be left unrecorded, which took place in England in the reign of King Stephen. And indeed I hesitated for a long time over this matter even though it was reported by many people, as it seemed to me that it was ridiculous to believe a thing of no or of the most obscure reason. Yet I was overwhelmed by the weight of so many and such witnesses, so that

---

1 Camden, *Britain*, 8.

2 William of Newburgh, *Rerum Anglicarum Libri Quinque* (Antwerp, 1567). For a complete English text see Joseph Stevenson, *The Church Historians of England*, vol. 4, part 2 (London: Seeley's, 1861), and for a more recent Latin/English parallel edition of Book I, see William of Newburgh, *The History of English Affairs: Book I*, ed. and trans. P.G. Walsh and M.J. Kennedy (Warminster: Aris & Phillips, 1988). The story also appears in Ralph of Coggeshall's *Chronicon Anglicanum*. Ralph was a younger contemporary of William and wrote after him; he reports that the Green Children were taken to the house of Sir Richard de Colne at Wakes in Essex and that Sir Richard told him this himself (Gransden, *Historical Writing in England*, 24, 330-31). The passage was reproduced in the commentary of the 1610 Paris Commelin edition of William. The story is still occasionally adapted for fictional pur-poses: e.g., Gary Russell, *Spiral Scratch* (London: BBC, 2005).

I am compelled to believe and to marvel, because I am not able by any strength of mind to understand or to investigate this matter.

There is a village in East Anglia four or five miles distant, it is said, from the well-known monastery of the blessed king and martyr Edmund. Nearby there can be observed certain ancient pits which are in English called "Vulputes," that is, "Wolf-Pits," and the nearby village is named after them. One harvest-time, when the reapers were busy in the fields gathering in the crop, there emerged from these pits two children, a boy and a girl, green from head to toe, and dressed in clothing of an unusual colour and of an unknown fabric. As they were wandering, stunned, about the fields, they were spotted by the reapers and taken to the village, where many assembled to see such a novelty. For several days they were confined without food. When they were almost expiring with hunger yet would not accept any food offered to them, it happened by chance that some beans were brought in from the fields. Instantly seizing hold of the vegetable, they searched among the stalks; but finding nothing inside the hollow of the stalks, they cried bitterly. Then someone present offered to them the vegetable peeled from the shell, which at once they eagerly took and ate.

For a number of months they were nourished with this food until they learned to eat bread. Eventually, they gradually changed their colour due to the influence of our food, became like us, and also learned our language. It was then decided by the wise that they should receive the sacrament of holy baptism, and so this was done. But the boy, who seemed younger by birth, living for only a short time after his baptism, succumbed to an untimely death. His sister however remained unharmed, and in no way differed from women of our kind. Indeed she married later on, at Lynn [*apud Lennam*], and she was said still to have been living a few years ago.

Since now they had the use of our language, they were asked who they were and where they came from, to which they are said to have replied, "We are people of the land [*terra*] of Saint Martin, who in the land of our birth is held in the highest veneration." When they were next asked where that land was, and how they had got from there to here, they replied, "We know neither answer. This is all we can recall. One day we were grazing our father's cattle in our field when we heard a noise just like that which we are used to hearing when they say the bells of St. Albans are ringing out [*apud Sanctum Albanum cum signa concrepare*]. When we turned our attention to the sound that we were marvelling at, it was as if we were suddenly put out of our minds, for we found ourselves among you in the fields where you were harvesting." They were asked whether they believed in Christ, and whether the sun rose in their land, to which they replied that their land was Christian, and had churches. "But," they said, "for us the sun does not rise, and our land is barely illuminated by its rays, and is content only with that measure of its brightness which with you precedes the rising or follows the setting of the sun. Furthermore, there is a certain shining land visible not far off from our own land, both separated by a huge river."

These and many other such things too time-consuming to repeat they are said to have replied diligently to their interlocutors. People can say and conclude whatever they are able about this, but I am not ashamed to have recounted this strange and wonderful event.

Book I, conclusion to chapter 28.

Some things [wicked angels] achieve by the power of their own angelic nature, if they be permitted by the Higher Power; some things they achieve by trickery and illusion, like that night-time feast inside the hill. But others are actually real, like those dogs, or the toad with the golden chain, or the cup [tales related in this chapter], by means of which people can be gripped by a profitless fascination. These wicked angels, when permitted, undoubtedly perform with great eagerness actions by which men are most perniciously deceived. But an explanation [ratio] of the green children who are said to have come out of the earth is more puzzling; the frailty of our intelligence is quite incapable of explaining this.

Appendix D: Arguments about Aliens (Philip Melanchthon, Tommaso Campanella, John Wilkins)

The orthodox theological position on extraterrestrial non-angelic life is represented by this extract from the famous Lutheran Reformer Philip Melanchthon's university textbook in physics, the *Initia Doctrinæ Physicæ*. It is noteworthy that Melanchthon considered the refutation of alien life of such importance that he was willing to break generic decorum and intrude arguments from theology into a textbook on physics, as he himself confesses:

> But for us Christians, it is both simpler and necessary to affirm that the world is unique, because divine doctrine asserts that this world in which God revealed himself, in which he delivered to men his doctrine, and into which he sent his Son to men, was created by God. [...]
>
> And let this corroboration, which is altogether trustworthy, be added to the previous argument concerning the singularity of the world. The Son of God is one, our Lord Jesus Christ, who when he had revealed himself in this world died once, and rose again. He did not disclose himself elsewhere, nor elsewhere did he die and rise again. So it must not be thought that there is a plurality of worlds, because it must not be thought that Christ often dies and is resurrected. Nor in any other world is eternal life restored to men without recognition of the Son of God. Even if these arguments technically do not belong to Physics, they must nevertheless be appreciated; nor if other worlds be fashioned should other religions be dreamed up, and other natures of men.[1]

It was this objection to Galileo that the systematically persecuted Dominican monk Tommaso Campanella rehearsed and rejected in a notorious passage of his *Apologia pro Galileo* (written 1616, published 1622). Campanella answers the orthodox objection by deciding that alien life can only exist entirely outside the Christian economy:

> I pass without comment the opinion that Galileo has revived the heresy that Christ must make atonement for the men who inhabit the stars and die there again; just as formerly it was said that Christ

---

1 Text translated from *Initia Doctrinæ Physicæ* (Wittenberg: the heirs of Johannes Crato, 1581), 69-70.

must be crucified a second time in the antipodes, if the men living there were to be saved as we have been saved.

[...]

If the inhabitants which may be in other stars are men, they did not originate from Adam and are not infected by his sin. Nor do these inhabitants need redemption, unless they have committed some other sin.[1]

John Wilkins reviewed this argument in his *Discourse Concerning a New World and Another Planet* shortly before his discussion of Godwin:

Wherefore *Campanella's* second conjecture may be more probable, that the inhabitants of that world, are not men as we are, but some other kinde of creatures which beare some proportion, and likenesse to our natures. Or it may be, they are of a quite different nature from any thing here below, such as no imagination can describe; our understandings being only capable of such things as have entered by our senses, or else such mixed natures as may bee composed from them. Now, there may be may other species of creatures besides those that are already knowne in the world; there is a great chasme betwixt the nature of men and Angels; It may bee the inhabitants of the Planets are of a middle nature between both these. Tis not improbable that God might create some of all kindes, that so he might more compleatly glorifie himselfe in the works of his Power and Wisedom.[2]

This possibility that the lunar aliens were indeed very alien had just been realised by Kepler in his *Somnium*, a text to which Wilkins had recently gained access but which was unknown to Godwin.[3]

---

1 Tommaso Campanella, *Apologia pro Galileo*, trans. Grant McColley in *Smith College Studies in History XXII* (1937), these extracts pp. 8, 66. The heresy of the Christ of the Antipodes refers to St. Virgilius, later Bishop of Salzburg (d. 784), denounced in 748 to Pope Zachary for having maintained that the Antipodean lands were also inhabited. See Johannes Aventinus, *Annalium Boiorum Libri VII* (Basel: Perna and Lecythus, 1580), 220, where Virgilius is treated as skilled in the mathematical disciplines, but misinterpreted by his denouncer Boniface to be asserting "another world, other men under the earth, and finally another sun and another moon."

2 John Wilkins, *A Discourse Concerning a New World and Another Planet* (London: John Maynard, 1640), 189-90. Compare Burton's "Digression," in Appendix G, below; and John Milton, *Paradise Lost*, 3.459-62.

3 Wilkins, *The Discovery of a World in the Moone*, 124, 186, 208; *Discourse Concerning a New World and Another Planet*, 82, 123; Wilkins also cited the *Somnium* in *Mathematical Magick* (London: Samuel Gellibrand, 1648), 201 (see Appendix H, below).

Appendix E: From Jan Huygen van Linschoten, Discours of Voyages into the Easte and West Indies *(1596)*

[Published originally in Dutch in 1596, Linschoten's celebrated *Discours of Voyages into the Easte and West Indies* was made available to English readers just two years later.[1] Godwin probably looked first and patriotically to the account of Thomas Cavendish's visit to St. Helena, the standard stopping-off point on voyages from Europe to the Far East (printed by Hakluyt, also reported by Linschoten), but for the sake of range, below is presented Linschoten's account of his own visit. Comparison of Cavendish and Linschoten will show how quickly a set of stock symbols was established, many gesturing toward St. Helena as an Earthly Paradise.[2]]

[171]

The *23* of Aprill we passed the Cape *de Bona Speranza*, with a great and generall gladnes, it being as then 3 months and three dayes after we set sayle from Cochun, not once seeing any land or sand at all, but onelie these assured tokens of the said Cape, which happened very seldome: for that the pilots doe alwaies vse what meanes they can to see the cape, and to know the land, thereby to know certainlie that they are past it: for then their degrees must lesse, and there they may as soone make towards *Mosambique*, as to the Iland of S. *Helena*: for although they can well perceiue it by ye water, yet is it necessary for them to see the land, the better to set their course vnto S. *Helena*, wherein they must alwaies keepe on the left hand: otherwise it were impossible for them to come at it, if they leaue that course: for if they once passe it, they can not come to it again, because there bloweth continually but one kind of wind, which is South east: and thus hauing passed the Cape, we got before the wind.

[...]

The *12* of May, in the morning betimes, we discouered the Island of S. *Helena*, where at there was so great ioy in the ship, as if we had bene in heauen: & as then we were about *2* miles from ye land, the Iland lying from vs West, south West: whereunto we sayled so close, that with a caliuer shot we might reach vnto the shore: being hard by it, we sayled

---

1   Text taken from Jan Huygen van Linschoten, *Discours of Voyages into the Easte and West Indies* (London: John Wolfe, [1598]), 171-74.

2   On St. Helena, with some discussion of Godwin, see Grove, *Green Imperialism*, 95-125, esp. 99-101.

about a corner of the land, that from vs lay Northwest, which hauing compassed wee sayled close by the land. West, North west: the land on that side beeing so high and still, that it seemed to be a wall that reached vnto the skyes. And in that sort we sayled about a mile and a half, and compassed about ye other corner that lay westward from vs, which corner being compassed, we presentlie perceiued the shippes that lay in the road, which were those ships that set sayle before vs out of *India*, lying about a small half mile from the foresaid corner, close vnder the land, so that the land as then lieth South east from them: and by reason of the high land the shippes lie there as safe, as if they were in a hauen: for they may well heare the wind whistle on the top of their maine yards, but lower it can not come: and they lie so close vnder the land, that they may almost cast a stone vpon the shore. There is good ground there, at *25* and *30* fadomes deep, but if they chance to put further out, or to passe beyond it, they must goe forward, for they can get no more vnto ye land: and for this cause we kept so close to the shore, that the height of the land took the wind from vs, & the ship wold not steer without wind, so that it draue vpon the land, whereby our boresprit touched ye shore, & there with we thought that shippe & goods had all [172] beene cast away: but by reason of the great depth, being 10 fadomes water, and with the help of the Boats, and men off the other ships that came vnto vs, we put off from the land, without any hurt, and by those Boates wee were brought to a place wher the other ships lay at Anker, which is right against a valley that lyeth betweene two high hilles, wherein there standeth a little Church called Saint *Helena*. There we found fiue shippes, which were, the ship that came from *Malacca*, and the S. *Mary* that had beene there about *15.* daies, which came both together to the Cape *de Bona Speranza*, the S. *Anthonie*, and the S. *Christopher* being Admiral, that had arriued there *10.* daies before, and the *Conception*, which came thether but the day before vs, so that ther wanted none of the fleet but the S. *Thomas*, and by the signes and tokens, that we and the other ships had seene at Sea, we presumed it to be lost, as after we vnderstoode (for it was neuer seene after) for the other shippes had seene Mastes, Deales, Fattes, Chestes, & many dead men that had bound themselues vpon boardes, with a thousand other such like signs. Our Admiral likewise had beene in great danger of casting away: for although it was a new ship, & this the first Viage it had made, yet it was so eaten with Wormes, that it had at the least *20* handfuls deepe of water within it, and at the Cape was forced to throw halfe the goods ouer bord, into the Sea, and were constrained continually to Pumpe with two Pumpes, both night and day, and neuer holde still: and being before the Iland of S. *Helena*, had ther also sunke to the ground, if the other ships had not holpen her. The rest of the shippes coulde likewise tell what dangers and miseries they had indured. About three Moneths before our arriuall at S. *Helena*, there had beene a ship which the yere before set out of *Ormus*, with the goods & men that remained in the S. *Saluador*, that had beene saued by the Portingal armie, vpon the coast of *Abex*, and brought vnto *Ormus*, as in an other place I haue declared. That ship had wintered in *Mosambique*, and had passed verie soone by the Cape, & so sayled without any companie vnto Portingall, hauing left some of her sicke men in the Iland, (as the maner is) which the next ships that came thether must take into them. These gaue vs intelligence, that about four monthes before our arriuall, there had beene an English ship at the Iland of Saint *Helena*, which had sayled through the Straights of *Magellanaes*, and through the south seas, & from thence to the Ilands of *Phillippinas*, and had passed through the Straights of Sunda, that lyeth beyond *Malacca*, betweene the Ilands of *Sumatra* and *Iaua*: in the which way she had taken a shippe of *China* (such as they call *Iunkos*) laden with Siluer and Golde, and all kind of Silkes, and that shee sent a letter with a small present to the Bishop of *Malacca*, telling him, that shee sent him that of friendship, meaning to come herselfe and visite him. Out of that ship of *China*, they tooke a Portingall Pilot, & so passed the Cape *de Bona Speranza*, and came to the Iland of Saint *Helena*, where they tooke in fresh water and other necessaries, and beate downe the Alter and the Crosse that stoode in the Church, and left behind them a Ketle and a Sword, which the Portingales at our arriual found there yet could they not conceiue or thinke what that might meane. Some thought it was left there for a signe to some other ships of his companie, but euerie man may thinke what he will thereof. In the ship of *Malacca* came for Factor of the Pepper, one *Gerrit van Afhuysen*, borne in *Antwarpe*, and dwelling in *Lisbone*, who had sayled in the same ship from *Lisbone* about two yeares before, for that they staied in *Malacca* at the least fourteene Monthes, by reason of the warres and troubles that were in that countrie, vntill *Malacca* was relieued, as I saide before: whereby they had passed great miserie, and beene at great charges. And because it is a very vnwholesome countrie together with ye constraint of lying there so long, of *200.* men, that at the first sayled from *Lisbone* in the ship, there were but *18.* or *20.* left aliue, and all the rest dyed, so that they were enforced to take in other vnskilfull men in *Malacca*, to bring the shipps home. This *Gerrard van Afhuysen*, being of mine acquaintance and my good friend, before my departure out of *Portingall* for *India*, maruelled and ioyed much to find me there, little thinking that we should meete in so strange a place, and there we discoursed of our trauels past. And of him among diuers other things, I learned many true instruction as well of *Malacca*, as of the countries and Ilands lying about it, both for their manner of dealing in trade of Marchandise, as in other memorable things.

[...]

[173] The Iland of Saint Helena is so named, because the Portingales discouered it vppon Saint *Helens* day, which is the twentie one of May. It is in compasse sixe miles, little more or lesse, and lyeth vnder sixteene degrees and a quarter, on the South side of the Equinoctall *550.* Spanish miles from the Cape *de Bona Speranza,* and from the coast called *Angola* or *Ethiopia 350.* miles, & from *Brasilia 510.* miles. These are the two neerest lands adioyning to it. It is a verie high and hillie countrie, so that it commonly reacheth vnto the clouds: the countrie of it selfe is verie ashie and drie: also all the trees that are therein, whereof there are great store, & grow of themselues in the woods, are little worth but only to burne: for it hath no special substance, but sheweth as if it were halfe consumed, so that it should seeme that some mines of Brimstone, hath in times past beene in that Iland, as commonly all the Ilands are all much subiect to the same: for that in some places thereof they find Sulphur and Brimstone. When the Portingales first discouered it, there was not any beasts, nor fruite, at all within the Iland, but onely great store of fresh water, which is excellent good, and falleth downe from the mountaines, and so runneth in great abundance into the Valley, where the Church standeth, and from thence by small chanels into the Sea, where the Portingales fill their vessels full of fresh water, and wash their clothes: so that it is a great benefit for them, and a pleasant sight to behold, how cleare & in how many streames the water runneth downe into the valley, which may bee thought a myracle, considering the drinesse of the country, together with the stonie Rockes and hilles therein. The Portingales haue by little and little brought many beastes into it, and in the valleyes planted all sorts of fruites: which haue growne there in so great abundance, that it is almost incredible. For it is full of Goates, Buckes, wild Hogges, Hennes, Partridges, and Doues, by thousands, so that any man that will, may hunt and take them & ther is alwaies plentie and sufficient, although there came as many shippes more into the Iland as there doe: and they may kill them with stones and staues by reason of the gret numbers of them. Now for fruits, as Portingall Figges, Pomegranets, Oranges, Lemons, Citrons, and such like fruites, there are so many, that growe without planting or setting, that all the valleyes are full of them, which is a great pleasure to behold, so that it seemeth to bee an earthly Paradise. It hath fruite all the yeare long, because it raineth there by showers at the least fiue or six times euerie day, and then againe the Sunne shineth so, that whatsoeuer is planted, there is groweth verie well: but because the Portingales are not ouer curious of new things, there groweth not of al sorts of fruits of Portingall and *India* in that Iland: for assuredly without any doubt [174] they would growe well in that land, because of the good temperature of the ayre, besides this, they haue so great abundance of Fish, round about

the Iland, that it seemeth a wonder wrought of God: for with crooked nayles, they may take as much Fish as they will, so that all the shippes doe prouide themselues of Fish, of all sorts in that place, which is hanged vp and dried, and is of as good a taste and sauor, as any Fish that euer I eate: and this euery man that hath beene there, affirmeth to be true. And the better to serue their turnes, vpon the Rockes they find salt, which serueth them for their necessarie prouisions, so that to conclude, it is an earthly Paradise for ye Portingall shippes, and seemeth to haue been miraculously discouered for the refreshing and seruice of the same, considering the smalnesse and highnesse of the land, lying in the middle of the Ocean seas, and so far from the firme land or any other Ilands, that it seemeth to be a Boye, placed in the midle of the Spanish Seas: for if this Iland were not, it were impossible for the shippes to make any good or prosperous Viage: for it hath often fallen out, that some shippes which haue missed thereof, haue endured the greatest miserie in ye world, and were forced to put into the coast of *Guinea*, there to stay the falling of the raine, and so to get fresh water, and afterwardes came halfe dead and spoyled into Portingall. It is the fashion, that all the sicke persons, that are in the shippes, and can not wel sayle in them, are left there in the Iland, with some prouisions of Rice, Bisket, Oyle, and some Spices, for Fish and flesh they may haue enough, for when the ships are gone, then all the beastes (which by reason of the great number of people fly into the mountaines) come downe againe into the valleyes, where they make take them with their handes and kill them as they list, those sicke men stay there till the next yeare, till other ships come thether, which take them with them, they are commonly soone healed in that Iland, as being a veryie sound and pleasant countrie: and it is verie seldome seene, that any of them dyeth there, because they haue alwaies a temperate ayre, and coole winde, and alwayes fruite throughout the whole yeare.

Appendix F: From Mark Ridley, A Short Treatise of Magneticall Bodies and Motions (1613)

[The sixth book of William Gilbert's *De Magnete, Magneticisque Corporibus, et de Magno Magnete Tellure, Physiologia Nova* ("A New Physics on the Magnet, Magnetic Bodies, and the Great Terrestrial Magnet"), published in 1600, turned to the cosmological consequences of Gilbert's terrestrial theory of magnetism.[1] Gilbert argued that the earth as a whole possessed magnetic power, and that this caused it to spin on its own axis. But Gilbert did not openly endorse the annual motion of the earth, although it is a possible inference left open to the reader. He also argued that magnetism is the soul of the earth (compare Ridley's "starlike vigor, or intelligence" below), an animistic emphasis quietly retired by his later followers, including Godwin.[2] Gilbert's noisiest English adherent was the physician Mark Ridley (1560-c. 1624), whose *A Short Treatise of Magneticall Bodies and Motions* (1613) furnished the general reader with Gilbert summarized in English, but with his cosmological consequences now front-loaded. Ridley claimed to have worked with Gilbert, but his publication greatly angered the cleric William Barlow (1544-1624), also a one-time colleague of Gilbert, but now in his seventies, who replied with his *Magneticall Advertisements* (1617), a work that had apparently circulated in manuscript for some time. The controversy centred on Gilbert's cosmology, which Ridley treated as both licit and integral, but which Barlow protested was heretical and an unnecessary appendix to Gilbert's orthodox first five books.[3] Below is presented the bulk of Ridley's third chapter, "Of the Earth."[4]]

---

1   There is an old and rather cavalier translation of Gilbert, published as *On the Lodestone and Magnetic Bodies*, trans. P. Fleury Mottelay (London: Quaritch, 1893), with many reprints. A better but very scarce translation was made by Sylvanus P. Thompson and others for the Gilbert Club and privately printed by the Chiswick Press in 1900 in an edition of only 250 copies. A facsimile, likewise scarce, of the Chiswick Press edition was published by Basic Books of New York in 1958. See further Duane H.D. Roller, *The "De Magnete" of William Gilbert* (Amsterdam: Menno Hertzberger, 1959).

2   J.A. Bennett, "Cosmology and Magnetical Philosophy, 1640-1680," *Journal of the History of Astronomy* 12 (1981): 163-77.

3   For Gilbert and his reception, see Gad Freudenthal, "Theory of Matter and Cosmology in William Gilbert's *De Magnete*," *Isis* 74 (1983): 22-37; Stephen Pumfrey, *Latitude and the Magnetic Earth* (Cambridge: Icon, 2002).

4   Text taken from Mark Ridley, *A Short Treatise of Magneticall Bodies and Motions* (London: Nicholas Okes, 1613), 12-17.

[12]
Of the Earth.

This great Globe of the Earth whereon we moue and trauell, is found to be a *Magneticall* body, by such as haue trauelled and sayled round about her, as Sir *Francis Drake* did, and M. *Candish* [i.e., Cavendish], whose *Magneticall* Compasses were always directed *Magnetically*, that is, the Lilly of their Compasses was turned always towards the North-pole in all places wheresoeuer they sayled, by the vertue *Magneticall*, and disponent faculty of the *Magneticall* Globe of the Earth. ... Also by such as haue made their course northerly and southerly, it hath bin obserued that the *Magneticall Inclinatory-needle* doth in euery eleuation of the pole conforme and apply it selfe, or rather is conformed and disponed vnto the *axis* of the Earth, according vnto certaine corre-spondent angles to the Latitude ... whereby it is demonstratiuely to be concluded, that the Earth is a *Magneticall* body, directing both her selfe and the other two *Magneticall* bodies into the North and South, by the vertue of her Meridian circles and parts ...

Moreouer, the Earth hath naturally two *Magneticall* poles; vnto the which these meridionall parts do direct, [13] bend & force, not only *Magneticall* bodies neere the Earth; but also her owne mighty and massie situation, stability, and firmnesse, and seateth her selfe so strongly vpon her two poles, by her naturall and *Magneticall* vigor, passing from her meridionall parts to the poles, as if she were tied by many mighty strong cables vnto two most firme pillars, farre stronger than any *Hercules* pillars, not to be remoued by any force from her nat-urall position; which thing, if it might chance that it should come to passe, yet certainely she would returne againe vnto her former firme seate and place, as all *Magneticall* bodies and directory needles do, as is demonstrated hereafter.

Thus we proue that the Earth is placed and firmed by her *Magnet-icall* vertue, and not by her grauity and waight, though the parts of the Earth do conioyne and adhere together by their grauity mouing to their Center. But the *Magneticall* nature moueth, conformeth, and firmely seateth it selfe to the poles and *Axis*.

Now for that the poles of the Earth do alwayes, by their natural vertues hold the Earth North and South in one certaine and vniforme situation, eleuation and place, there is no doubt but that the whole globe of the Earth, inwardly stored with many materials and rich min-erals, & outwardly adorned with many trees and excrescences, all for the vse of man, with liuing creatures innumerable, as also in reason it is an vnfallible certainty, that the Earth hath, at her first creation, bestowed vpon her a globous and starlike vigor, or intelligence, whereby she may, hauing her whole parts vnited together, by the vertue of grauity vnto the center, and her place made sure *Magnetically* by her [14] poles vnmoueable; yet moue naturally, keeping her place circularly & diurnally out of the West into the East, to the end that all creatures should receiue the comfortable and liuely beames of the Sunne, and the influences of the rest of the Planets and Starres.

This motion many learned men haue attributed vnto the Earth, for the benefit of calculating the motion of the Planets the better, which naturally she hath in her selfe; for euen as it were needlesse for a wheele to haue her naue, spokes and rimme about her, if it should not be vsed to turne about; so it were to no purpose that the Earth should naturally haue a globous body, two poles, an *axis*, meridians and æquator, as shall be demonstrated hereafter, parts fit for circular motion, and not for to turne her æquator and paralels about, as the wheele doth.

Although these arguments will hardly perswade vs to beleeue the earths motion; yet because that it is lately obserued vnto our sences by helpe of the trunke-spectakle, both by *Galileus* and *Kepler*, famous Mathematitians, that the great body of the globe of *Iupiter*, being twelue times greater then the Earth, doth turne about in lesse time then a day vpon his *axis* and poles, who also haue obserued foure Moones, attendant on *Iupiter*, which moue round about him, the slowest in 14 dayes, the next in seuen dayes, and the rest in shorter time. So likewise *Iohn Fabricius* hath obserued, that the great globe of the Sunne, hauing three great spots, like continents in him, and being sixty times greater then the Earth, to moue about his *axis* and poles neere the time of ten dayes, or thereabouts, so *Galileus* and *Kepler* haue seene the Planet of *Venus* to moue about the Sunne in ten moneths, and to haue her light [15] from the Sunne in this time increased and diminished vpon her body, as we see the Moone here neerer vnto vs to haue; therefore it being certaine by obseruation, that the globe of *Iupiter* and the Sunne do turne about their *axis* and poles, whose materials we know not, we need not doubt that the Earth should haue a circular motion for her great good. But how the Earth doth turne circularly we cannot well see it, with the sence of our eyes, vnlesse we had them placed in another globous body and starre, as if they were in the Moone, where we might see the spots of the Earth to turne about, as well as now we see the spots in the Sunne, and *Iupiter* to moue circularly in their place. And as contrariwise our eyes here on the Earth do see that the Moone doth not turne about, by the placing of her spots, alwayes in one fashion vnto vs: for we may obserue with our eyes, that the Moone hath poles of a kind of *Magneticall* nature, which do alwayes hold her to behold the center of the Earth, and so stayeth and conformeth her, that howsoeuer she moue, higher or lower, or wheresoeuer she be, yet alwaies the spots of halfe her globe be alike apparent vnto our eyes, and conforme her to behold the center of the Earth with one pole: neither doth the Moone turne about her body vpon two poles, as the Earth doth vpon hers, but is kept firme and vnmoueable from circular motion about her *axis*, by other two poles that be vpon the edges and æquator of her body, because her spots be always alike on her East and West side, that hold her firmely & stiffely that she can by no meanes turne about vpon her first two poles: For it is the vertue polar and *Magneticall* that holdeth all globes in the position what-soeuer. Besides, the Moone hath [16] another vertue giuen her at her first creation, whereby beholding alwayes the center of the Earth, and mouing neerer and further from the Earth, as tied with an axletree, she moueth, slideth, and passeth monethly about the Zodiacke, that all the parts of her globe may be illuminated and refreshed with the beames of the Sunne, and influences of the Starres: for as a ship vpon the water is directed euen forward by the sterne and ruther [i.e., rudder], which hath not only a right line to direct forward, but also a right angle descending downewards, that she waue not sidelings or turne about, yet hauing this position, if ankors be layd out, either forward, or back-ward, or sidelings, with their cables on boord, if their be force or vertue on boord to hale forward, she moueth forward, if drawne back-ward, she goeth backward, if pulled by the cable on the left hand, yet keeping her position, she betaketh to that hand, and so to other parts. Euen so the Moone being seated, as afore is said, doth moue on her *axis*, higher or lower, on this side or on that, according to the vertue & strength of the multiplicity of her axletrees, being her limbes to stay and moue withall, as the body hath armes and legges, with variety of muscles to moue on all hands.

But the Earth, whereon we liue and trauell, hath neuer bene found by any to haue any poles in the æquator of her body, or neere the same: for if we were so happy as to find any in the East or West of the earth, then the matter of longitude would be perfectly attained vnto, which hath so greatly busied all the ingenious wits of the world: and therefore we affirme that the Earth doth turne about, because there are no poles in the æquator to hinder her, as there is in the [17] Moone, from circular motion.

Appendix G: From Robert Burton, The Anatomy of Melancholy *(1621, 1628)*

[The section of Robert Burton's famous and immediately popular *Anatomy of Melancholy* (1621, many subsequent, expanded editions) that particularly caught Godwin's eye was the dazzling "digression of the Ayre," as the extracts below demonstrate.[1] Burton and Godwin coincide in every particular; we may note below especially the stray anecdote of the Green Children, imitated by Godwin too. Burton constantly added material to his text, and so bold type below represents material added between the 1621 and 1628 editions. I also replace planetary symbols with their names in brackets, and any Latin phrases not immediately translated by Burton I supply in English between square brackets too.]

[230]
Ayre rectified. With a digression of the Ayre.

AS a long-winged Hawke when hee is first whistled off the fist, mounts aloft, and for his pleasure fetcheth many a circuit in the Ayre, still soaring higher and higher, till he bee come to his full pitch, and in the end when the game is sprung, comes downe amaine, and stoopes vpon a sudden: so will I, hauing now come at last into these ample fields of Ayre, wherein I may freely expatiate and exercise my selfe, for my recreation a while roue, and wander round about the world, mount aloft to those ætheriall orbes and celestiall spheres, and so descend to my former elements againe.
[...]
[237] If as *Tycho* proues the Moone to bee distant from vs 50 and 60 Semediameters of the Earth: and as *Peter Nonius* will haue it, the aire be so angust, what proportion is there betwixt the other three Ele-

---

1 Text taken from Part 2, Section 2, Member 3, Subsection 1 of the 1628 edition, the one Godwin probably used (see the Introduction [p. 20]). For reasons of space I have suppressed explanatory notes, which can be found in J.B. Bamborough's excellent commentary for the Clarendon edition of Burton, vol. 5 (Oxford: Clarendon P, 2000), 130-53. The whole "Digression" comprises 2.33-67 of the Clarendon edition. Discussions of the "Digression" include J. Max Patrick, "Robert Burton's Utopianism," *Philological Quarterly* 27 (1948): 345-58; R.M. Browne, "Robert Burton and the New Cosmology," *Modern Language Quarterly* 13 (1952): 131-48; Barlow, "Infinite Worlds."

ments, and it? to what vse serues it? is't full of spirits which inhabit it, as the *Paracelsians* and *Platonists* hold, the higher, the more noble, full of Birds, or a meere *Vacuum* to no purpose? It is much controverted betwixt *Tycho Brahe*, and *Christopher Rotman* the *Lantsgraue* of *Hassias* Mathematitian, in their Astronomicall Epistles, whether it bee the same *Diaphanum*, cleerenesse, matter of aire and heauens, or two distinct Essences? *Christopher Rotman, Iohn Pena, Iordanus Brunus*, with many other late Mathematicians, contend it is the same, and one matter throughout, sauing that the higher, still the purer it is, and more subtile. *Tycho* will haue two distinct matters of Heauen and Ayre, but to say truth, with some small qualification, they haue [238] one and the selfe same opinion, about the Essence and matter of Heavens, that it is not hard and impenetrable, as *Peripateticks* hold, transparent of a *quinta essentia, but that it is penetrable and soft as the aire it selfe is, and that the Planets moue in it, as Birds in the Aire, Fishes in the Sea.* This they proue by motion of Comets, and otherwise, which are not generated, as *Aristotle* teacheth, in the aëriall Region of an hot and dry exhalation, and so consumed; but as *Anaxagoras* and *Democritus* held of old, of a celestiall matter: & as *Tycho, Helisæus Roeslin, Thaddeus Haggesius, Pena, Rotman, Fracastorius,* demonstrate by their expresse Paralaxes, refractions, motions **of the Planets which enterfeire and cut one anothers orbs, now higher, and then lower, as [Mars] amongst the rest, which sometimes, as *Kepler* confirmes by his owne, and Tycho's accurate obseruations, comes neerer the earth then the [Sun], and is againe eftsoones aloft in *Iuppiters* orbe**; And other sufficient reasons, farre aboue the Moone: exploding in the meane time **that Element of fire**, those **monstrous Orbes of** *Eccentricks*, and **Eccentre** *Epicycles.* Which how soeuer *Ptolomy, Alhasen, Vitellio,* **Purbachus**, *Maginus, Clavius*, and many of their associats stiffely maintaine to be reall orbes, excentricke, concentricke, circles æquant &c. are absurd and ridiculous. For who is so mad to thinke, that there should be so many circles, like subordinate wheeles in a clock, all impenetrable and hard, as they faine, adde and substract at their pleasures. *Maginus* makes eleuen Heavens, all subdiuided into their orbes and circles, and all too little to serue those particular appearances, *Fracastorius* 72. Homocentricks, *Tycho Brahe, Nicholas Ramerus, Heliseus Roeslin,* haue peculiar hypotheses of their owne inventions, and they be but inventions, as most of them acknowledge, as we admit of *Æquators, Tropicks, Colures,* **Circles Artique and Antartique**, for doctrines sake (though *Ramus* thinke them all vnnecessary) they will haue them supposed only for method and order. *Tycho* hath fained, I knowe not how many subdiuisions of Epicycles in Epicycles &c. to calculate and expresse the Moones motion: But when all is done, as a supposition, and no otherwise; Not (as he holds) hard, impenetrable, subtile, transparent, &c. or making Musicke, as *Phythagoras* maintained; **but still quiet, liquid, open, &c.**

If the Heauens be penetrable, as these men deliuer, & no lets, it were not amisse in this aeriall progresse, to make wings, and flye vp, as that *Turke* in *Busbequius*, made his fellow Citizens in *Constantinople* beleeue he would performe: and some new-fangled wits, me thinkes, should some time or other finde out: or if that may not be, yet with a *Galilies* glasse, or *Icaro-menippus* wings in *Lucian*, command the Spheares and Heauens, and see what is done amongst them. Whether there bee generation and corruption, as some thinke, by reason of ætheriall Comets, that in *Cassiopea* 1572. **that in *Cygno* 1600, that in *Sagittarius* 1604.** &c. and many like, or that they were created *ab initio* [from the beginning], and shew themselues at set times: and as *Heliscæus Rœslin* contends, haue Poles, Axeltrees, Circles of their own, and regular motions. *An coelum sit coloratum?* [Whether the sky be coloured?] Whether the starres be of that bignesse, distance, as Astronomers relate, so many in number, 1026. or 1725, as *I. Bayerus*; or as some *Rabbins* 29000 *Myriades*; or as *Galilie* discouers by his glasses, infinite, **and that *via lactea* [Milky Way], a confused light of small starres**; the least **visible** star in the eighth Spheare, 18 times bigger then the earth; whether they be thicker [239] parts of the Orbs, as *Aristotle* deliuers, or so many habitable Worlds, as *Democritus*: whether they haue light of their owne, or from the Sunne, or giue light round, as *Patritius* discourseth. Whether light be of their Essence; **and that light be a substance or an accident**; whether they bee hot by themselues, or by accident cause heat? whether there bee such a Pre- cession of the Æquinoxes, as *Copernicus* holds, or that the eighth Spheare moue? *An bene Philosophentur, R. Bacon, & I. Dee, Aphorism. de multiplicatione specierum.* [Whether they philosophise well, Roger Bacon, and John Dee, *Aphorisms on the multiplication of appearances*.] Whether there be any such Images ascending with each degree of the Zodiack in the East, as *Aliacensis* faines. *An aequae super cœlum* [Whether there be waters above the heavens], as *Patritius*, **& the Schoolmen will, a Cristalline watry heauen.** *An terra sit animata?* [Whether the world is alive?] **Which some so confidently beleeue with *Orpheus* and *Hermes*, and euery starre a soule, Angell, or Intelligence to animate or moue it** &c. Or to omit all smaller controuersies, as matters of lesse moment, to examine that maine Paradoxe of the Earths motion, now so much in question, *Pythagoras* maintained it of old, *Democritus*, and many of their Schollers, **Didacus Astunica, Antony Fascanius, a Carmelite, and some other Commentators will haue *Iob* to insinuate *cap*. 9. *vers*. 4. *Qui commovet terram de loco suo*** [He who disturbs the Earth from out of its place], **&c. and that this one place of**

Scripture makes more for the earths motion, then all the other proue against it. Whom *Pineda* confutes, most contradict: how soeuer, it is reviued since by *Copernicus*, not as a truth, but a supposition, as he confesseth himselfe in the Preface to Pope *Nicholas*, but now maintained in good earnest by *Calcagninus, Telesius, Kepler, Rotman, Gilbert, Digges, Galileus, Campanella, Origanus*, and some others of his followers. For if the Earth be the Center of the World, stand still, and the Heauens moue, as the most receaued opinion is, *Quis ille furor?* &c. What fury is that, saith Dr *Gilbert*, that shall driue the Heauens about with such incomprehensible celerity in 24 houres, when as every point of the Firmament, and in the *Æquator* must needs moue (as *Clavius* calculates) 176660 in one 246th part of an houre: and an arrow out of a bowe, must goe seauen times about the Earth, whilst a man can say an *Ave Maria*, if it keepe the same space, or compasse the earth 1884 times in an howre, which is *supra humanam cogitationem*, beyond humane conceipt. A man could not ride so much ground going 40 miles a day, in 2904 yeares, as the Firmament goes in 24 houres, **or so much in 203 yeares, as the said Firmament in one minute**, *quod incredibile videtur* [which seems astonishing]: And the Pole starre, which to our thinking scarce moueth out of his place, goeth a bigger circuit then the Sunne, whose Diameter is much larger then the Diameter of the Heauen of the Sunne; **And 20000 Semidiameters of the Earth from vs, with the rest of the fixed Starres, as** *Tycho* **proues.** To avoid therefore these impossibilities, they ascribe a triple motion to the earth the Sunne immoueable in the Center, **(or as** *Origanus* **and others will, one single motion to the earth, still placed in the Center of the world, which is most probable) a single motion to the Firmament, which moues in 30 or 26 thousand yeares, and so the Planets,** *Saturne* **in 30 yeares absolues his sole and proper motion,** *Iupiter* **in 12,** *Mars* **in 3, &c.** and so solue all apparances better then any way whatsoeuer; calculate all motions, much more certaine then by those *Alphonsine*, or any such tables, which are grounded from those other suppositions. Now if the Earth moue, it is a Planet, and shines to them in the *Moone*, and to the other Planetary inhabitants, as the *Moone* & they [240] doe to vs vpon the Earth: but shine she doth, as *Galilie, Kepler*, and others proue, and then *per consequens*, the rest of the Planets are inhabited, as well as the *Moone*, which he grants in his dissertation with *Galilies Nuncius Siderius, that there be Iouiall and Saturnine Inhabitants, &c.* and that those severall Planets, haue their severall *Moones* about them, as the Earth hath hers, as *Galileus* hath already evinced by his glasses, foure about *Iupiter*, two about *Saturne* (though *Sitius* the *Florentine* cavell at it) yet *Kepler*, the Emperours Mathematician, confirmes out of his experience, that hee saw as much, by the

same helpe. Then **(I say)** the Earth and they be Planets alike, inhabited alike, moued about the Sunne, the common center of the World
alike, **and it may be those two greene children, which** *Nubri-*
gensis **speakes of in his time, that fell from Heauen, came from**
thence.[1] And we may inferre with *Campanella and Brunus,* that
which *Melissus, Democritus, Leucippus* maintained in their ages, there be
infinite Worlds, and infinite Earths, **or systemes,** because infinite
starres and planets, like vnto this of ours. *Kepler* betwixt iest and
earnest in his Perspectiues, Lunar Geography, *dissertat cum nunc: syder.*
seemes in part to agree with this, and partly to contradict; for the
Planets he yeelds them to be inhabited, he doubts of the Starres: and
so doth *Tycho* in his Astronomicall Epistles, out of a consideration of
their vastity and greatnesse, breake out into some such like speeches,
that he will neuer beleeue those great and huge Bodies were made to
no other vse, then this that we perceaue, to illuminate the Earth, a
point insensible, in respect of the whole. But who shall dwell in these
vast Bodies, Earths, Worlds, *if they bee inhabited? rationall creatures,* as
Kepler demands? *Or haue they soules to be saued? Or doe they inhabit a*
better part of the World then we doe? Are we or they Lords of the World? And
how are all things made for man? Difficile est nodum hunc expedire, eò quòd
nondum omnia quæ huc pertinent, explorata habemus [It is hard to loosen
this knot, especially as we have not yet researched everything that
pertains to it], 'tis hard to determine: this only he proues, that we
are in *præcipuo mundi sinu,* in the best place, best World, nearest the
Heart of the Sun. **Thomas Campanella, a Calabrian Monke,**
in his second book *de sensu rerum,* **c. 4. subscribes to this of**
Keplerus, **that they are inhabited hee certainly supposeth, but**
with what kinde of creatures he cannot say, he labours to proue
it by all meanes, and that there are infinite worlds, hauing
made an Apologie for *Galileus,* **and dedicates this tenent of his**
to Cardinal *Caietanus.* **Others freely speake, mutter, and would**
perswade the World (as *Marinus Mersennus* **complaines) that**
our moderne Divines are too severe and rigid against Mathe-
maticians, ignorant and peeuish, in not admitting their true
Demonstrations and certaine obseruations, that they tyrannize
ouer arte, sciences, and all Philosophy, in suppressing their
labours, forbidding them to write, to speake a truth, all to
maintaine their superstition, and for their profits sake. As for
those places of Scripture which oppungne it, they will haue
spoken *ad captum vulgi* [according to the common person's under-
standing], **and as** *Otho Casman Astol. cap.* **1.** *part.* **1. notes,**

---

1 This anecdote was only referred to in a note in the 1621 edition; here it is
integrated into the main text.

many great Divines, besides *Porphyrius, Proclus, Simplicius,* and those Heathen Philosophers, *doctrinâ & ætate venerandi, Mosis Genesin mundanam popularis nescio cuius ruditatis,* [241] *quæ longa absit à vera Philosophorum eruditione insimulant.* [... venerable in doctrine and antiquity, who accuse Moses' Genesis of I know not what vulgar unsophistication, subsisting far apart from the true learning of the Philosophers.] **Read more in him, in *Grossius* and *Iunius*. But to proceed**, these and such like **insolent and bold attempts**, prodigious Paradoxes, inferences must needs follow, if it once be granted, which *Rotman, Kepler, Gilbert, Diggeus,* **Origanus**, *Galilie,* & others maintaine of the Earths motion, that it is a Planet, and shines as the Moone doth, which containes in it *both land and sea as the Moone doth,* for so they find by their glasses, that *Maculæ in facie Lunæ* [the spots in the Moon's face], *the brighter parts are Earth, the duskier Sea,* which **Thales**, *Plutarch,* and *Pythagoras* formerly taught: and manifestly discerne hills and dales, and such like concauities, if we may subscribe to and belieue *Galilies* obseruations. [...]

[243] But hoo? I am now gone quite out of sight, I am almost giddy with rouing about: I could haue ranged farther yet, but I am an infant, and not able to diue into these profundities, not able to vnderstand, much lesse to discusse. I leaue the contemplation of these things, to stronger wits, that haue better ability, and happier leisure to wade into such Philosophicall mysteries: my melancholy spaniels quest, my game is sprung, and I must **suddenly** come downe and follow.

Appendix H: From John Wilkins, Mathematicall Magick (1648)

[In 1648 Wilkins wrote a chapter on "the Art of Flying," in which he placed Godwin's Gansas alongside all the other ways humans have claimed to have been able to fly. The chapter is reproduced below.[1] The notes are based largely on Wilkins's own annotations, hence their occasional obscurity. Biblical references are incorporated into the text.]

Concerning the Art of Flying.
The severall ways whereby this hath been or may be attempted.

I have formerly in two other Discourses[2] mentioned the possibility of this art of flying, and intimated a further inquiry into it, which is a kind of engagement to some fuller disquisitions and conjectures to that purpose.

There are four severall ways whereby this flying in the air, hath beene or may be attempted. Two of them by the strength of other things, and [200] two of them by our owne strength.

1. By spirits or Angels.
2. By the help of fowls.
3. By wings fastned immediately to the body.
4. By a flying chariot.

1. For the first, we read of divers that have passed swiftly in the air, by the help of spirits and Angels,[3] whether good Angels, as *Elias* was carried unto heaven in a fiery chariot [2 Kings 2:11]: as *Philip* was conveyed to *Azotus* [Acts 8:39], and *Habbacuck* from Jewry to Babylon, and back again immediately [Daniel 39]: Or by evill Angels, as our Saviour was carried by the Devill to the top of a high mountain, and to the pinacle of the Temple [Luke 4]. Thus witches are commonly related to passe unto their usuall meetings in some remote place; and as they doe sell windes unto Mariners, so likewise are they sometimes

---

1   Text taken from *Mathematicall Magick* (London: Samuel Gellibrand, 1648), 199-210.

2   *Discourse concerning a New World*, 203-42; *Mercury*, 36.

3   Zanchius, *De operibus dei*, 1.4. ("On the heaven of the blessed") = *Operum theologicorum ... tomus tertius* ([Geneva]: Stephanus Gamonetus, 1605), cols. 46-58.

hired to carry men speedily through the open air.[1] *Acosta* affirms that such kind of passages are usuall amongst divers Sorcerers with the Indians at this day.[2] [201]

So *Kepler* in his Astronomicall dream, doth fancy a witch to be conveyed unto the Moon by her Familiar.[3]

Simon Magus was so eminent for miraculous sorceries, that all the people in *Samaria* from the least to the greatest, did esteem him *as the great power of God* [Acts 8:10]. And so famous was he at *Rome*, that the Emperour erected a statue to him with this inscription, *Simoni Deo Sancto.*[4] 'Tis storied of this Magician, that having challenged Saint *Peter* to doe miracles with him, he attempted to fly from the Capitoll to the Aventine hill.[5] But when he was in the midst of the way, Saint *Peters* prayers did overcome his sorceries, and violently bring him to the ground, in which fall having broke his thigh, within a while after he died.

But none of all these relations may conduce to the discovery of this experiment, as it is here enquired after, upon *natural* & *artificial* grounds.

2. There are others who have [202] conjectured a possibility of being conveyed through the air by the help of fowls; to which purpose that fiction of the *Ganza's,* is the most pleasant and probable. They are supposed to be great fowl of a strong lasting flight, and easily tamable. Divers of which may be so brought up as to joyn together in carrying the weight of a man, so as each of them shall partake his proportionable share of the burden; and the person that is carried may by certain reins direct and steer them in their courses. However this may seem a strange proposall, yet it is not certainly more improbable, then many other arts, wherein the industry of ingenious men hath instructed

---

1   Thomas Erastus, *Repetitio disputationis de lamiis, seu strigibus* (Basel: Peter Perna, [1578]).

2   Acosta, *The Naturall and Morall Historie of the East and West Indies,* 406 (book 5, chapter 26).

3   Kepler, *Somnium;* Rosen, ed. and trans., *Kepler's Somnium.*

4   Hegesippus, *Historia* (Paris, 1511), sgs. Eiir-Eiiir (bk. 3, ch. 2).

5   Polydore Vergil, *De inventoribus rerum,* book 8, chapter 3. English translation in Polydore Vergil, *The Works of the Famous Antiquary, Polidore Virgil* (London: Simon Miller, 1663), 286-90 ("... as he was by his Magical exorcisms lifted up, and flying in the Ayre, he had such a fall that he brake his Leg, and it cost him his life in Aretia, where he lay at Surgery for the healing of his leg" [287]). Wilkins adds that Petrus Crinitus, *Comentarii de honesta disciplina* (Florence, 1504), sgs. [e7]v-[e8]r (bk. 8, ch. 1), "mistrusts this relation as fabulous. *Non enim Lucas hoc [antiochenus] omisisset* [For otherwise Luke had not omitted it]."

these brute creatures. And I am very confident, that one whose genius doth enable him for such kind of experiments upon leisure, and the advantage of such helps as are requisite for various and frequent trials, might effect some strange thing by this kind of enquiry.

'Tis reported as a custome amongst [203] the *Leucatians*, that they were wont upon a superstition to precipitate a man from some high cliffe into the sea, tying about him with strings at some distance, many great fowls, and fixing unto his body divers feathers spread, to break the fall; which (saith the learned *Bacon*, if it were diligently and exactly contrived) would be able to hold up, and carry any proportionable weight; and therefore he advises others to think further upon this experiment, as giving some light to the invention of the art of flying.[1]

3. 'Tis the more obvious and common opinion that this may be effected by wings fastned immediately to the body, this coming nearest to the imitation of nature, which should be observed in such attempts as these. This is that way which *Fredericus Hermannus* in his little discourse *de Arte volandi*, doth onely mention and insist upon.[2] And if we may trust credible story, it hath been frequently attempted not without some successe.[3] [204] 'Tis related of a certaine English Munk called *Elmerus*, about the Confessors time, that he did by such wings fly from a Tower above a furlong; and so another from Saint *Marks* steeple in *Venice*; another at *Norinberge*; and *Busbequius* speaks of a Turk in *Constantinople*, who attempted something this way.[4] M. *Burton* mentioning this quotation, doth beleeve that some new-fangled wit ('tis his cynicall phrase) will some time or other find out

---

1 Bacon, *Sylva Sylvarum* (London, 1627), exp. 886.

2 Fridericus Hermannus Flayderus, *De Arte Volandi* (Tübingen: Theodoricus Werlinus, 1628). Later in the century, attention would turn to Francesco Lana, *Prodromo* (Brescia, 1670), a work containing accounts of mechanical birds and airships, which latter account Robert Hooke translated and refuted (*Philosophical Collections* 1 [1679]: 14-29).

3 Wilkins comments, "So the ancient British Bladuds," i.e., King Bladud, mythical King of England and father of King Lear. See, e.g., John Stowe, *A Summarie of English Chronicles* (London: Thomas Marsh, 1566), sg. C2r: Bladud "decked hymselfe in fethers, and presumed to flye in the ayre, and fallynge on hys temple of Apollo, brake his necke, when he had reigned .xx. yeares."

4 Johan Ernst Burggravius, *Achilles Panoplos Redivivus, seu Panoplia Physico-Vulcania* (Amsterdam, [1612]), 52; Busbequius' "flying Turk" was recalled by numerous writers in this period, including Wilkins here and his protégé Hooke. Actually, Busbequius recounted no such anecdote, all references to it deriving from Burton's first, erroneous reference. Burton presumably meant the anecdote in the thirteenth-century chronicler Nicetas Acominatus, recounted in Richard Knolles, *A General History of the Turkes* (London: Adam Islip, 1603), 37. The flying Turk crashed and broke all his bones.

this art.[1] Though the truth is, most of these Artists did unfotunately miscarry by falling down and breaking their arms or legs, yet that may be imputed to their want of experience, and too much fear, which must needs possesse men in such dangerous and strange attempts. Those things that seem very difficult and fearfull at the first, may grow very facil after frequent triall and exercise. And therefore he that would effect any thing in this kind, must be brought up to the constant practise of it from his youth. Trying [205] first onely to use his wings in running on the ground, as an Estrich or tame Geese will doe, touching the earth with his toes; and so by degrees learn to rise higher, till hee shall attain unto skill and confidence. I have heard it from credible testimony, that one of our own Nation hath proceeded so far in this experiment, that he was able by the help of wings in such a running pace to step constantly ten yards at a time.[2]

[...]

[208] But now because the arms extended, are but weak and easily wearied, therfore the motions by them are like to be but short and slow, answerable it may be to the flight of such domestick fowl as are most conversant on the ground, which of themselves we see are quickly weary, and therefore much more would the arm of a man, as being not naturally designed to such a motion.

It were therefore worth the inquiry [209] to consider whether this might not be more probably effected by the labour of the feet, which

---

1 Burton, *Anatomy*, 2.2.3.1 (2.48), included in the extract in Appendix G, above.

2 Compare John Aubrey on Sir Jonas Moore: "I remember Sir Jonas told us that a Jesuite (I think 'twas Grenbergerus, of the Roman College) found out a way of flying, and that he made a youth performe it. Mr. Gascoigne taught an Irish boy the way, and he flew over a river in Lancashire (or therabout), but when he was up in the ayre, the people gave a shoute, wherat the boy being frighted, he fell downe on the other side of the river, and broke his legges, and when he came to himselfe, he sayd that he thought the people had seen some strange apparition, which fancy amazed him. This was anno 1635, and he spake it in the Royall Societie, upon the account of the flyeing at Paris, two yeares since" (John Aubrey, *Brief Lives*, ed. Andrew Clark, 2 vols. [Oxford: Clarendon P, 1898], 2.80. Gascoigne is William Gascoigne (1612?-1644) the astronomical inventor. For the Royal Society and human flight, see Thomas Birch, *The History of the Royal Society of London*, 4 vols. (London: A. Millar, 1756-57), 2.59; 3.181, 481-82 (minutes of the 1679 meeting to which Aubrey refers), 487, 489. The Paris contraption was Besnier's "Engine for Flying," upon which Robert Hooke again commented ("An Account of the Sieur Bernier's Way of Flying," *Philosophical Collections* 1 [1679]: 14-18). This is the import of Wesley's phrase on "the *French* Smith's wings" cited in the section on Godwin's Reception, above, p. 47.

are naturally more strong and indefatigable: In which contrivance the wings should come down from the shoulders on each side as in the other, but the motion of them should be from the legs, being thrust out and drawn in again one after another, so as each leg should move both wings, by which means a man should (as it were) walk or climbe up into the air: and then the hands and arms might be at leisure to help and direct the motion, or for any other service proportionable to their strength. Which conjecture is not without good probability, and some speciall advantages above the other.

4. But the fourth and last way seems unto me altogether as probable, and much more usefull then any of the rest. And that is by a flying chariot, which may be so contrived as to carry a man within it; & though the strength of a spring might perhaps [210] be serviceable for the motion of this engine, yet it were better to have it assisted by the labour of some intelligent mover as the heavenly orbs are supposed to be turned. And therefore if it were made big enough to carry sundry persons together, then each of them in their severall turns might successively labour in the causing of this motion; which thereby would be much more constant and lasting, then it could otherwise be, if it did wholly depend on the strength of the same person. This contrivance being as much to be preferred before any of the other, as swimming in a ship before swimming in the water.

Bibliography and Works Cited

Primary Sources

Francis Godwin

The Man in the Moone

Below is supplied a full entry for the first edition, followed by more basic bibliographical entries. For the continental vernacular editions, omitted here, see the section on Godwin's Reception in the Introduction (pp. 49-50). The bibliography of *The Man in the Moone* was first discussed by H.W. Lawton in an appendix to his "Bishop Godwin's 'Man in the Moone,'" *Review of English Studies* 7 (1931): 23-55; this was corrected and expanded by Grant McColley in his "The Third Edition of Francis Godwin's 'The Man in the Moone,'" *The Library* 17 (1937): 472-75.

THE | MAN IN THE | MOONE: | *OR* | A DISCOVRSE OF A | Voyage thither | BY | [rule] | DOMINGO GONSALES | [rule] | *The speedy Messenger* | [Printer's device: McKerrow 26] | LONDON | Printed by JOHN NORTON, for | *Ioshua Kirton,* and *Thomas Warren,* 1638.

Collation: 8°: A^4 B-I^8 [$4 signed (-A1, 2, 4; D3 signed "D5")].
Pagination: [8], 126, [2].
Imprimatur, often missing from surviving copies: I8a, signed by Mathew Clay, dated "Iulij. ultimo. 1638"; entered into the Stationers' Register 1 August 1638.
Surviving copies in the British Library, London; the Bodleian, Oxford; John Rylands, Manchester; Harvard University Library; the Folger Shakespeare Library, Yale University Library; the Bibliothèque Nationale, Paris. Surviving copies are often mutilated: e.g., British Library *caret* A1, I8; Folger *caret* A1; Harvard *caret* I8; Yale *caret* A1; BNF *caret* C6.

The Man in the Moone, or a Discourse of a Voyage Thither by F. G. B. of H. To which is added Nuncius Inanimatus, written in Latin by the same author, and now Englished by a Person of Worth. London: Joshua Kirton, 1657. Reset from the 1638 edition. The translator of the *Nuncius Inanimatus* was the scholar Thomas Smith (1638-1710).

R.B. [Nathaniel Crouch], *A View of the English Acquisitions in Guinea, and the East Indies* (London: Nathaniel Crouch, 1686), 74-131. Bowdlerised text of *The Man in the Moone,* and the basis for most subsequent editions until McColley. ESTC lists five editions between 1686 and 1728, and compare *A Description of the Famous New Colony of Georgia* [with *A View*] (Dublin: James Hoey, 1734). "Crouch 'thought fit to republish the Substance' of Godwin's narrative, and, in so doing, made the preface part of the text proper, generally abridged and slightly altered the content, and established the paragraph divisions found in the *Harleian Miscellany* (and *Anglia*) text" (McColley, "Third Edition," 472-73).

A Voyage to the Moon. Stamford: W. Thompson and T. Baily, 171[8]. Date conjectured by ESTC, copy in Senate House Library, London.

A View of St. Helena ... with an account of the ... voyage of Domingo Gonsales. The Harleian Miscellany 8 (1746): 332-48. Second edition, London, 1811. Based on the Crouch text.

The Strange Voyage and Adventures of Domingo Gonsales. London: John Lever, [1768]. Described as "The Second Edition." This edition includes a spurious continuation in which Gonsales arrives back home and reveals his secrets to the Spanish king, "who held several Cabinet Councils to deliberate on a proper Use to be made of these Discoveries." ESTC also lists a 1790[?] edition (London: T. Sabine), described as "The Fifth Edition."

MODERN EDITIONS AND FACSIMILES

The Voyage of Domingo Gonzales to the World of the Moon. Ed. E. Hönncher, and followed by his "Bemerkungen zu Godwins 'Voyage of Domingo Gonsales to the Moon.'" *Anglia* 10 (1888): 428-56. Hönncher's text is based on the Harleian Miscellany.

The Man in the Moone and Nvncivs Inanimatvs, ed. Grant McColley in *Smith College Studies in Modern Languages* 19 (1937). The major scholarly intervention.

The Man in the Moone: A Story of Space Travel in the Seventeenth Century. Hereford: Nagrom c/o the Hereford Times, 1959. A reprint of McColley's text with a forward by "F.C.M." and no notes.

The Man in the Moone, retrieved from obscurity, introduced, edited and annotated by Ivan Volkoff. Los Angeles: Advertisers Composition Company, 1961. Based on the 1657 edition.

Short Fiction of the Seventeenth Century, ed. Charles C Mish. New York: New York UP, 1963, and subsequent editions. Based on the 1657 edition.

The Man in the Moone. London: Albion P, 1969. Facsimile of the 1638 edition, copy unspecified, with no editorial material.

The Man in the Moone. Menston: Scolar P, 1971. Facsimile of the 1638 edition, from the Bodleian copy, with no editorial material.

The Man in the Moone: An Anthology of Antique Science-Fiction and Fantasy, ed. Faith K. Pizor and T. Allan Comp. London: Sidgwick and Jackson, 1971. The editors print an excerpt from the 1638 text.

The Man in the Moone. Amsterdam: Theatrum Orbis Terrarum, 1972. Facsimile: The English Experience no. 459.

The Man in the Moone/L'Homme dans la Lune, notes et introduction de
Annie Amartin-Serin. Nancy: Presses universitaires de Nancy, Collec-
tion "Textes Oubliés," 1984. An excellent edition, placing Baudoin and
Godwin's texts in parallel.
The Man in the Moon, ed. John A. Butler. Ottawa: Dovehouse Edition,
1995. But see Robert M. Philmus, "Murder most Fowl: Butler's
Edition of Francis Godwin," *Science Fiction Studies* 23 (1996): 260-69.
The Man in the Moon. With a modern introduction by Andy Johnson and
Ron Shoesmith. Woonton Almeley, Herefordshire: Logaston P, 1996.

Godwin: Major Works Other than Man in the Moone *(only contemporary editions are listed)*

*A Catalogue of the Bishops of England, since the First Planting of Christian
Religion in this Island.* London: [Eliot's Court Press] for George Bishop,
1601.
*A Catalogue of the Bishops of England, since the First Planting of Christian
Religion in this Island.* London: [Eliot's Court Press] for Thomas
Adams, 1615.
De Praesulibus Angliae commentarius omnium episcoporum. London: [William
Stansby and Eliot's Court Press] for John Bill, 1616.
*Rerum Anglicarum Henrico VIII. Edwardo VI. et Maria Regnantibus, Annales
Nunc primùm editi.* London: John Bill, 1616.
De Praesulibus Angliae commentarius omnium episcoporum. London: [William
Stansby and Eliot's Court Press] for John Bill, 1621.
*The Succession of the Bishops of England since the First Planting of Christian
Religion in this Island.* London: [Eliot's Court Press] for Andrew Hebb,
1625.
Rerum Anglicarum Henrico VIII. Edwardo VI. et Maria regnantibus, annales.
London: John Bill, 1628.
Nuncius Inanimatus. In Vtopia [i.e., London]: [J. Bill], 1629.
*Annales of England Containing the Reignes of Henry the Eighth. Edward the
Sixt. Queene Mary ... Thus Englished, corrected and inlarged with the
Author's consent, by Morgan Godwyn.* London: Printed by A. Islip, and
W. Stansby, 1630.

Other Primary Materials

Manuscripts

London, The British Library

MS Add. 11812. *The Lunarian* (c. 1681)
MS Add. 45140, fols. 6r-9v. Autograph inserts to Godwin's *Rerum Angli-
carum ... Annales* (c. 1616)
MS Add. 46370. Sir John Harington's *Supplie or Addicion to the Catalogue*

of Bishops (1608) to Godwin's *Catalogue*; his biography of Godwin himself occupies fols. 43v-45v

MS Cotton Julius C. V, fols. 57v, 197v. Godwin-Camden letters
MS Cotton Julius F. VI, fols. 296r-300v. Godwin-Camden letters
MS Cotton Titus C. XI. Fair copy of Godwin's *Rerum Anglicarum ... Annales* (c. 1616)
MS Stowe 76, Roger Lea/Ley, *Gesta Britannica praesertim Anglorum* (1664)
Royal MS 17 B XXII. Sir John Harington, final presentation copy to Prince Henry of *A Supplie or Addicion ot the Catalogue of Bishops* (1608)

LONDON, THE NATIONAL ARCHIVES

SP 14/120/17, Godwin's 1621 telegraphic petition

OXFORD, BODLEIAN LIBRARY

MS Aubrey 1, fol. 88v. John Aubrey's comments on Edmond Halley's theory of the hollow earth (1691)
MS Gough Eccl. Top. 52. Thomas Delafield, Life of Francis Godwin (1734), following a printed copy of Godwin's *Catalogue*
MS Tanner 36, fol. 16. Letter of Morgan Godwin to Archbishop Sancroft, 23 April 1681

OXFORD, CHRIST CHURCH LIBRARY

MS 162, Papers of George Dalgarno, including "That there is both a diurnal and annual motion, either in the Heaven, or Earth, nothing can be more certain ..." (c. 1660-87)

Selected Printed Books

Note: Classical texts unless otherwise referenced are cited from the Loeb Classical Library.

Acosta, José. *The Naturall and Morall Historie of the East and West Indies.* London: Edward Blount and William Apsley, 1604.
[Pseudo-]Albertus Magnus. *The Boke of Secrets of Albertus Magnus, of the Vertues of Herbes, Stones, and certayne Beastes.* [London]: [John King], 1560.
Apuleius. *Opera Omnia Quae Exstant.* Paris: Michael Sonnius, 1601.
Aventinus, Johannes. *Annalium Boiorum Libri VII.* Basel: Perna and Lecythus, 1580.
Bacon, Francis. *Of the Proficience and Advancement of Learning.* London: Henrie Tomes, 1605.
——. *Sylva Sylvarum.* London: William Lee, 1627.
Baker, Thomas. *Reflections upon Learning.* London: A. Boswell, 1699.
Barlow, William. *Magneticall Advertisements.* London: Timothy Barlow, 1616.

Behn, Aphra. *The Emperor of the Moon* (1687). In *The Works of Aphra Behn*. Vol. 7. Ed. Janet Todd. London: William Pickering, 1996.

Birch, Thomas. *The History of the Royal Society of London for the Improving of Natural Knowledge from its First Rise*. 4 vols. London: A. Millar, 1756-57.

Blundeville, Thomas. *M. Blundevile his Exercises*. London: John Windet, 1594.

Bourne, William. *Inventions and Devises*. London: Thomas Woodcock, 1590.

Bright, Timothie. *Characterie*. London: John Windet, 1588.

Breydenbach, Bernhard von. *Opusculum sanctarum peregrinationum ad sepulchrum Christi*. Mainz: Erhard Reuwich, 1486.

Burton, Robert. *The Anatomy of Melancholy*. Ed. Thomas C. Faulkner *et al.* 6 vols. Oxford: Clarendon P, 1989-2000 [1621 etc].

Busbequius, A.G. *Itinera Constantinopolitanum et Amasianum*. Antwerp, 1581. Trans. as *The Four Epistles ... concerning his Embassy into Turkey*. London: J. Taylor and J. Wyat, 1694.

Camden, William. *Britain*. Trans. Philemon Holland. London: George Bishop and John Norton, 1610.

Campanella, Tommaso. *Apologia pro Galileo*. Trans. Grant McColley. *Smith College Studies in History XXII* (1937).

Carpenter, Nathanael. *Geographie Delineated Forth in Two Bookes*. Oxford: Henry Cripps, 1635.

Cavendish, Margaret. *The Description of a New World, Called the Blazing World*. London: A. Maxwell, 1666.

"Chrysostom Trueman." *The History of a Voyage to the Moon*. London: Lockwood & Co., 1864.

Clark, Andrew, ed. *Register of the University of Oxford*. Oxford: Clarendon P, 1887.

Comes, Natalis. *Mythologiæ ... libri decem*. Geneva: Samuel Crispinus, 1612.

Copernicus, *De Revolutionibus/On the Revolutions*. Ed. and trans. Edward Rosen. Baltimore: Johns Hopkins UP, 1992 [1543].

[Crouch, Nathaniel] 'R. B.' *A View of the English Acquisitions in Guinea, and the East Indies*. London: Nathaniel Crouch, 1686.

Cyrano de Bergerac. *Selenarchia, or the Government of the World in the Moon a Comical History*. Trans. Thomas St. Serf. London: Humphrey Robinson, 1659.

Democritus Turned States-Man. London: n.p., 1659.

Digges, Leonard. *A Prognostication Everlastinge*. London: Thomas Marsh, 1576.

Drayton, Michael. *Poems Lyrick and Pastorall*. London: N.L. and I. Flasket, [1606].

D'Urfey, Thomas. *Wonders in the Sun, or the Kingdom of the Birds: A Comick Opera*. London, 1706.

Eden, Richard, ed. and trans. *The Decades of the Newe Worlde or West India Conteynyng the Navigations and Conquestes of the Spanyardes*. London: William Powell, 1555.

Erasmus, Desiderius. *Literary and Educational Writings 2: De Copia and De Ratione Studii.* Ed. Craig R. Thompson. Toronto: U of Toronto P, 1978.

Fleyderus, Fridericus Hermannus. *De Arte Volandi.* Tübingen: Theodoricus Werlinus, 1628.

Foigny, Gabriel du. *A New Discovery of Terra Incognita Australis.* London: John Dunton, 1693.

Frende, Gabriel. *An Almanacke and Prognostication for this Yeere of Our Lord Jesus Christ MDXCIX.* London: Richard Watkins and James Roberts, 1599.

Fuller, Thomas. *The History of the Worthies of England.* London: Thomas Williams, 1662.

Galilei, Galileo. *Sidereus Nuncius, or the Sidereal Messenger.* Ed. and trans. Albert Van Helden. Chicago: U of Chicago P, 1989.

Gilbert, William. *De Magnete.* London: Peter Short, 1600.

——. *De Mundo nostro Sublunari Philosophia Nova.* Amsterdam: Ludovicus Elzevir, 1651.

Greene, Robert. *The Honorable Historie of Frier Bacon, and Frier Bongay.* London: Edward White, 1594.

Hakewill, George. *An Apologie for the Power and Providence of God.* 2nd ed. Oxford: William Turner, 1630; 3rd ed. Oxford: William Turner, 1635.

Hakluyt, Richard. *The Principal Navigations.* 2 vols. London: George Bishop *et al.*, 1599-[1600].

Hariot, Thomas. *A Brief and True Report of the New-Found Land of Virginia.* Frankfurt: Wechel, 1590.

Harley, Brilliana, *Letters of the Lady Brilliana Harley.* Ed. Thomas Taylor Lewis. London: Camden Society, 1854.

The Hartlib Papers. Ed. Judith Crawford *et al.* 2 CD-ROMs. Ann Arbor, MI: UMI Research Publication, 1995.

Herbert, Sir Thomas. *A Relation of Some Yeares Travail Begunne Anno 1626 into Afrique and the Greater Asia.* London: William Stansby and Jacob Bloome, 1634.

Hieronymus de Sancto Marco. *Opusculum de Universali Mundi Machina ... editum ad mentem Aristotelis necnon aliorum philosophorum peritissimorum.* London: Richard Pynson, 1505.

The Historie of the Damnable Life, and Deserved Death of Doctor John Faustus. London: Edward White, 1592. [Ed. John Henry Jones as *The English Faust Book.* Cambridge: Cambridge UP, 1994.]

[Hooke, Robert]. "An Account of the Sieur *Bernier's* Way of Flying [etc]." *Philosophical Collections* 1 (1679): 14-18.

——. "A Demonstration [by Francesco Lana, with animadversions by Hooke], how it is practically possible to make a Ship, which shall be sustained by the Air, and may be moved either by Sails or Oars." *Philosophical Collections* 1 (1679): 18-29.

H[ooke], R[obert]. "Some Observations, and Conjectures Concerning the Chinese Characters." *Philosophical Transactions* 180 (1686): 63-78.

[Hooke, Robert]. *Bibliotheca Hookiana sive Catalogus Diversorum Librorum ... R. Hooke.* London, 1703.

Hopton, Arthur. *A Concordancy of Yeares*. London: Company of Stationers, 1612.

Jonson, Ben. *The Works*. London: H. Herringman *et al.*, 1692.

Kepler, Johannes. *Kepler's Conversation with the Starry Messenger*. Ed. and trans. Edward Rosen. New York: Johnson Reprint Corporation, 1965.

——. *Somnium, seu opus posthumum de astronomia lunari*. Sagan/Frankfurt: The Heirs of Kepler, 1634.

——. *Kepler's Somnium: The Dream, or Posthumous Work on Lunar Astronomy*. Ed. and trans. Edward Rosen. Madison: U of Wisconsin P, 1967; repr. New York: Dover, 2003.

Kircher, Athanasius. *Mundus Subterraneus*. 2 vols. Amsterdam: J.J. van Waesberge, 1678.

Knolles, Richard. *A General History of the Turkes*. London: Adam Islip, 1603.

Lana, Francesco. *Prodromo Ouero saggio di alcune inuentioni nuoue premesso all'arte maestra opera*. Brescia: Li Rizzardi, 1670.

Leo Africanus, Johannes. *A Geographical Historie of Africa*. Trans. John Pory. London: George Bishop, 1600.

Linschoten, Jan Huygen van. *Discours of Voyages into the Easte and West Indies*. London: John Wolfe, [1598].

Lucian of Samosata. *Certaine Select Dialogues*. Oxford: William Turner, 1634.

Lyly, John. *Endimion, The Man in the Moone*. London: For the Widow Broome, 1591.

——. *The Woman in the Moone*. London: William Jones, 1597.

Maclean, John, ed. *Letters from George Lord Carew to Sir Thomas Roe, Ambassador to the Court of the Great Mogul 1615–1617*. London: Camden Society, 1860.

Macrobius. *Commentary on the Dream of Cicero*. Ed. and trans. William Harris Stahl. New York: Columbia UP, 1990 [1952].

Magirus, Johannes. *Physiologiæ Peripateticæ Libri Sex*. London: John Bill, 1619.

Marlowe, Christopher. *The Tragicall History of Doctor Faustus*. London: Thomas Bushell, 1604.

Melanchthon, Philip. *Initia Doctrinæ Physicæ*. Wittenberg: The Heirs of Johannes Crato, 1581.

Mendoza. Juan Gonzáles de. *Historie of the Great and Mightie Kingdome of China*. London: Edward White, 1588.

[Mendoza, ?Diego Hurtado de.] *The Plesant Historie of Lazarillo de Tormes a Spaniarde*. Trans. David Rouland. London: Abel Jeffes, 1596.

Meteren, Emmanuel van. *Historia Belgica*. [Antwerp]: [n.p.], c. 1600.

More, Thomas. *Utopia*. Trans. Ralph Robynson (1556). Ed. J.H. Lupton. Oxford: Clarendon P, 1895.

Mosellanus, Petrus. *Tabulae de Schematibus et Tropis*. Antwerp: Martin Caesar, 1532.

Neville, Henry. *The Isle of Pines*. London: Allen Banks and Charles Harper, 1668.

Le Petit, Pierre/Emmanuel van Meteren. *A Generall Historie of the Netherlands*. London: Adam Islip, 1627.

Plutarch. *The Philosophie, commonlie called the Morals*. Trans. Philemon Holland. London: Arnold Hatfield, 1603.

Poole, Mrs Reginald Lane. *A Catalogue of Portraits in the Possession of the University, Colleges, City, and County of Oxford*. 3 vols. Oxford: Clarendon P, 1912-25.

Porta, Giambattista della. *De Occultis Literarum Notis*. Montbéliard: Lazarus Zetsnerus, 1593.

Prynne, William. *The Antipathie of the English Lordly Prelacie*. London: Michael Sparke, 1641.

Ptolemy. *Ptolemy's Almagest*. Trans. and annotated G.J. Toomer. Princeton: Princeton UP, 1998.

Purchas, Samuel. *Purchas His Pilgrimes*. 4 vols. London: Henry Fetherstone, 1625.

——. *Purchas His Pilgrimage*. London: Henry Fetherstone, 1626.

Ray, John. *Philosophical Letters*. London: William and John Innys, 1718.

Ricci, Matteo. *De Expeditione Christiana apud Sinos*. Trans. Nicholas Trigault. Ausburg, 1615.

Riccioli, Jean-Baptista. *Almagestum Novum*. Bologna, 1651.

Ridley, Mark. *A Short Treatise of Magneticall Bodies and Motions*. London: Nicholas Okes, 1613.

Salusbury, Thomas. *Mathematical Discourses and Demonstrations*. London: William Leybourn, 1665.

Savile, Henry. *A Libell of Spanish Lies found at the Sack of Cale*. London: John Windet, 1596.

Settle, Elkanah. *The World in the Moon: An Opera*. London: Abel Roper, 1697.

Smith, Thomas. *V. Cl. Gulielmi Camdeni et Illustrium Virorum Ad G. Camdenum Epistolae*. London: Richard Chiswell, 1691.

Stowe, John. *A Summarie of English Chronicles*. London: Thomas Marsh, 1566.

Suetonius. *The Historie of Twelve Caesars*. London: Matthew Lownes, 1606.

Swift, Jonathan. *Gulliver's Travels*. Ed. Robert A. Greenberg. New York: W.W. Norton, 1970.

Sylvester, Josuah. *Bartas: His Devine Weekes and Workes*. London: Humfrey Lownes, 1605.

Tacitus. *The Annales of Cornelius Tacitus*. Trans. Richard Greneway. London: Bonham and John Norton, 1598.

Vega, Garcilaso de la. *The Royal Commentaries of Peru in Two Parts*. Trans. Paul Rycaut. London: Richard Tonson, 1688.

Vergil, Polydore. *The Works of the Famous Antiquary, Polidore Virgil*. London: Simon Miller, 1663.

Vigenère, Blaise de. *Traicté des Chiffres ou Secretes Manieres d'Escrire*. Paris: Abel L'Angelier, 1586.

Ware, James. *De Praesulibus Lageniae*. Dublin: Societas Bibliopolarum, 1628.

———. *De Praesulibus Hiberniae Commentarius.* Dublin: Samuel Dancer, 1665.

Wells, H.G. *The First Men in the Moon.* Ed. David Lake. Oxford: Oxford UP, 1995.

Wesley, Samuel. *Maggots, or Poems on Several Subjects.* London: John Dunton, 1685.

Wilkins, John. *The Discovery of a World in the Moone.* London: Michael Sparke and Edward Forrest, 1638.

———. *A Discourse Concerning a New World, and Another Planet.* London: John Maynard, 1640.

———. *Mercury, or the Secret and Swift Messenger.* London: John Maynard and Timothy Wilkins, 1641.

———. *Mathematicall Magick.* London: Samuel Gellibrand, 1648.

———. *An Essay Towards a Real Character, and a Philosophical Language.* London: Samuel Gellibrand and John Martyn, 1668.

William of Newburgh. *Rerum Anglicarum Libri Quinque.* Antwerp, 1567.

Wood, Anthony. *Athenae Oxonienses.* Ed. Philip Bliss. 4 vols. London: Rivington *et al.*, 1813-20.

———. *Fasti Oxonienses.* Ed. Philip Bliss. 2 vols. London: Rivington *et al.*, 1813-20.

Zuñiga, Diego de. *In Iob Commentaria.* Rome: Franciscus Zannettus, 1591.

Selected Secondary Sources

Adams, John. "Outer Space and the New World in the Imagination of Eighteenth-Century Europeans." *Eighteenth-Century Life* 19 (1995): 70-83.

Aït-Touati, Frédérique. "La découverte d'un autre monde: fiction et théorie dans les oeuvres de John Wilkins et de Francis Godwin." *Etudes Epistémè* 7 (2005). Available online: <http://www.etudes-episteme.org/ee/articles.php?lng=fr&pg=78>.

Applebaum, Wilbur. "Kepler in England: The Reception of Keplerian Astronomy in England, 1599-1687." Ph.D. diss., SUNY Buffalo, 1969.

Apt, Adam Jared. "The Reception of Kepler's Astronomy in England: 1596-1650." D. Phil. Thesis, Oxford U, 1982.

Bachrach, A.G.H. "*Luna Mendax*: Some Reflections on Moon Voyages in Early Seventeenth-Century England." In Dominic Baker-Smith and C.C. Barfoot, eds. *Between Dream and Nature: Essays on Utopia and Dystopia.* Amsterdam: Rodopi (DQR studies in literature 2), 1987.

Beech, Martin. "Resolving some Chronological Issues in Bishop Godwin's *The Man in the Moone*." *The Observatory* 121 (2001): 255-59.

Bürger, Thomas. "Francis Godwin's *The Man in the Moone* oder: Der Fliegende Wandersmann nach dem Mond." In Francis Godwin, *Der Fliegende Wandersmann nach dem Mond: Facsimiledruck der ersten deutschen Übersetzung.* Wolfenbüttel: Herzog August Bibliothek, 1993.

Campbell, Mary Baine. "Impossible Voyages: Seventeenth-Century Space

Travel and the Impulse of Ethnology." *Literature and History* 6:2 (1997): 1-17.

Carey, Daniel. "Henry Neville's Isle of Pines: Travel, Forgery, and the Problem of Genre." *Angelaki* 1 (1993): 23-39.

Copeland, Thomas A. "Francis Godwin's 'The Man in the Moone': A Picaresque Satire." *Extrapolation* 16 (1975): 156-63.

Cornelius, Paul. *Languages in Seventeenth- and Early-Eighteenth-Century Imaginary Voyages.* Geneva: Librarie Droz, 1965.

Cressy, David. "Early Modern Space Travel and the English Man in the Moon." *American Historical Review* 111 (2006): 961-82.

Davies, H. Neville. "Bishop Godwin's 'Lunatique Language.'" *Journal of the Warburg and Courtauld Institutes* 30 (1967): 296-316.

———. "'Symzonia' and 'The Man in the Moon.'" *N&Q* 213 (1968): 342-45.

Elsner, H. "Grimmelshausen, *Der fliegende Wandersman nach dem Mond.*" *Archiv* 32 (1914): 1-35.

Empson, William. "Godwin's Voyage to the Moon." In John Haffenden, ed., *Essays on Renaissance Literature.* Vol. 1, 220-54. Cambridge: Cambridge UP, 1993.

Freudenthal, Gad. "Theory of Matter and Cosmology in William Gilbert's *De Magnete.*" *Isis* 74 (1983): 22-37.

Grant, Edward. *Physical Sciences in the Middle Ages.* Cambridge: Cambridge UP, 1977.

———. "Celestial Orbs in the Latin Middle Ages." *Isis* 78 (1987): 152-73.

———. *Planets, Stars, and Orbs: The Medieval Cosmos, 1200-1687.* Cambridge: Cambridge UP, 1994.

Grove, Richard. *Green Imperialism: Colonial Expansion, Tropical Island Edens, and the Origins of Environmentalism 1600-1860.* Cambridge: Cambridge UP, 1995.

Grewell, Greg. "Colonizing the Universe: Science Fictions Then, Now, and in the (Imagined) Future." *Rocky Mountain Review of Language and Literature* 55:2 (2001): 25-47.

Guthke, Karl S. *The Last Frontier: Imagining Other Worlds, from the Copernican Revolution to Modern Science Fiction.* Trans. Helen Atkins. Ithaca, NY: Cornell UP, 1990.

Harley, Timothy. *Moon Lore.* Wakefield: EP Publishing Limited, 1973 [1885].

Harrison, Thomas P. "Birds in the Moon." *Isis* 45 (1954): 323-30.

Hönncher, E. "Bemerkungen zu Godwins 'Voyage of Domingo Gonsales to the Moon.'" *Anglia* 10 (1888): 452-56. [Preceded by his edition]

Hutton, Sarah. Review of Anke Jannsen, *Francis Godwins "The Man in the Moone."* *Isis* 74 (1983): 267.

———. "The Man in the Moone and the New Astronomy: Godwin, Gilbert, Kepler." *Etudes Epistémè* 7 (2005) Available online: <http://www.etudes-episteme.org/ee/articles.php?lng=fr&pg=77>.

Jannsen, Anke. *Francis Godwins "The Man in the Moone": Die Entdeckung des Romans als Medium der Auseinandersetzung mit Zeitproblemen.* Frankfurt: Lang, 1981.

——. "A Hitherto Unnoticed Allusion to Francis Godwin's *The Man in the Moone* in Swift's *The Battel Between the Antient and the Modern Books.*" *N&Q* 32 (1985): 200-01.

——. "Wirkung eines Romans als Inspirationsquelle: Francis Godwins *The Man in the Moone.*" Arcadia: Zeitschrift für vergleichende Literaturwissenschaft 20 (1985): 20-46.

Jardine, Nicholas. "The Significance of the Copernican Orbs." *Journal for the History of Astronomy* 13 (1982): 168-94.

Knight, David. "Science Fiction of the Seventeenth Century." *The Seventeenth Century* 1 (1986): 69-79.

Knowlson, James R. "A Note on Bishop Godwin's 'Man in the Moone': The East Indies Trade Route and a 'Language' of Musical Notes." *Modern Philology* 55 (1968): 357-61.

Lach, Donald. "The Chinese Studies of Andreas Müller." *Journal of the American Oriental Society* 60 (1940): 564-75.

Lawton, H.W. "Notes sur Jean Baudoin et sur ses traductions de l'anglais." *Revue de Littérature Comparée* 6 (1926): 673-81.

——. "Bishop Godwin's 'Man in the Moone.'" *Review of English Studies* 7 (1931): 23-55.

McColley, Grant. "The Seventeenth-Century Doctrine of a Plurality of Worlds." *Annals of Science* 1 (1936): 285-430.

——, ed. The Man in the Moone and Nvncivs Inanimatvs. In *Smith College Studies in Modern Languages* 19 (1937).

——. "The Date of Godwin's 'Domingo Gonsales.'" *Modern Philology* 35 (1937): 47-60.

——. "The Pseudonyms of Bishop Godwin." *Philological Quarterly* 16 (1937): 78-80.

——. "The Third Edition of Francis Godwin's 'The Man in the Moone.'" *The Library* 17 (1937): 472–75.

Menner, Robert J. "The Man in the Moon and Hedging," *JEGP* 48 (1949): 1-14.

Merchant, W.M. "Bishop Francis Godwin, Historian and Novelist." *Journal of the Historical Society of the Church in Wales* 5 (1955): 45-51.

Nicolson, Marjorie Hope. *Voyages to the Moon.* London: Macmillan, 1960 [1948].

Parrett, Aaron. *The Translunar Narrative in the Western Tradition.* Aldershot: Ashgate, 2004.

Philmus, Robert M. "Murder Most Fowl: Butler's Edition of Francis Godwin." *Science Fiction Studies* 23 (1996): 260-69.

——. *Into the Unknown: The Evolution of Science Fiction from Francis Godwin to H.G. Wells.* 2nd ed. Berkeley: U of California P, 1983.

Pioffet, Marie-Christine. "Godwin et Cyrano: deux conceptions du voyage." *Canadian Review of Comparative Literature* 25:1/2 (1998): 144-57.

Ponnau, Gwenhaël. "Sur quelques modalités du voyage imaginaire." *Littératures* 11 (1984): 55-64.

Poole, William. "The Origins of Francis Godwin's *The Man in the Moone* (1638)." *Philological Quarterly* 84 (2005): 189-210.

———. "*Nuncius Inanimatus*: Telegraphy and Paradox in the Seventeenth Century: the Schemes of Francis Godwin and Henry Reynolds." *The Seventeenth Century* 21 (2006): 45-71.

Pumfrey, Stephen. *Latitude and the Magnetic Earth*. Cambridge: Icon, 2002.

Roberts, Adam. *The History of Science Fiction*. Basingstoke, Palgrave Macmillan, 2006.

Rubiés, Joan-Pau. "Travel Writing as a Genre: Facts, Fictions and the Invention of a Scientific Discourse in Early modern Europe." *Journeys* 1 (1996): 5-35.

Scholes, Robert E., and Eric S. Rabkin. *Science Fiction: History, Science, Vision*. Oxford: Oxford UP, 1977.

Sellin, Paul R. "The Performances of Ben Jonson's 'Newes from the New World Discover'd in the Moone.'" *English Studies* 61 (1980): 491-97.

Shimada, Takao. "Gonzáles de Mendoza's *Historie* as a Possible Source for Godwin's *Man in the Moone*." *N&Q* 34 (1987): 314-15.

Suvin, Darko. *Metamorphoses of Science Fiction: On the Poetics and History of a Literary Genre*. New Haven, CT: Yale UP, 1979.

Tempera, Mariangela. "'Their usual voyage': il viaggio con i cigni in *The Man in the Moone* di Francis Godwin." In Raffaella Baccolini, Vita Fortunati, and Nadia Minerva, eds. *Viaggi in Utopia*. Ravenna: Longo, 1996: 121-29.

Urban, Raymond. "Why Caliban Worships the Man in the Moon." *Shakespeare Quarterly* 27 (1976): 203-05.

Weber, Alan. "Changes in Celestial Journey Literature 1400-1650." *Culture and Cosmos* 1:1 (1997): 34-50.

Whitaker, Ewen A. *Mapping and Naming the Moon*. Cambridge: Cambridge UP, 1999.

Williams, Sparkes Henderson. "Domingo Gonsales." *Notes and Queries* 5th Series, 3 (1874): 209-10.